THAT
CH

Adam and Jocelyn

A novel about young friendship,
adventure and exploration
over the summer of 1969

By Paul Money

I

COPYRIGHT NOTICE

ACKNOWLEDGEMENTS

The author would like to acknowledge the support and help of his wife, Lorraine, in listening to the idea for this book how it developed and giving both invaluable advice, encouragement and editing ideas as the story progressed.

He would also like to thank the following for their advice, informed wisdom, patience and encouragement as this book progressed from a few pages to a full-blown novel:

Gill Hart
Mary McIntyre
Julian Onions

CONTENTS

PREFACE

Adam was a quiet, shy, nine year old bookworm having to spend the summer at his aunt and uncle's farm.

He was not looking forward to it.

Jocelyn was an outgoing and adventurous twelve year old also coming to stay for the summer at her godparent's farm.

She was eagerly looking forward to it.

Neither expected to see the other at Ashton Wood Farm in the Lincolnshire Wolds, and it didn't start well!

******

Jocelyn pushed hard and the swing soared higher and higher as Adam tried to get her attention, but she was annoyed at him for being there at the same time as her and she wasn't listening.

Higher and higher until suddenly Adam lost his grip and plunged forward, crashing to the ground, screaming in pain as he hit the hard surface. Jocelyn stood paralysed and shocked at what she'd done as Aunty Karen and Uncle Gary raced out of the farmhouse to discover what the commotion was about.

It didn't bode well for the start of their holiday of the summer of 1969 …

PROLOGUE
March 18th 2020

"Ahh, here he is at last. About time too. We thought you were going to stand us up!" Gordon said as he and Mary smiled on seeing Adam step through the door of the small café on the seafront at Skegness.

"As if. Train was cancelled due to a signal fault, so last leg of the journey was by replacement bus from Boston!"

"Explains that then. Come on, get your coat off and take a seat. What'll you have?" Mary pointed to the menu.

"White, flat coffee, three sugars, I need the caffeine boost!"

The waitress had seen him come in as she had been forewarned the couple were expecting a guest. As Adam took the proffered seat, the coffee was quickly rustled up, brought to him and he blew on it then took a sip of the hot drink, "I needed that."

"So, sixty then!" Gordon chuckled.

"Well, you can rub it in all you like but you two are just a few months behind me!" Adam retorted but in a humorous way.

"Shucks, we've been caught out. Well, I think what makes this poignant is the sad fact that we three are what's left of our class. I can't believe we've lost so many in the last five years" Mary said shaking her head with sadness.

"Yeah, quite sobering isn't it. What's with the universe? Too many gone well before their time," Gordon added looking into his empty cup.

Mary smiled at Adam sadly. "We're sorry we couldn't get to the funeral but when we heard, we were on a cruise down the Nile so couldn't get back. Did you get our card and flowers?"

"Yes, thanks. It was quite a shock and completely out of the blue. Can't believe the chances of it being a crash, Mum's parents were killed in a car crash too. Mum and Dad wouldn't have known or felt a thing as it was so quick. HGV veered out of control, across the reservation on the M18 and that was it. The funeral was really hard. Lots were there as they were popular. Even Aunty Karen made it despite her poor health."

"You were always fond of her weren't you? Often talked about your holidays at the farm, Ashton Wood Farm, Scrawford wasn't it?" asked Mary.

"Yes, compared with home it was a breath of fresh air. At least to me as a nine to fourteen year old. Good times. Dear Aunty Karen, I thought the world of her, but Uncle Gary now. Didn't like him as much in his later years, too so called manly, a real old fart. Couldn't cope with the fast progress of the modern world. Always came out with awkward things like 'woman's place is in the kitchen', and such like. However, when I was there as a boy, he was strict but had his fun moments.

Later years, not so much and I did at times wonder why Aunty stayed with him."

"I guess that's what they call old fashioned love," offered Mary wistfully.

"Nah. More like she knew he wouldn't last a day without her. Despite it all she was a very loyal and loving woman. He was lucky to have her in his life and I guess I was lucky enough to know him when I was a boy visiting the farm," Adam took another sip of his coffee and a small bite from the custard cream the waitress had brought out with the coffee.

"So, did you take early retirement from that government job you'd been moaning and complaining about for years?" asked Gordon.

"Yes, last day was a week ago and boy does it feel good. That's why I'm now free for today, I couldn't always get the time off when I wanted, except for things like funerals of course. Bringing us back to my parent's funeral, I mentioned to Aunty Karen that I'd be here today, so I was hoping she'd pop in. We are here for a few hours aren't we?"

Mary nodded. "Yes, I phoned the café up and confirmed we could meet here as long as we bought some food and drink."

"Well, here comes the waitress. Ahh, I'm going to be boring and have fish, chips, small portions please, mushy peas, lots of vinegar and salt and I see there's only one sachet of tomato sauce. If you could top them up please, I do like my sauce!" Adam flashed a smile at the waitress and she smiled back at him.

"No comment," Gordon grinned.

"Cheeky. What about you two?"

Gordon didn't need to look at the menu. "Same for me."

Mary however had to be different. "Do you do battered sausage here?"

"Of course, small medium or large?"

Gordon sniggered. "She prefers 'em large."

"Oi! Mind yer manners! But yes, make mine a large one, a little vinegar, chips, lots of them and beans. Any mushrooms or tomatoes?"

"Yes, which or both?"

"Ooh, both please."

"Well, I for one am happy we have separate beds in the B&B!" Gordon retorted and Adam had to shake his head at the pair of them. Still, it was good to see them now that they were the only ones left from their school class of '76.

"Shame about Bobby wasn't it?" mused Adam.

"Yeah, nasty way to go, caught up in his harvester. Mind you he never did mince his words did he!"

"Oh, that's cheap, Gordon. He was one of the fittest of us all. I always thought he'd be an athlete. Had a nice body …" Mary had a good memory.

"That's right, you had a crush on him until that Jackie sunk her claws into him."

"He deserved better. That's all I can say."

"And you ended up with me!"

"No comment!"

"Who's being cheeky now? You married me, didn't you!"

"What's the saying, beggers can't be choosers," they all three burst out laughing and a younger couple diagonally across from them towards the front frowned at the noise. Gordon and Mary had their backs to the couple so made a face to Adam who had to keep a straight face. He mouthed 'sorry' to the other couple but they just shook their heads and carried on eating. There were three others in the cafe all sitting facing away from the trio and scattered at various tables including one directly behind Adam, but none of them seem bothered.

"Back to the good old days, talking of my first crush, did you ever find out what happened to that girl you fell for before we all met up in big school?"

"Oh, you mean Jocelyn. Ahh, the holiday at Aunty Karen's, the summer of '69," Adam stared misty eyed into the distance as memories came flooding back.

"You still carry a torch for her!" Gordon exclaimed and Mary raised her eyebrows as if in agreement.

"Don't be daft, it was puppy love and all

that. Anyhow, other than her, I met Tracey at university and we married and had three kids so I had no time for looking back at what could have been."

"Yeah, but didn't she run off with that economics lecturer from Yale?" Mary wondered as she eyed up Adam's reaction.

"Charming, nice one bringing that up. Yes, took the kids with her to the States and that was that. Haven't seen them since," Adam sighed as it brought back sad memories.

"Mary, fancy bringing that up, sorry Adam, she doesn't always think before she speaks."

"Now who sounds like my Uncle Gary!" noted Adam, however, Mary was determined to find out more about Adam's love life, or by the sounds of it, lack of …

"Didn't you marry again though? I'm sure we got an invite but were away so couldn't come."

"Story of our lives, eh Mary?" Gordon couldn't escape the light slap on the arm she gave him.

"Yes. Miranda," he went quiet. "Twenty three years then, gone, breast cancer. We found out too late."

There was an awkward silence only broken when their food arrived and they began to tuck in after Adam had snaffled up four sachets of tomato ketchup.

Mary changed tack as she took a bite out of her battered sausage, relishing it. "Back to this here Jocelyn and your holidays with her …"

"Holiday, it was just one summer. At Aunty Karen and Uncle Gary's farm, Ashton Wood Farm, Scrawford, you remembered well. She's still there you know, Aunty Karen, that is. Her daughter Carol and Jonathon, the son in law, moved in recently to help care for her I gather. She's still fairly mobile for an old 'un but doesn't go out much."

"So, back to this Jocelyn girl. I seem to remember you wrote a piece about that holiday in English Lit class. She was the first girl you kissed …"

"'Cider with Rosie' by Laurie Lee. That was the book we had to read and give our own interpretation of. I made the mistake of writing about it quite naively not realising old Hannerty would make me stand up and read parts of it out to the class. God, I was so embarrassed."

"But it was true, wasn't it?" Mary pressed further.

"Yes, Jocelyn, ahh sweet Jocelyn. She was three years older than me. I was just nine and quite innocent. It was really an accident us being there at the same time, mum and dad had to work at a government research facility up in the arctic circle during the summer. Aunty Karen and Uncle Gary agreed I could stay with them for the six weeks over the summer that they would be away.

By accident, Aunty Karen forgot she had also

agreed that her goddaughter, her best friend's daughter, could stay over the summer as well and so we were almost destined to meet. If I'm honest, she was my soul mate and the one I should have been with all these years but that's the sort of thing life throws at you, isn't it?"

"Yeah. So, was what I remember of your English lit take on the book, true?" Mary was eager to hear more and even Gordon leant closer and looked like he'd want to hear the full story.

"Yes, pretty much, but there was a lot more, a lot, lot more that happened during that summer.

It was the summer of '69, the first moon landing had just taken place, they'd left the moon, splashed down and were in quarantine before heading back home. I was a real nerdy sort and very quiet back then when I arrived at Ashton Wood Farm ready for the summer holiday. Little could have I have known that it would be a real eye opener and certainly make me mature quicker than I expected.

It all began ..."

CHAPTER 1: ARRIVAL
Friday, July 25th 1969

The bright red Austin 1100 Mk.I trundled up the country lane and finally came to a halt in the old flagstone courtyard of Ashton Wood Farm, two miles, as the crow flies, from the nearest village, Scrawford in mid Lincolnshire. Three people got out just as the farm owners opened the front door to greet them.

"Finally made it then. Ooh a very red car! What happened to the black Mini?" Gary was inquisitive as Bob and Marion, followed by their son Adam walked up to the couple. Bob was carrying a suitcase as Adam looked nervously around, unsure of what to expect. He'd never visited the farm before.

"We needed something a bit more spacious and after the promotion I got, I figured it was time to get something else. You don't like the colour then?" replied Bob as he shook Gary's hand and the two ladies kissed cheeks.

"Could have been worse I guess, black is boring!" Gary chuckled. "So here he is then. Good to see you young man."

"Yes sir." Adam had been taught that kids like him should be seen and generally not heard. However, he did manage a smile to his aunty, who returned it and gave him a hug and a kiss on the cheek, as all aunties do.

"So, it'll be fun, won't it Adam, out here in the country with us for the summer?"

"Yes, I guess so Aunty Karen."

By now they were passing through the hallway and Gary pointed up the stairs.

"Adam'll be in the first room to the right at the top of the stairs. It's the only other bedroom we have, as we've had a bit of a disaster with the roof on one side of the farmhouse. The other bedroom is somewhat damp as the roof leaks. Karen has been busy getting the other bedroom ready for him, so if you want to take his suitcase up there now?"

"Fine, give me a minute and I'll join you all in the living room," Bob quickly disappeared upstairs with the suitcase. The rest went into the combined living and dining room, the intervening wall having been taken out to make a much larger, spacious room. Karen asked if anyone wanted a drink.

"Tea for me and Bob, no sugar for me and just one for Bob though, but milk in both.

"What about you Adam?" asked Karen and he nervously looked at his mother.

Marion looked expectantly at Adam who shrugged his shoulders. Karen saw his reticence and knew he was not much of a talker but very quiet and a bookworm to boot as well.

"Hey, Adam, I make my own lemonade, fancy some?"

Adam's eyes lit up and he looked at his

mother for her approval.

"Well, to be fair, as I explained in my letter, we've read so much about such sweet things being the cause of tooth decay that I prefer him to stick to tea, only one sugar though and only a little milk."

Karen smiled but couldn't help but feel sorry for Adam who was clearly not impressed that he wasn't allowed the lemonade. But Karen knew that at the moment, she would, let's say, have to follow his parents guidance, for now anyway. Once they left then that would be a different matter.

Bob joined them and without thinking turned to Karen.

"Any chance of a coffee, I wouldn't be surprised if you've got that new Nescafé Gold Blend? You and Gary always seem to be ahead of the curve. You got a refrigerator before we did!"

Before Karen could utter a word, Marion cut in.

"Karen is making us a nice pot of tea, aren't you Karen?"

"Yes sis, looks like it." Karen gave a sly look at Bob but Gary spoke up.

"Well I for one will have a coffee, Maxwell in this house, so Bob, if you want one you can have it."

Marion grimaced, she was not very keen on her sister's choice of a husband. A farmer and general labourer and not at all the sort of person she thought her sister should have married, how did that saying go? She married beneath her station, Marion remembered it and again slightly grimaced.

Bob, however, knew which side he had to be on. "Thanks Gary, but tea will be fine."

Marion's 'glow' of satisfaction at winning her way was evident. Adam was sat down and began kicking his legs up and down in boredom.

"Now you can stop that Adam. You're going to be a guest here for the next six weeks, so you are to be on your best behaviour. You will be representing your family whilst here, so be good for your aunty and uncle as they have been so kind as to take you in whilst we have to be away."

Adam stopped swinging his legs and deep down Karen felt sorry for him. She left them to go make the drinks and hoped Gary behaved himself as she knew her husband and Marion didn't quite see eye to eye.

"So," Gary began, "what's with this trip that's so important?"

Bob looked about to begin to speak but as usual Marion jumped in first. Despite her long skirt, Gary could have sworn she was wearing the trousers!

"You know both our jobs deal with climatology. We're part of a team going up to the Scandinavian arctic circle to study the wildlife, fauna and environment. There has been some talk that things could change over the coming decades. We're to conduct a detailed survey for the records as a baseline for future generations."

Bob was determined not to be left out of the conversation. "Yes, it could just be natural, but a minority of scientists in the field have begun to raise concerns, we've got a placement based in northern Norway. There's eight of us up there doing sample analysis and collection of temperature, pressure readings and the such like. But there's no provision for children so we really are grateful that you are happy to have Adam for the summer."

"No worries. He's most welcome here and I'm sure, Marion, he will be on his best behaviour. Karen will tell you I am quite strict but I do like to think I'm a fair person too."

"Indeed. Well, we'll see what he's like on our return. I'm sure Karen will probably spoil him rotten if I know my sister!" Marion retorted just as Karen entered with a tray in her hands and placed it on the small table.

"Well now Marion, someone's got to haven't they?"

Marion just grimaced. "I'm sure you will do a good job," she knew she had to take care as they had no other option other than Karen and Gary, so she had to keep her comments civil for the remainder of their short visit.

Marion stood up and seemed to give Karen an odd look, appearing to indicate with her eyes that she wanted her to follow her out into the kitchen. Karen smiled and got up.

"Just excuse us boys, girl talk I think!"

Bob and Gary looked at each other and shrugged. Bob handed over an official looking letter with their institution on the letterhead.

"Keep this just in case, as it officially confirms we're asking you to look after Adam for the summer holidays. Shouldn't be needed but in the very unlikely event there's an accident then we're authorising you both to be his guardians for the duration he is here."

"Gosh, was this really necessary? For heavens sake, it's a summer holiday for him! Bet Marion came up with this."

"Nope. It may amaze you to hear this but I do sometimes take control!"

"Sorry, I only ..."

"Forget it, we all know that Marion loves to think she's in charge, sometimes it's best to let her get on with things but in this case I felt you ought to be covered. Not that Adam will be any bother, will you Adam?"

"No Dad."

Adam went back to being quiet and watched how his father and Gary got on without the two women there to keep an eye on them. In the end they just chatted amicably enough about everything except the one thing that Adam was interested in, the moon men!

In the kitchen Karen eyed up her rather stuffy sister and gave her a look as much to say

'Well?'

"I, I know I can be a bit tough on Adam and I can at times be a bit over protective. But that's what mothers do. We've got a development that's just happened this week and it's thrown me and Bob as it's so close to us going away. Under normal circumstances then there wouldn't be an issue him staying with you all summer but as your Gary would probably put it, we've been thrown a spanner in the works.

Adam, well, Adam, he's, he's," Marion hated talking about intimate things to anyone but she knew that as Adam was going to spend six weeks with her sister and brother-in-law, then they should be put in the picture. Marion looked downwards at Karen's crotch and made a face that Karen almost burst out laughing at.

"Spit it out sis, he's what?"

"Developing down there!"

"Oh. Isn't he a bit young for that to be happening? He's only nine!"

"Err, yes, and no, it can happen early apparently but for a while now he baths himself and sheepishly came to me worried last week. He's now got hair down there just starting and they've got bigger."

"What the hair?"

"No you twillock. You know, what's down there!"

"Oh!"

"You see, so he might start getting moody

and heaven knows when his voice will break but our doctor said it can happen early so, well, I thought you ought to know. It couldn't have come at a worse time and you know how useless men are when it comes to anything to do with the birds and the bees, my Bob may be brilliant but not when it comes to something like this!"

"Oh. Bless Adam, does he understand what's happening to him?"

"I'm not sure, he does like reading an awful lot, but I haven't plucked up the courage to see if there are any guide books out there that can help him."

"You're over thinking things, he'll be alright I'm sure. If Adam comes to me or Gary with a problem do you want us to help explain what's happening?"

"As I won't be here, if you would sis. I know I'm not always kind to you but I do love you, I feel right out of my depth and didn't want to leave you in the dark if something happened."

"And you think that I won't be out of my depth? I don't have kids!"

"But I do know you are really good with them, you've had a kid stay with you sometimes over the summer, that goddaughter if I remember rightly, so I assume that helps. I hope he won't be any trouble for you as it won't be easy to get in touch with Bob or myself being up in the arctic, so I hope you are okay with the situation?"

Something tried to come to the forefront of

Karen's subconscious but faded away and she shook her head. "Leave it with me, Adam and I have always got on like a house on fire so don't worry. I'll keep an eye on things and do what I can."

"Love you sis."

"Love you too Marion. Now, I suspect you two have to be getting off soon so best say your goodbyes as you will be away for quite a few weeks."

Together they walked back into the living room and the men were none the wiser as to what they'd been discussing.

#

They waved goodbye to his parents as the very red car disappeared behind the farm outbuildings and Karen tapped Adam on the shoulder.

"Fancy that lemonade then?" Adam's eyes lit up and she took that as a yes as the three of them walked back indoors.

"You're inscrutable, you are. I'll have a glass too if you don't mind," Gary winked at Adam who managed a smile at this unexpected side to his uncle. Perhaps he wasn't so bad after all. His mother had often said bad things about Uncle Gary, hence Adam having bad feelings about spending almost six weeks with them over the summer. But there was something else on his mind.

"Uncle Gary, did the moon men get back all right?"

"Oh, that palaver, waste of money I say. But I'll give the Yank's credit, they said they'd do it and they have. Yes, the three are in quarantine. If you are good, then I always watch the news at teatime, but I have rules mind you, no talking whilst I am watching the television. I work hard all day and like to keep abreast of events. Like to think I am a man of the world and better for knowing what's going on. Not that we can do anything about it, mind. So you know the rule, be seen and not heard, got it?"

"Yes Uncle. Can I go upstairs and unpack?"

He didn't get a reply as Karen tapped him on the shoulder to lead him upstairs. "Uncle Gary may think he's in charge but when it comes to the house, it's me. Come on, let's get you unpacked and I'll show you your room and where you can go whilst upstairs."

Adam nodded and meekly followed her, as Gary ruffled his hair; shaking his head as he grabbed his wellingtons from just inside the door to go out to his tractor.

Upstairs, Adam now got the tour.

"Here's your room. We only have the one spare bedroom as the second has a leaking roof. Uncle Gary is supposed to be getting it fixed but so far hasn't. Naughty Uncle eh?"

"I guess so," Adam didn't want to say the

wrong thing in case it got him into trouble.

"Across the hallway and off to the right is our room, which you only enter if you knock first when we are in there; wait for a reply. We only recently had mains running water put in to the farmhouse and the bathroom across next to our room is small but has a bath in it with, would you believe, hot and cold taps and a wash basin. How posh are we eh? There is a toilet with a pull chain to flush but I would ask that you make sure for tinkles you use the outside privy if you have to get up in the night.

That's so you don't flush the toilet up here otherwise it'll wake us up and we always get up early. This is a farm and farmers are often up at the crack of dawn. But outside going in the privy won't be a problem. We have a small torch that I've put on the bedside table for you for that purpose, but don't point it towards our bedroom door in case it wakes up your Uncle as he is a light sleeper."

Adam looked into the bathroom and was impressed but was a little worried.

"What about if, if I need to do the other at night?"

"Also use the outside privy. You'll be alright, it's summer and so far they reckon it'll be a good one and might even be quite warm and sunny. Oh of course, not at night although it won't get very dark until the end of your stay with us."

Adam looked at her as he undid the

fastenings on his suitcase and they both clicked open at the same time. He began to pull out a few of his clothes along with several books and several recent newspaper cuttings all covering the manned landing on the moon.

"Aunty, what time do I have to go to bed?"

"Well, let's see, what time do you go when you are at home?"

"Seven thirty."

"Goodness! That's a little early, especially when it is so light outside in the summer. How about …" she paused for dramatic effect, "nine o'clock?"

Adam's eyes went wide and he grinned, nodding eagerly.

"Now, Uncle Gary has to be up at the crack of dawn so he and I will be up by four am as I always cook him breakfast," Adam now looked at her in shock and she quickly continued, "but don't worry, I'll come and knock on your door at, say seven, how's that for you?"

He smiled and she took him across the landing and opened the bedroom door to the room that was unusable.

He could see why, there was several buckets which for now were not needed as it was a dry day. The room was in a poor state with wallpaper peeling off the walls and several holes above exposing the wooden latticework of the ceiling.

"Pretty rough isn't it. Anyway, I reckon I should get on with cooking tea. It'll be at five thirty sharp so make sure you have washed your hands and are promptly sitting at the table. You'll know Uncle Gary's place as he has a thick set chair that has been handed down through the ages by his ancestors so don't sit in it. I sit across from him so you can sit on his right side. You got that?"

"Yes Aunty."

"Good boy. Now, I guess you'll stay up here reading won't you?"

"Yes Aunty, if that's alright with you?"

"No problem sweetie. See you at the dinner table then later."

She gave him a light kiss on his forehead and then left as Adam carried on emptying his suitcase then settled down to read his book, 'From the Earth to the Moon' by Jules Verne.

CHAPTER 2: A SURPRISE AND SHOCK

Adam was as good as his word and at the dinner table he kept quiet, eating his dinner carefully so as not to make too much noise, but he was also in his element.

Uncle Gary was known to be quite a serious person and didn't suffer fools lightly, being very old fashioned in his views. Aunty Karen forewarned Adam that his uncle believed that boys should be outside, exploring, climbing trees, rough and tumble and happy to get stuck in helping with the chores around the farm.

So, he was already a little disappointed when he found out Adam was a bookworm and preferred to find out about the world through reading and whenever possible watching the TV, devouring whatever he could get his hands on.

But on this occasion with the historic moon landing still quite fresh, both Adam and his uncle watched the news coverage that seemed to keep going. This despite the successful splashdown of the astronauts a few days before Adam arrived.

Suddenly Adam realised his uncle was actually talking to him, at the dinner table no less!

"Bet it'll be Mars next, what do you think boy?"

Karen coughed and looked sternly at Gary. "He's got a name and is your nephew so if you want him to respect you, then show a little decency to him too!"

Gary's eyes widened as he looked at his wife then looked at Adam who stopped eating and waited nervously for the argument to begin.

Uncle Gary shook his head, looked at Adam and actually smiled at him.

"She is of course right Adam, and I am sorry, but do you think they'll go to Mars next?"

It had to be a trick question. He wasn't supposed to talk at the table so this had to be a test to see if he would speak or not? Adam took a chance to talk about one of his favourite things, space.

"They have quite a few more planned Uncle, but there is talk that there will be space stations and a moonbase after this and then on to Mars, but I don't know how long it'll be before they do those other things."

"Interesting. Clever boy. I may not be into reading like you as such, but I get my information from the news coverage and the pundits do seem to talk a lot like that. But you see, here's the problem, The US of A is at war with the Vietcong and it's not popular and it's costing them a whole lot of money. My guess is that they might not be able to afford to carry on. Anyhow, here's the weather, I need to hear this so let's be quiet."

"Yes sir," Adam lowered his head and picked at his carrots, slicing a large one up so he could manage it. But he had to admit he had been surprised by his uncle. Perhaps this holiday was going to be alright after all ...

#

Adam didn't sleep too well that first night. A different bed was always odd and affected his sleep, although he didn't go to many places other than his home in Cambridge. The bed was also huge as it was a double bed and he was able to roll all over it to find the most comfortable position.

This, however, was somewhere called Lincolnshire and it had felt like a long drive, so although he had cat napped in the car on the way up, he finally drifted off into a deep sleep. He seemed to join his uncle and aunt on the moon as they explored it in his dreams. Oddly enough none of them had spacesuits on, but for some reason they didn't seem to care as they bounced across the lunar surface.

He came awake at an odd sound then realised it was a cockerel crowing and he could hear footsteps on the landing and someone pulling the toilet chain, he assumed it had to be close to four in the morning. The room was quite light as the curtains were thin so he ducked under the bedcovers and eventually drifted off again to sleep. However for some reason he kept thinking the cockerel was huge and began to chase him around the room. He did tend to have very imaginative dreams and sometimes nightmares too.

He awoke to a light knocking on the door and then Aunty Karen entered with a glass of milk and some buttered toast.

"I'm sure you don't need a full cooked breakfast but just for this morning I thought you could have milk and toast here. Then from now on you can come down to the kitchen and have breakfast there, once you have done all you need to do. Do you have a toothbrush?"

"Yes, and toothpaste."

"Good, I expected nothing less from your mother as she does think we live out in the wilds here with no civilisation. I'll see you downstairs soon. It's not bad outside, some breaks in the cloud and ideal for your uncle, but I have got some good news. He doesn't expect you to help out on the farm and if you want to explore, just be careful of the machinery, some of it can be quite deadly. On a farm there are many dangers so be careful, alright?" Adam nodded as he took a drink of milk.

"There are several footpaths that either go out from the farm or pass through our land. The ones to the north east of us eventually lead to the village nearby, but that's a bit of a walk. Do you have any wellies?"

"No, just my shoes and some slippers."

"Oh, well I've had youngsters stay over in the past so I'll see if there are any that might fit you if you decide to go off exploring whilst you are here."

Again, she had the feeling that she should be remembering something but it slipped away.

"Is it alright if I read, I don't like going outdoors."

"Now, Adam, you can't come up to us in the countryside and not do a little exploring. Perhaps on a fine day when I'm not so busy, we can go for a walk together?"

"Oh, yes, alright but as long as I can read either up here or downstairs in the living room?"

"It's a deal. Now, eat up your toast and I'll see you downstairs soon."

She patted him on the head and walked out as Adam wondered if he was a pet dog or something.

#

Mid morning.

The blue Ford Cortina slowed down as it entered the farmyard and Karen heard the vehicle arrive and stop. She was puzzled, as she had not been expecting visitors and Gary was out on the tractor in the top field; that would have been unmistakable had it been the one to arrive.

Adam had gone back upstairs and was reading in his room so she opened the front door and then stared in surprise at the visitors.

"Beryl, Henry, Jocelyn, err, nice to see you again, everything alright?"

Henry fished out a suitcase from the boot of the car as Jocelyn ran up to Karen and gave her a hug.

"Glad to be back again Aunty, sorry I couldn't come last year, I was poorly, but back to normal now."

"Hmn, back to normal? Suitcase?"

"Yes," Beryl laughed, "you remember, we said we'd bring Jossy to stay for the summer whilst we go on that Caribbean cruise we won at Christmas. You know she loves to stay with you and Gary and so we were delighted that you said she could stay all summer."

"Yes, yes, of course, gosh, when was that again?"

"Back in April, don't say you forgot Karen, that'd be most unlike you!" quipped Henry as they all stood outside the door wondering if Karen was going to let them in.

Karen hoped Adam was still upstairs and she stood to one side as the new arrivals trouped indoors.

"Shall I take Jossy's case upstairs then?" asked Henry as he was about the walk up the stairs.

"No! Sorry, we're in a bit of a state upstairs as we've got a leaky roof in her usual room so I need to do some tidying up. Leave it in the hallway here and when I'm ready I can take it up."

"OK, *suit* yourself, geddit, *suit* yourself, *suit*case eh? Oh never mind," Henry's jokes were always bad, thought Karen. Beryl was thinking it too. Jocelyn shook her head, knowing what her father was like.

Karen indicated to the front living room and they went in as she suggested tea or coffee for the adults and lemonade for Jocelyn.

"Ooh, tell you what, can I have your lemonade as well as it's been a bit of a warm drive," Beryl asked and Henry nodded in agreement.

"Three lemonades coming up," Karen went out to the kitchen, her mind buzzing as to what she could do. They only had the one functional bedroom and just the one bed in it with no room for another bed.

Beryl spotted something on the sideboard and examined it as Karen came back in with the tray of drinks.

"Your Gary becoming educated then?" Beryl held up the Boys Book of Astronomy and Space, much to Karen's horror but she quickly recovered.

"You could say that. He's surprised me to be honest, as he's watched the news about the moon landing over the last few weeks like a hawk. Just for fun I found that in Louth library for him. Hasn't even started reading it."

"Oh, funny that as there's a rocket shaped

bookmark halfway in it. Someone must have left it in there when they returned it. Name of Adam."

"I guess so," Karen quickly changed tack, "My, Jocelyn, you've grown since you were last here!"

"I was only ten last time I was here but now I'm twelve and in the senior school!"

"Ahh, things are changing I see, you're taller if I'm not mistaken?"

"Four inches!"

"Wow, anything else I need to know about?"

"Err, I'm just going to check the oil and water before we head back, as you're into female things!" declared Henry and promptly put his now empty glass down, smiled and left the three of them to talk on a more personal level.

Beryl smiled and shook her head. "He's useless when it comes to our little girl. Actually that's my point. Although Jossy is beginning to, let's say, grow a little 'up top' she isn't big enough for a bra but I bet by next year that may well have changed. She's pretty mature and quite with it, aren't you sweetie?"

"Yes mom. Had the pep talk and know all about the birds and the bees, have done it all at school at special lessons. Anyway, more importantly, the weatherman last night seemed to suggest we might have a good summer so I can't wait to get out and explore like I used to do. Is the swing still up on the back lawn, Aunty?"

Karen always liked it when Jocelyn called

her that even though they were not technically related. She and Beryl had been best friends since primary school days and once Jocelyn arrived on the scene, Karen had always been a part of her life as she and Gary were her godparents.

"I'm sure you will and yes the swing is still in the same old place. Oh, Henry, ready to go then?"

Henry had walked in and he nodded to them both and then gave Jocelyn a hug.

"Now, you be on your best behaviour and we'll see you in around five or so weeks time."

"Yes Daddy, hope you have a nice trip," Jocelyn hugged her mum.

"Be good sweetie for Aunty Karen and Uncle Gary."

"I will, promise."

Beryl turned back to Karen and handed her a letter.

"What's this?"

"As we're away for several weeks out of the country, OK almost six weeks, Henry thought it prudent to write a formal letter confirming Jossy is staying with you whilst we are away and you have our permission to not only look after her but take whatever action is needed. Personally, I can't see the need, but I guess as this is different from a week or two's holiday, it's perhaps best to be on the safe side."

"Oh, okay. Funny that Marion did the same … oh, never mind, my mind wandered to something else."

Henry was already getting into the car as Karen tapped Beryl on the arm and she turned back to her, puzzled.

"Hey, we had some good times when we were kids didn't we?"

Marion smiled. "We sure did."

"Yeah, remember when we had to share beds with Aunty Irene's two boys because there was nowhere to put us up?"

"Hah! Yes, they were fun days and the boys didn't know what to make of us. Why?"

"Nothing, just had that memory pop into my head and I wanted to see if you remembered it too."

"O...kay, anyhow, bye Karen, give Gary our love won't you and you young lady, have a good time over the summer and be good for Aunty Karen and Uncle Gary!"

"Yes Mom! Bye Dad!"

Together they waved them off and headed indoors as Karen wondered what she was going to do and how to explain it to Gary once he got back from the fields ...

#

Karen decided to take the plunge and get the introductions over with first, then face the wrath of Jocelyn as the young girl would surely be furious.

She motioned to Jocelyn to follow her

upstairs as Karen picked up her suitcase. "Let's go upstairs, but I have to tell you that I had indeed forgotten you were coming and I have a bit of a problem, indeed a surprise. I really hope you can forgive me."

"Aunty Karen, you look pale, what do I have to forgive you for?" Jocelyn was puzzled as they reached the top of the stairs.

"We're here," Karen hesitated, knocked lightly on the door, then opened it. Adam was lying on his front on the bed reading his book. He turned round and looked up, then his eyes went wide open as he stared at the newcomer.

"Erm, Adam, this is Jocelyn, Jocelyn, this is my nephew, Adam."

"Oh, hi Adam, you're staying too then. This might be fun, someone to explore the farmland with."

Adam was still staring at Jocelyn with his mouth open catching flies, as if she were an alien from a far off distant world, which to him, she was.

"Aunty Karen, I think he's broken!"

"You'd best sit on the bed Jocelyn, I need to explain something and I'm just figuring out what we can do.

So, the thing is, your usual bedroom across the landing is a mess as there is water coming through from the roof and there's a lot of damage so you can't sleep in there.

I had honestly forgotten you were coming to

stay but I didn't want to let your parents down. But I will tell you this, when your mother and I were young girls, much the same age as yourself, we stopped over at your Great Aunty Irene's in Exeter. It was when your grandparents were taking us down to Cornwall on holiday but the car was giving them trouble. Great Aunt Irene didn't have any other bedrooms so me and your mother had to sleep with Great Aunt Irene's two boys …

… in the same bed. She did the sheets folded over so that we girls couldn't accidentally mix with the boys and we were all under strict instructions to behave ourselves."

Jocelyn joined Adam in staring at Karen as it began to dawn on her what was probably coming.

Karen continued, "So, I'm sort of stuck with the same situation and need you two to be very good and share this bedroom. I'll bring in extra sheets and if you can help me change the bed, we'll do two folded over sheets to form like two single beds, but on this one with a sort of barrier in the middle made of pillows until Uncle Gary can come up with something better. Understand?"

Adam, and even more so, Jocelyn, looked horrified.

"I, I, I have to sleep in here with her?"

"I have to sleep in here with him?" Jocelyn looked incredulously at Karen, who shook her head in sadness.

"Oh dear, you both really don't like this do you. And before you start arguing, I agree with you, but I'm at a loss of what else to do. You see, the lounge settee is quite short and would be useless for six weeks and quite cramped. Plus we are up at 4am each morning and would always disturb whoever was sleeping there.

If you can't cope then I'll have to telephone your parents. The nearest telephone is a telephone box in Scrawford and by now I doubt we'd be able to get either of your parents. Yours Adam were due to fly out this morning and yours Jocelyn will be on the way to Heathrow for their early morning flight with no way of calling them.

I love you both but I'm stuck. Will you try for me? Please? I'm not asking you to get undressed in the same room, you'll have to decide who gets dressed and undressed here and in the bathroom, but I'm so sorry. I really think you two will get on great, so will you try for me? Pretty please?"

Jocelyn kept shaking her head, wandered out into the bathroom and closed the door. Then she began to shriek and both Karen and Adam raced into the bathroom worried sick that Jocelyn was doing something awful to herself.

Instead, she was pointing to a huge spider on the toilet seat and was shaking.

Adam looked at it and had to smile.

"It's a giant house spider. It's harmless and is more scared of you squashing it than you are of it."

Jocelyn stepped back but seemed to calm down a little. Aunty Karen wasn't keen on spiders either but knew that no matter what she did with them, other than kill them, they always managed to get back in the farmhouse, so as a rule, she just left them alone and ignored them.

Adam just walked over and scooped it up quickly holding it carefully in his hand and nodded to the bathroom window. Aunty Karen quickly opened it, Adam looked around and saw a small stool which he dragged over whilst keeping the spider trapped and then he climbed up and deposited it outside.

Karen gave out a sigh of relief as Adam walked up to Jocelyn. "Are you OK now?"

She looked at him, turned her back and walked out muttering something under her breath. Adam just looked at his aunty wondering what he should do. She quickly walked after Jocelyn, following her down the stairs and into the living room. Jocelyn sat down heavily on the settee with tears in her eyes.

She heard the front door open and Jocelyn rushed out into the hallway in the vain hope her parents somehow knew there was a problem and had miraculously come back for her. Instead there stood Uncle Gary and his happy expression changed to shock as he saw Jocelyn run towards him and fling her arms around his waist.

"Hello Jocelyn, what are you doing here then?"

"I don't want to share a room or bed with a boy!"

"Sorry, *what*?"

Karen reached the bottom of the stairs with Adam quietly following behind her, not knowing what his uncle was going to say or think about the bizarre situation.

"Honey, I've made a right mess. I'd forgotten I'd said Jocelyn could stay for the summer whilst her parents go on that cruise they won at Christmas."

"Sharing bedroom, and a bed?" he asked incredulously.

"Well, when I was little we did it in the past. Wasn't a big deal."

"Maybe with your folks but, well, it's not fair on either of them."

He turned to Jocelyn and Adam.

"Look you two, go out and play on the swing whilst Aunty Karen and I try to sort something out."

They both just stood there and didn't move.

"NOW!" he urged a little more loudly that he'd intended.

That did it and Jocelyn walked quickly down the hallway, into the kitchen towards the back door as Adam followed in a daze. This was bad, very bad, he thought.

Not knowing the exact same thoughts were going through Jocelyn's mind as well.

#

"What the hell Karen! What were you thinking?"

"Listen, we all make mistakes, forget things, you do too at times so don't give me that face! Look we have no way of contacting either parents so my plan is the best option. I'll make sure the beds are made up so they can't mingle by accident and they'll have to promise to behave themselves and get changed in different rooms.

Jocelyn is the more mature of the two, although at this moment she's understandably upset and angry. But I reckon they'll be OK and settle down once we have a proper routine in place."

"You'd better be right about this. But I can tell you now for one thing. You will be the one to explain to both their parents when they get back as to what's happened, so help you!"

"I know. I'll-"

There was a shout and scream from outside and they rushed out wondering what had happened.

#

Jocelyn had reached the swing first and, refusing any help from Adam, she began to swing higher and higher before slowing down, then doing it again. It was her way of trying to calm down and come to terms with the situation.

Adam waited patiently. He wasn't a big fan of swings as normally the ones at school were fraught with danger, usually from the bullys that tried to push you higher and higher until you fell off.

Jocelyn slowed down and stopped herself by using her feet, then jumped off and walked past Adam without saying a word. He got on it and waited until she was far enough away so he wouldn't catch her with his feet.

He began swinging but didn't go too high and watched Jocelyn as she stood there looking serious and studying the ground beneath her feet intently.

"It's not my fault," he said quietly.

She looked at him and scowled but did look a little less serious. He tried again.

"It's not my fault. I love Aunty Karen and she wouldn't do this deliberately, would she?"

Jocelyn stamped her right foot down hard then seemed to relax a little more.

"She's never mentioned me to you then?" he asked on the next upswing.

"No."

"This is my first time here so I was a bit nervous as I don't like being outdoors," Adam slowed a little as Jocelyn moved a bit closer to him but still clear of his swings.

"Who comes on holiday to a farm and doesn't like the outdoors?" she taunted Adam.

"I didn't ask to come. Mum and Dad have to be away over the summer, something to do with their jobs and there was no one else who could look after me."

Jocelyn seemed to settle down a little more. "Sort of same thing for me. My parents won a trip for two to somewhere called the Caribbean and they managed to have the holiday extended by paying extra to the prize. So they were in the same boat they ..."

Adam laughed. "Ha ha, same boat!"

"Silly boy. They had no one else who could have me for such a long time, except for Uncle Gary and Aunty Karen. I've been here for holidays before but missed last year, I was ill. I usually come here for a couple of weeks in early August so this is a bit different."

She wandered around to the back of the swing and began to gently push Adam and although she couldn't see it, he smiled.

Higher, a harder push, she began to talk about her previous visits but wasn't paying too much attention. With each push, Adam began to go higher and he tried to tell her to stop, but she was in a world of her own now.

Harder yet again until suddenly Adam lost his grip and fell forwards off the swing crashing onto the ground and crumpled up screaming in pain. Jocelyn stood frozen in horror then ran over to him just as Gary and Karen came running out on hearing him scream.

#

They got back from Louth County Hospital after several hours of physical examination, an x-ray of his legs and extensive questioning of Gary and Karen, as they weren't Adam's parents. In the end he was sent home with nothing more than a few cuts and bruises but with good sized sticking plasters on his head and knees with instructions that someone slept in his room and kept an eye on him overnight.

That turned out to be easier than expected. Jocelyn was so overcome with remorse that she insisted Aunty Karen put her plan into place and Jocelyn would keep a eye on Adam for them.

Gary was furious with the overall situation, but Karen pointed out that their own doctor had been consulted as to their suitability for looking after the two children. That and they had remembered to take the letters from both parents which they were now grateful for. They were lucky as the doctor was familiar with Jocelyn, two years earlier she had been running a temperature and the doctor had been called out.

It felt to all like a narrow escape from having to get in touch with both sets of parents and explain what had happened which could have wrecked their plans and probably caused a breakdown in relations.

Uncle Gary took himself to bed as he kept reminding them that he had to be up early in the morning. Farm chores were never done, but an ongoing process.

Aunty Karen set about preparing the bed and folding two sets of sheets and blankets to form two single beds on the double bed base. Adam immediately claimed the left hand side so Jocelyn had no choice but to have the side closest to the window. Jocelyn waited until Uncle Gary had finished in the bathroom then went in and hurriedly changed into her nightie before heading back to the room, but waited outside until she heard Aunty Karen come to the door.

The door opened quietly. "Adam is tucked up now and sleeping on his side. What a day! I am so sorry Jocelyn, I should have told your parents the situation but I was pleased to see you and if I'm honest, I think Adam having someone else nearer his age here, will help him overcome his shyness and maybe even bring him out of his bookworm trance!"

Jocelyn put her arms around Karen.

"I shouldn't have been so nasty to him. He didn't deserve it. It's my fault we ended up having to go to the hospital but I hope he will be alright. I'll do my best and keep an eye out in case he has a bad night. Do I fetch you as I don't want Uncle Gary to be angry with me."

"Trust me, he's more angry with me than you

at what's happened. Yes. If Adam does have a bad night then get me straight away. Anyhow young lady, get yourself into bed and hopefully we'll all get some sleep and have a laugh about this in the coming days."

Karen kissed her lightly on the forehead and Jocelyn entered the bedroom and got into her side of the bed. Adam was awake but quiet, keeping himself under the bedsheets lest he saw her!

"Night night Adam, I'm really sorry and I won't do that again, I promise."

There was a faint sound from Adam, difficult to work out if it was a grunt or an acknowledgement.

Jocelyn turned out her bedside light and hoped it would be an uneventful night.

CHAPTER 3: A REVELATION
July 27th

Morning. As Adam slowly awoke he tried to roll over onto his back and stretch out across the bed as he had done the morning before.

Only to be rudely reminded he was no longer the sole occupant.

"You alright?" asked Jocelyn sleepily and Adam bolted upright in bed, wide awake now. Then the events of the previous day and evening came drifting back and he turned back onto his side facing away from 'the girl'.

"Adam, are you OK? Otherwise I'll have to fetch Aunty Karen."

He relented. "Yes, slight headache, but I'm alright."

Jocelyn sat up in bed and turned to look at him, leaning over the pillow barrier Aunty Karen had put between them. She nudged him gently on the shoulder.

"Headache? I wonder if I should fetch Aunty anyway?"

"NO! I'm alright, honest. Just didn't sleep much. I can normally spread out all over the bed but someone's taken it over!" he said a little more grumpily than he'd intended.

The reply was almost a whisper but was well intended. "Sorry."

Adam realised there were muffled sobs and

Jocelyn was crying.

"I didn't mean to hurt you, I was upset and confused and I shouldn't have taken it out on you."

Adam lay there thinking she was right, she shouldn't have done, but as is their wont when young girls cry, it was having the desired effect, especially considering the fact the tears were genuine.

He softened. "You don't have to cry, I know you didn't mean it. Friends?"

"Friends."

"I don't know what time it is ..."

"That's OK, I brought an alarm clock with me and it's set for seven am."

"But what time is it, something feels wrong as it's very light."

Jocelyn turned over and grabbed her alarm clock.

"Oh, it's almost six in the morning."

"Funny, it's very quiet. Uncle Gary isn't very good at being quiet when get gets up, that's at about four in the morning." Adam hesitated, "I, I need a wee."

"Don't just lie there then, go to the toilet. I'm sure Uncle Gary has been up for hours, so you can use the new bathroom!"

Adam pushed his bedsheets off, made sure nothing was trying to escape to embarrass him, then he stood up but swayed a little. Jocelyn saw this and immediately got out of bed and held his hand as he steadied himself. He looked down at her holding his hand and carefully pried it away.

"You're not coming. You can't come in with me!"

"Of course not, silly, but I'll feel better if I come with you and I'll stand outside the bathroom so I can make sure you are OK, then we'll come back. It's the least I can do."

Adam eyed her and thought the nightdress looked quite cute. He'd never seen a girl in a nightdress before and didn't quite understand what it was he was feeling.

"OK then. Uncle Gary will be outside by now so I'm glad I don't have to use the privy outside."

They managed to open the door quietly and walked across the landing to the bathroom where Jocelyn took up station outside whilst Adam went in. A few seconds later and the sound of him tinkling into the toilet almost made her burst out laughing, but she managed to contain herself.

Then she noticed something.

Uncle Gary and Aunty Karen's bedroom door was still shut. All the years she had visited in the past, she knew that once they had got up, the door was almost always left slightly open.

She realised something, Uncle Gary must have overslept! Then the toilet flushed and she realised, with horror, how loud it was.

Muffled angry sounds struck up inside the adult's bedroom and then she head someone stomping around before the door was flung open quickly and there was Uncle Gary, just in pyjama bottoms sporting a very hairy chest. He stared at her as if seeing an alien, then it dawned on him and he rushed back inside.

Various noises, muffled sounds from aunty Karen, then Uncle Gary once again came out of the bedroom this time dressed with his pyjama top on as well.

"I've overslept!!!" Who's in the bathroom?"

Jocelyn couldn't help but think it had to be obvious but she replied meekly, "Adam, he needed the toilet and we thought you were already up."

"Oh, yes, err no, is he done?"

Jocelyn really wanted to ask how she could possibly know that when the bathroom door opened and Adam came out, then stood stock still when he saw his uncle.

"Good boy, feeling better?"

"Err, yes sir."

"Finished in there?"

"Yes."

"Good. Back to your bedroom you two as I'm late!"

They did as they were told, Jocelyn grabbing Adam by the hand and leading him quickly back into their room, whereby Adam let go and grimaced at being led by a girl.

As Jocelyn closed the door she burst out laughing trying to be as quiet as she could.

"Eh?" wondered Adam.

"Uncle Gary has a very hairy chest!" she replied as she jumped onto the bed and slid under her side of the sheets. Adam grinned as he'd spotted uncle Gary's pyjama top buttons were open and he'd seen how hairy he was. He got in on his side of the bed but lay on his back looking up at the ceiling.

"Hairy Uncle Gary," he chuckled.

"Hairy Uncle Gary," Jocelyn repeated.

"Uncle Gary is an ape!"

"Uncle Gary is a very hairy ape!" Jocelyn said and they both giggled until Aunty Karen suddenly opened the door, making then stop and try to hide under the bedsheets.

"Shush you two! Your uncle is angry enough without you two adding to things. As we've all had quite a day and night of it. I'll expect you down for breakfast at eight instead of seven. And remember, no getting dressed in the same room! Your parents would skin me alive!"

She closed the door as both children thought they wouldn't be seen dead dressing together and settled down to try to get back to sleep.

#

"I'm telling you Karen, those two in the same bedroom and indeed bed, is wrong and it's thrown my routine. Yesterday is a bad omen I tell you! We've lied to their parents, or rather you have, the boy's had an accident and we've had to take him to the hospital, and then this morning for the first time I'm late up. And all that's happened in just the first two days!"

"Now Gary, you've been late getting up more times than a cow shakes it's tail, so don't go blaming the children. Jocelyn already feels very bad and it was an accident. Even Adam seems to have forgiven her.

We've no room to put one of them downstairs as the settee is too small. I said we should have got a bigger one but oh no, 'why spend all that money on something larger when it's hardly going to be used'. Your exact words."

"But she's twelve and he's nine!"

"So? Jocelyn is more grown up than you at times and has her head screwed on. Adam is a typical boy and is not yet interested in girls, so won't be letting her influence him. You need to have more faith and trust in them. Even if we put a camp bed downstairs in the living-dining room we'd always disturb them every morning at an ungodly hour so that won't work."

"We haven't got a camp bed!"

"Exactly! Anyway, I did remind Beryl that as fifteen year old girls we had to share a bed with her Aunty Irene's two thirteen year old boys and we were top to toe with them. The boys absolutely hated it but had no choice!"

"Well, it's on your head, so make sure nothing else happens."

"Yes dear. Thank you for your support!"

Gary just grunted and grabbed his coat and headed out to work on the north field.

Karen sighed, she knew the next few weeks were going to be testing, but she had to hope Adam and Jocelyn would settle down and become friends. Only time would tell if she would regret letting Jocelyn stay under the circumstances.

#

Adam stirred as he felt the bed rocking slightly and he turned over to see what was going on, just in time to catch Jocelyn finishing putting her skirt on and pulling it up to her waist then seeing he was looking at her.

"Cheeky! Lucky I was finished dressing!"

"I didn't know, why didn't you go out to the bathroom and dress?"

"You were fast asleep and snoring so I figured I could get dressed here but as I pulled on my skirt I fell back a little and bumped the bed. Sorry if I woke you," she came round to his side of the bed and looked at his forehead. "How does it feel?"

"Headache's almost gone, just a bit sore on my knees and that cut on my head."

"Adam, I really am sorry. I'll go to the bathroom now, when I come back will you be up and dressed?"

"Guess so. Well, go on then as I'm not getting dressed with you in here!"

Jocelyn smiled at him and almost skipped out of the bedroom, closing the door behind her. Adam slid out of bed and began rummaging in the lower drawer for his clothes, dressed, then sat on the bed waiting. Several minutes later there was a light knock on the door and without waiting Jocelyn entered.

"Hey! I didn't say you could come in. I might have still been getting dressed!"

"Liar, liar, pants on fire! You were sat waiting so must have finished as you're fully dressed!"

Adam looked at her warily, then smiled having been sussed out by her. "OK Jossy, we'd best go down otherwise Aunty Karen will begin to fuss!"

"DON'T call me Jossy! Mum and Dad calls me that and I hate it! Never again, right?"

"Alright Jocelyn, sorry."

With that they hurried downstairs to see Aunty Karen putting out two plates of bacon sandwiches and two empty bowls with a packet of cornflakes at the side with a jug of milk and the sugar bowl all ready for them.

It didn't take long for them to polish off breakfast.

"So, what are you two going to do today? It's not too bad a day and they say it will be mainly sun and cloud but no rain, not that we trust the forecast mind you!" Aunty Karen said as she cleared away their plates and bowls onto her tray.

"We can go out and I can take Adam to explore the footpaths nearby."

"Nope, not doing that!" retorted Adam as Aunty Karen came back and examined the plaster on his head.

"Looks like the doc was right, just a minor scratch. You feeling alright this morning then Adam?"

He seized his chance. "I have a bit of a headache and told Jocelyn about it."

"THAT was when we woke up Uncle Gary, not when we finally got up and you said to me you were feeling better!"

"Adam?" asked Karen as she looked at him expectantly.

"I sort of feel alright but my knees do hurt a little now I've come downstairs," he said meekly and looked down at the table.

"Let me see them." Aunty Karen stooped down as Adam rolled up his right trouser leg and she nodded. "Small cuts will smart for a while and you'll soon have the bruises appearing. I was expecting that so I guess the other knee is the same?"

"Yes. The other one doesn't hurt quite as much."

"Alright. If you want to read then the living room is nice and bright and gets a bit of sun when it is out in the morning. What are you going to do then, Jocelyn?"

"Can I go outside to the swing please?" Adam gave her a nasty look but she ignored it, although it did dawn on her she perhaps hadn't been very tactful.

"Very well, but do be careful after yesterday. Can't have me calling for uncle Gary to come away from his work to take you to hospital if you fall off! Promise?"

"Yes, Aunty, I promise."

She gave Adam a sideways look as if expecting him to say something, but he kept quiet. Jocelyn smiled at Karen then walked out to get her shoes on as Adam watched her leave.

"You're not her aunty, are you?"

"No, but I am her godmother and have known her since birth, so she's always known me as Aunty Karen. Just like I've known you since you were a wee little baby and we're family as your mother is my sister."

Adam tilted his head taking in this information, then shuffled off his chair and wandered out of the kitchen and into the living room. Although to him it was one long room, Uncle Gary had taken down the wall between two rooms to create a large living-dining room which took up three quarters of the northern half of the somewhat large farmhouse.

On the small coffee table, he spotted his book, 'The Boys Book of Astronomy and Space' and picked it up, settling on the settee to read.

Aunty Karen came in with a glass of

lemonade and set it down as she winked at him. "Don't tell Jocelyn, I think as you're the injured party and recovering you are deserving of this lemonade. Oh, that's the book I had to tell a little white lie about to Jocelyn's parents and say it was Uncle Gary's!"

Adam burst out laughing at the thought his uncle would read his book. He couldn't imagine his uncle reading anything, let alone a book about space and the stars.

Karen sussed what he was thinking. "Now young man, your uncle does read sometimes, he just prefers to get his information from the news and the TV or radio."

"Sorry Aunty, it just felt odd to think he would read my book."

"Well, he didn't and as far as I know he hasn't even looked at or noticed it. Now, will you be alright as I'm going to be busy for the next few hours as a woman's work is never done?"

He nodded and turned back to his book.

She left him to read undisturbed, still wondering how the next few weeks were going to pan out.

#

An hour later and Adam didn't hear Jocelyn enter as he was so engrossed in studying the cutaway diagram of the Apollo capsule.

"Whatcha doing?" she asked, startling him

and he gave her an angry look but didn't reply as it was obvious he was reading.

"Sorry, I got bored being on the swing on my own. You still reading?"

He gave her another stern look and shook his head. Jocelyn then spotted the empty glass and looked at it wide eyed.

"You've had lemonade! Aunty Karen, Aunty Karen!" Jocelyn walked out of the room calling for Karen as Adam went back to his book. A short while later Jocelyn came back in with a glass filled almost to the brim and in danger of spilling. She took a sip and smiled.

"That's good! When I've finished this, come with me, I want to show you something in the back garden."

Adam shook his head and grunted, something to which Jocelyn decided to interpret as a 'yes' although she knew it was really a 'no'.

But she had to do something as she was bored. Normally it hadn't bothered her on past holidays as she'd known she would be on her own so had happily explored the surrounding countryside.

But that was two years earlier and she was only allowed to go so far. The woods to the north and northeast had terrified her when she had tried to follow a path that passed through them and she'd given up. It felt this could be a good time to try again, with someone with her this time. But now she had someone to explore with, all he wanted was to be boring and read!

She quickly downed her lemonade making sure she made a noisy slurping sound at the last drops, then set the glass down next to his empty one. She looked at him, then the glasses, before promptly picking them up and taking them out to the kitchen.

"Aunty Karen has enough to do without cleaning up after us two!"

She came back into the front room and scowled at Adam who was still engrossed in his book. "Come on Adam, just do this one thing for me. You'll like it, promise!"

"NO!"

Karen walked in at that moment. "Everything okay?"

"Adam has his nose stuck in that book and won't come outside with me."

Karen smiled at her sweetly as she had an idea. "Tell you what Jocelyn, you have the rest of the morning playing outside," Karen leaned in and whispered into her ear, "and I'll see if I can twist his arm in the meantime," she winked at Jocelyn as Adam looked up, a little suspicious at hearing them whispering, but he was non the wiser.

Jocelyn gave him a sad look then walked out much to Adam's relief, but Aunty Karen came over and sat next to him.

"Listen Adam. I know you are a bookworm and that you're not an outdoorsy type, but trust me when I tell you that us girls never give up. Jocelyn will keep asking until you give in. So after lunch I want you to go outside with her and see what it is she wants to show you. Then at least you can say you've done as she wanted and you can go back to your reading. Is that fair?"

Adam looked at her and nodded quietly. He knew deep down that Jocelyn wasn't going to let him off the hook, so perhaps it was best to get it over with, after lunch of course!

Karen left him to his book as she went out to the utility room to sort the laundry out. The mangle was waiting for her and she had a lot to do.

Lunchtime came and went with just a little chit chat, mainly between Karen and Jocelyn. Adam was puzzled that Uncle Gary didn't come in for lunch until Aunty Karen told him she always packed him a big lunch with beef and horseradish sandwiches, a sausage roll and a hefty slice of Farmhouse cake along with a large flask of tea.

It was true that a farmer's work was also never done and she told them both how hard their uncle worked to keep the farm going.

"Adam, you've had a good morning resting and reading so just for me, will you go and let Jocelyn show you the back garden?"

He looked over to Jocelyn who looked at him with her soft brown eyes, pleading with him to say yes.

"Alright. As long as we don't go near the swing!"

Jocelyn was all smiles now. "No, of course not. I got bored with the swing this morning so don't want to play on it for a while. Thanks Adam. You'll only need your shoes as it's dry outside," by now she was standing up and looked back at him, "You coming?"

Adam sighed and nodded reluctantly.

They put their shoes on in the hallway and she headed for the back door with Adam following on a little slower, until Aunty Karen gave him a look that said, *be good and go with her!*

Outside she held out her hand for him to take but he looked at her horrified. Be led by a girl? No way!

She shrugged. "Be like that then. Come on, follow me," she retorted and set off following the farmhouse wall until they reached an archway and, stepped through into a large allotment surrounded by a tall brick wall with a fairly large greenhouse at the far end.

"Aunty Karen and Uncle Gary grow their own food all year round, so everything we have is fresh. Over on the far side there is a large section for potatoes, broccoli and cauliflower, all growing for the autumn and winter. They grow carrots, peas on the vine on that side too, and beans, several types in fact. On this side is all the salad crops, look how much lettuce there is. That's why there is a brick wall surrounding us, so the rabbits can't get in and ruin them. Looks like there's radishes, oh, turnips, and over there looks like there's strawberries and raspberries."

"Some look half dead!"

"They're for later in the year. Do you like the Beatles?" she suddenly changed topic.

"Err, bugs?"

"Noo, the pop group. I fancy Paul myself."

"Eh?"

"Paul McCartney, he's really good looking!"

"What's this got to do with the garden?"

"Nothing. Just wanted to change the subject."

"Oh."

"Mum fancies someone called Lonnie Donegan. He sings that song, 'My Old Man's a Dustman'. Dad thinks she's barmy, but he once told me he liked Connie Francis - but I've no idea who she is. Do your mum and dad like anyone?"

"I, I don't know. I don't listen to music and I can't remember them saying who they like."

"Everyone has a favourite pop group or singer!"

"Boring!"

"Says the bookworm!"

He looked at her and laughed. "Uncle Gary is hairy!"

"Uncle Gary is a hairy ape!"

They burst out laughing as they reached the back wall near to the greenhouse. There was a bench and they sat down, but not before Adam noticed a little plaque affixed to its wooden back.

"Dedicated to both our parents who loved this garden and wished to be remembered here."

"Yes, that's what I wanted to show you. Uncle Gary put this bench in to remember his parents, Mollie and Geoffrey and Aunty Karen's parents, Mary and Douglas. I gather that they died within weeks of each other, Gary's parents were killed in an air crash and not long afterwards Karen's were killed in a car crash, it was just a few years ago, 1965.

Uncle Gary's parents originally owned this farm and Aunty Karen's parents, your grandparents on her side, used to visit here often. They loved the garden, so Uncle Gary and Aunty Karen put this bench in to remember them by. It's a special place that sometimes they come to and sit here when it's a nice sunny evening in the summer and think about their parents."

Adam thought about this and something like a distant memory surfaced in a vague form.

"Mum's parents, Grandad and Grandma, I was very little, seems like a long time now. We were at a church sat near the front and Mum was crying whilst Dad held her hand. The other grandad was there too."

"That'll be on your Dad's side then. Can you remember them much?"

"No, not much. Grandma did have a smell, Mum said it was the scent of a flower but I can't remember it now. Now I remember, Aunty Karen and Uncle Gary were there as well. They were sat further along the long wooden seat-"

"Pew."

"No, don't go on about how Grandma smelled!"

"No silly, the wooden seats in churches are called pews."

"Oh."

"You were too young I'd say. That's why it's vague. Must have been very sad and they all must have meant a lot to Aunty Karen and Uncle Gary."

"And mum too. She has a picture of them on the mantle piece. Jocelyn …"

"Yes?"

"Thank you for bringing me here. I didn't know."

She held his hand and gently squeezed it.

He grimaced a little. "You're not too bad for a girl."

She let go of his hand and shook her head at him but smiled.

"Uncle Gary is hairy," she giggled.

"Uncle Gary is a hairy ape," he replied and they both split their sides giggling.

Up on the landing with the window partly open, Karen had been watching them and listening as Jocelyn explained everything to Adam. She had a tear in her eye and couldn't help but smile at how the two appeared to be bonding.

She had a good feeling about them.

CHAPTER 4: SHENANIGANS

Adam had to admit that being in the walled garden and hearing stories about his grandparents from Jocelyn as they sat on the bench had been enjoyable. They'd then looked inside the greenhouse to find loads of tomato plants, lots with green tomatoes and some red ones ripened almost ready for harvesting.There were cucumbers, melons and many seedlings they couldn't identify.

Uncle Gary was clearly very busy until they finally went back indoors. Karen smiled at them. "I spotted you two out in the walled garden. Lot's growing well there isn't there! I'm really pleased."

"Why's that then Aunty?" asked Adam, puzzled.

"It's my garden! Your uncle has enough on his plate working the farm and so I have the garden and it helps me relax. You found the memorial bench then?" she stated rather than asked, having seen them sitting together deep in conversation.

"Yes. I told Adam about it as he didn't know."

"Hmm, I guess his mother doesn't talk much about me and your uncle. What made you both break up in fits of giggles then?"

Jocelyn looked quickly at Adam who looked at her and shrugged.

"Adam didn't know who the Beatles are! He thought I was talking about the bugs!" Jocelyn knew it wasn't quite a lie but had to think quickly and Adam surprisingly cottoned on and nodded enthusiastically.

"Doesn't surprise me. I expect in his home it's all Bach, Mozart and the like!"

Adam seemed to think for a moment then nodded. "I think I've heard those names talked about by Mum. Dad likes lots of band music which I think is loud and noisy!"

"The Glenn Miller Band, I suspect. It's his favourite. They're OK actually, I quite like their tunes. Anyhow you two, go upstairs and have a wash and be back down in half an hour as I'll be setting the table for when his lord and master gets in. He'll be hungry and will want to watch the news, so remember, keep quiet at the dinner table!"

#

They sat obediently at the table, Uncle Gary in his usual place at the head of the table with Adam on his right and Jocelyn on the left facing him, while Aunty Karen sat at the other end opposite Gary.

The news was on but Adam was disappointed that this evening there was no mention of the moon mission. He sat and quietly munched on his broccoli and cut a thin slice of chicken ready to cram it into his mouth. Jocelyn kept looking around; she too knew she had to keep quiet but even though she was enjoying dinner, she was bored with the television always being on for the news.

She slightly raised her right leg under the table, dropped it back then raised her left leg before bringing it back down. She did it again but raised it higher and suddenly Adam's face scrunched up and he looked about wondering what was going on. He kept quiet as she noted his reaction and tentatively lifted her left leg high enough to again catch Adam on his knee.

He glared at her as Uncle Gary didn't seem to notice as he was concentrating on the news and Aunty Karen was enjoying her meal. He kicked back and caught her on the ankle but she kept her cool and kicked back in retaliation.

Back and forth they continued, but Aunty Karen was becoming aware that something was going on.

Jocelyn kicked again causing Adam to kick back and he struck her leg ...

... or so he thought, as Aunty Karen winced and let out a stifled cry at which point Uncle Gary seemed to lose his fixation with the TV and began to look at Adam, as Karen was staring at him, annoyed.

"What's going on? Adam?"

Adam looked mortified. Rather than blaming it on Jocelyn for starting it, he looked meekly at his aunty.

"Sorry Aunty Karen. I was swinging my leg and didn't mean to kick you."

Gary, however, had been paying more attention than anyone realised.

"You kids can't pull the wool over my eyes. I noticed the subtle tell-tale signs that you were kicking each other under the table. And look what happened, you kicked your aunty which is downright naughty."

Both of them lowered their heads knowing they were spoiling their stay. It was about to get worse.

"Adam, for kicking your aunty, up to your bedroom now, no more dinner for you."

Adam looked at him in horror, "But, bu-"

"NO ARGUMENTS OR TALKING BACK. GO NOW!"

Adam was in shock and looked at his aunty for help.

"You heard what your uncle said. Up to your room."

Gary glared now at Jocelyn as Adam fled upstairs in tears. "Don't think I didn't spot who started it first. Go to your room and no more dinner for you either!"

Jocelyn didn't answer back or look at either of them but pushed away from the table and rushed out, bursting into tears as she did so.

"Gary …"

"Don't 'Gary' me. They know the rules about dinner time and deliberately ignored them.

Jocelyn may have started it, but Adam should have moved his seat a little further away so she couldn't reach him. Instead he wilfully chose to kick back. The result? He kicked you instead. He may not have intended to do so but a lesson has to be taught here and hopefully they will learn it. We have over five more weeks with them so discipline is vital if we are to get through the next month or so."

"I know love, but they're only being kids."

"No excuse. And Karen, I don't want you to pamper them after this. They have to learn their place and behave if they're staying here."

"And what if they don't and misbehave again?"

"I have their parents emergency contacts, there's a telephone box in Scrawford and I'm quite prepared to go down there and make the calls."

"My dearest hubby, I do agree that they should be told off and I think you know deep down this will have an effect on them and they will behave after this.

But really, calling their parents? Adam's are in the arctic circle doing vital research and Jocelyn's parents are somewhere on a cruise ship in the Caribbean! All that effort to get hold of them and for what?

I can just see Marion and Bob's faces now when you say you can't cope with their unruly and naughty boy. Adam? Adam, unruly?

Naughty? They'd be gob smacked at the thought.

As for Beryl and Henry, again, that girl is one of the nicest and politest of girls, and quite mature for her age too. They'd be highly puzzled that you were unable to cope with her and had to ruin their holiday.

We all have our off days, my god, you have enough of them. So, yes, tonight is a good lesson for both kids, but mark my words, it's time you started acting like a human being and not spending every dinner time glued to that box in the corner of the room. There's more to life than that box.

You proved it the first evening Adam was here when you talked to him about that moon mission malarkey. You initiated the conversation whilst the news was on and he was clearly in shock, knowing that you didn't like to talk at the dinner table. But did you notice how much it boosted his confidence when his uncle took an interest in what he finds fascinating?"

Gary grimaced at her, but she'd hit a nerve or two and deep down he had to admit that much of what she'd said was true.

"You always were good in an argument. The punishment still stands tonight though as they have to learn to behave at all times."

"Yes, love. I quite agree - to an extent. Now, I think the bigger person should show some compassion and let me go to them and bring them back. They will have to apologise to you and mean it as I've not cooked this meal and slaved over a hot stove for it to go to waste. Agreed?"

Gary nodded. Karen took both unfinished plates out into the kitchen and placed saucepan lids on them as she put them in the still warm oven.

She and Gary finished their dinners but before desert Karen looked at Gary and he again nodded.

She left and he waited patiently. At least it was now only the local news and then the weather so there was nothing to disturb.

A few minutes later he heard soft footsteps on the hallway tiled floor, then some mutterings, presumably Karen having words with the two children.

She entered the room with both of them keeping their heads down as she brought them round to their respective places at the table, then Karen coughed.

They looked up then burst into tears and rushed to each side of Gary, crying that they didn't mean to upset him and they were really sorry and they would be on their best behaviour from now on.

Gary sat there slightly taken aback but held them around their waists and gave them a gentle hug.

"So, you'll be good?"

In unison: "Yes Uncle Gary."

"Promise?"

Again in unison: "Yes Uncle Gary."

"Very well. Now, both of you apologise to Aunty Karen as she was the one who was kicked!"

They both rushed round the table and hugged her too.

In unison: "Sorry Aunty Karen."

"Good. Now, your aunty has slaved over a hot stove to make us dinner and so far these last few days I haven't heard anyone offer to help her. So from now on, both of you will help with the washing and drying up and if she needs any help with the household chores you will help without question. Understood?"

They both nodded as Aunty Karen brought in their dinners for them to finish.

"When you've eaten all that and cleared your plates mind, I don't want to see anything left, Aunty Karen might let you have her homemade chocolate sponge pudding with custard. That's if you are good!"

Adam and Jocelyn eagerly nodded and tucked in to the remains of their main course, relishing the prospect of pudding.

Karen looked at Gary and smiled with satisfaction. Calling the parents had been scuppered she hoped, as she fetched the pudding and jug of custard in to serve up.

CHAPTER 5: COMPROMISES!

The rest of the week took a downturn with the weather as several light storms passed over the county and for a while it felt like the rain wouldn't stop. Fortunately, they weren't heavy downpours, more a consistent drizzle, but Uncle Gary was concerned about the crops in the field, as well as the state of the front bedroom with it's leaky roof.

He'd convinced the kids to keep an eye on the buckets and bowls in the affected bedroom and empty them before they got too full by tipping them into the bath, easier for them to do that than in the wash basin.

Mid week and he was standing looking out of the living room window at the sky, having returned from the fields and was enjoying a large cup of coffee. Adam and Jocelyn had smaller cups of weak sweet milky tea as the weather was also cold for the time of year. They were sitting on the settee as their uncle bemoaned the conditions.

"It's not good I tell you kids. Rain is one thing when it helps the crops to grow, but too much of it at one time can cause the wheat to collapse and lie flat on the ground. Terrible for harvesting towards the end of this month. I could do with a spell of warm, sunny weather, you know, the sort of thing you expect in August!"

Jocelyn got up, turned round and knelt on

the settee just to Gary's right looking out the window and shook her head.

"Anything we can do Uncle?"

"No love. We're at the mercy of the elements I'm afraid, nowt any of us can do except hope for a change in the weather."

"Is it really serious, Uncle? Will we have to leave?" Adam could see the weather was bothering his uncle but would it mean they couldn't stay, he wondered.

"Oh Adam, no my boy, it is more of a nuisance as I have a wide range of crops. I have sheep and a few beef cattle and your aunty sells some of her garden produce to villagers in Scrawford, so we're okay. We had quite a few lambs last spring and we did well with them, they fetched a good price. It's just annoying that's all. You tend to feel helpless and at the mercy of the weather.

Now, I know you two still have plenty of time staying here it would seem, but trust me it'll pass by so quickly, you'll be wondering what happened to the summer holiday. The long-range forecast implies it may be a better week next week, so I'd like to suggest something to you both.

You can't tell your parents, they don't understand the ways of the countryside and are far too cautious, especially yours Adam, but do you want to ride in the tractor and trailer? It'd just be for a few hours. We'd go up to the fields and scatter some turnips and swedes for the sheep as they love 'em they do. What do you say?"

Jocelyn was virtually buzzing with excitement, as for Adam …

"I'd be in a lot of trouble with Mum and Dad if they found out."

"Well Adam, don't tell them!" Jocelyn retorted and looked at him as much to say, 'don't say no to this'.

Uncle Gary chuckled. "There is a catch … you both have to say yes or neither of you can do it."

Jocelyn gave Adam such a stare that he meekly nodded and said no more.

Uncle Gary just winked at Jocelyn as much to say 'good girl'. They turned back to looking out the window as the rain seemed to get harder and they could hear it splashing against the windows. Time to check on the buckets and bowls in the bedroom, Jocelyn nudged Adam and lifted her eyes to the ceiling, their little sign to do their duty.

#

Next day it was still persisting it down as Uncle Gary had called it that morning, before having to go out in it. Jocelyn had finished her breakfast and took her dirty dishes out to the kitchen and washed them up, placing them on the drying rack.

Aunty Karen came down the stairs and into the kitchen and stopped as Jocelyn seemed as if she wanted to say something.

"What's on your mind Jocelyn?"

"I didn't bring any wellies this time as I forgot as it was two years since I was last here. I don't mind the rain and Adam is being boring again and reading his book. Why are boys so boring?"

"Oh my dear, each to their own. Lots of boys his age love doing the things you do when you're here. Exploring, going out and making your own fun. You're a tom-boy when all is said and done whereas Adam just happens to be a bookworm and loves finding out about things, he follows his parents like that. You know that Adam's mother is my sister? Well, she was the bookworm in our family and I was like you, a tom-boy. I'd go out and play no matter what the weather was like. Give me my wellies and coat and I'd be outside for hours, jumping in and out of puddles, making mud pies, you name it."

"But I thought you were from somewhere down south?"

"Ahh, we lived on the outskirts of Gloucester in a village called Painswick. Those were the days, I must have explored almost every nook and cranny and ranged over many a field in my time."

"Is that how you met Uncle Gary then?"

"Oh no. He's a yellowbelly."

"Huh?"

"That's what someone who's born in Lincolnshire is called, a yellowbelly. No, I can see your mind working. No one has an actual yellow belly. It's a bit of a mystery as some say it's down to an unusual rare newt with a yellowish belly only found in the county fens. Others say it was the yellow waistcoats of the Royal North Lincolnshire Militia, some say it's down to the long shaggy wool of the Lincoln Longwool breed of sheep. When they grazed in fields of mustard their bellies became covered in the yellow pollen of the mustard flowers.

So, who knows the real reason for the nickname, but the golden rule is that you have to be born here."

"So Uncle Gary was born here?"

"Actually, yes, in this very farmhouse. It's been in his family since the eighteen hundreds and he inherited it from his father. Actually, his parents, you know, Mollie and Geoffrey who passed away a few years ago. They decided to hand over the farm to Gary and me so they could retire from all the hard work.

They had worked so hard, they made sure they saved every penny so were able to buy a bungalow on the outskirts of Horncastle and let us move in here and manage the farm. When they passed away in that awful air crash, Gary inherited the farm and its lands, so it's ours."

"It's sad that they had to pass away like that,

but if Uncle was always local then how did you two meet?"

"My father knew Geoffrey, so a bit like you, I would come up as a young girl and stay for a week here. Naturally I would see a young Gary, although he is two years older than me. Strapping lad he was. I fell instantly for him and when I went back home we began to write to each other, which was quite challenging for him as his writing was awful. But the thrill of seeing I had another letter from him, ahh, those were the days. He really tried his best to win me over with his letters and the rest as they say, is history."

"That's nice, I know Uncle Gary is strict but I'm glad you two got together."

"Yes, it's not all plain sailing, but life is about compromises. I tell him what to do, and he does it!"

Jocelyn giggled. "Like the other night?"

"Exactly!"

"So changing the subject, do you have any wellies?"

"Good point, we got waylaid didn't we! Yes, I'm sure I have a few pairs, one must fit you."

"Do you think there's a pair for Adam?"

"Seriously?"

"I'll be like you, it's a compromise, I'll tell him he's going out in the rain and he'll do it!"

"Oh Jocelyn, how innocent you can be. Gary and I are married."

"And?"

"Sweetheart, you can't go ordering Adam about, you're not married and you're not family!"

"Oh. Perhaps it's worth a try?"

"Good luck with that but don't forget, you two have to get along as we've nowhere else to put you!"

"Oh well, worth thinking about."

They walked through the kitchen and out the back door, across the yard to one of the outhouses. Karen opened the door and began to rummage through several piles of old clothes, footwear and finally – a pair of wellies that she placed next to Jocelyn's feet and sized them up.

"A little on the big size but if we add in some thick socks of your uncle's then you should be alright."

They headed back indoors and Karen went upstairs for a short while before coming down smiling, holding a pair of socks. "There you are."

Jocelyn took them and went out into the hallway to the small chair that was just next to the door. She'd sometimes wondered about the chair but it all came clear now as she sat down, took her shoes off, donned the socks and slipped the wellies on. Almost perfect fit.

Aunty Karen had fetched her raincoat and handed it over as Jocelyn gleefully put it on then playfully shouted, "Thanks Aunty Karen, I'm going outside to enjoy myself now!"

Adam just ignored her and carried on reading.

#

He was getting annoyed now. It kept happening and he couldn't concentrate.

Once again Jocelyn was in the front yard and was jumping in and out of puddles, especially those she knew were outside the front living room window. Guaranteed to annoy a certain bookworm!

However, Aunty Karen was beginning to notice that Adam was becoming upset. After all, what he was doing was not affecting or hurting anyone else and it seemed Jocelyn was being a little selfish. She opened the front door, just keeping back enough not to get wet from the rain and as soon as Jocelyn came past, she looked at her sternly. Jocelyn stopped and came up to her.

"Everything alright Aunty?"

"Now Jocelyn, I think you know what the matter is."

"No?"

Karen tilted her head at her. "Let me put it like this. How would you feel if Adam deliberately hid your wellies and socks so you couldn't go outside in the rain? What if he also hid your raincoat? How would you feel?"

"I, I'd be upset and angry with him! It would be mean!"

"So, with that in mind, how do you think Adam feels with you jumping about deliberately outside the window distracting him? Is that fair do you think?"

Jocelyn looked down at her wet wellies.

"I, oh."

"Penny dropped has it?"

Jocelyn meekly came in, sat on the chair and took off her wellies and socks, put her slippers back on and walked into the living room before standing, swaying slightly to get Adam's attention.

"What?" he asked a little grumpily.

"Sorry for the noise I was making outside the window. I've come in now and I'll be quiet, promise."

"Huh!" Adam went back to his Boys' Book of Astronomy and Space.

Meanwhile, Karen had an idea.

"Look you two, the weatherman got it wrong and it is looking bad for a few days, so you need to be considerate to each other. I have an idea. There are quite a few board games stashed away upstairs in the small room next to the bathroom. It's filled with all sorts of stuff but if you can find the games, why not play with them together whilst it's wet outside. That will mean that Jocelyn will be indoors rather than exploring as it's not a good idea with this weather, BUT, Adam, when the weather clears up, then you must be good and go out exploring with her – it's only fair! Am I clear?"

In unison – "Yes Aunty Karen."

Karen smiled inwardly. A result!

CHAPTER 6: THE COTTAGE NEAR THE WOOD
Saturday August 2nd

The living room was normally quiet with Adam reading but now ...

Karen shook her head as she heard the laughter and occasional shouts coming from the room as Jocelyn and Adam played, first KerPlunk, Jocelyn winning three of the four games before Adam became bored, then onto Frustration where they both won three games each before Karen found them her favourite, the game of Mousetrap.

The noise of laughter, giggles, and finally "MOUSETRAP" shouted triumphantly by Jocelyn, seemed to indicate they were having a good time that managed to last all through the day. Then the next, and the following morning. Gary was most impressed with Karen's quick thinking as both kids had become so well behaved at the evening mealtimes that he had peace and quiet. The small black and white TV they watched was usually only on for the news for Gary, but both Jocelyn and Adam knew that it was on later on in the evenings when they retired to bed as they could sometimes hear it.

But it was now the weekend and with all his work done, Gary was looking forward to sitting down and watching Grandstand on BBC1 later that day, so they had instructions to keep quiet. Which is why, that morning, with no rain and the skies sunny with occasional fluffy clouds, Adam now had to endure going outside to explore the countryside with Jocelyn. Unlike Jocelyn's parents, Adam's had packed his coat and wellies, although they suspected they would hardly be used.

Well, now they would be.

Jocelyn led the way out of the front courtyard and down the dirt track, following it as it wound its way roughly towards the west. Adam had no idea where they were going or what the plan was, but then Jocelyn found the place where the old footpath began.

"Found it, thought I remembered it! We can follow this, there's a spooky old cottage on the edge of the woods. Let's see if we can get in and explore."

"Why?"

"Why what?"

"Go in a spooky house, doesn't sound fun!"

"Because this is what I want to do, remember what Aunty Karen got us both to promise? I would play games with you indoors when it was raining but when the weather cleared, you were to explore outside with me."

Adam grimaced. "Nothing was said about a spooky house!"

"Adam's getting frightened, Adam's getting frightened! Frighty pants! Frighty pants!"

"Stop it! I'm not! Let's go!"

Jocelyn's ploy had worked and before she knew it, Adam was up and over the stile but then looking about as he couldn't see the path, to him the field was just grass with a few sheep in it. Jocelyn climbed over the stile, wishing she had trousers on instead of a mid length skirt. She saw Adam's confusion so pointed across the field to a hedge with a gap in it and another wooden stile. "There you are," she briskly began to walk towards it and Adam ran to keep up.

They walked in silence across the field as the few sheep there just watched them, then went back to grazing. Over the second stile and there was a faint path that headed off to the northwest towards a thin stretch of woodland and in the distance, there was the rather sad looking cottage.

They reached it but didn't try to enter. Jocelyn looked at it thoughtfully, "It's worse than I remember from my last holiday here."

"Well, I'm not going in there!" declared Adam as he surveyed the rundown cottage. The roof had partially collapsed on the left-hand side, but Jocelyn was intrigued and sidled up to the partially collapsed wall and, picking her footfall carefully, she stepped on the bricks that looked stable and peered in.

She climbed a bit higher and tested the remains of the wall before leaning over it to look inside. A slight breeze had picked up and wafted her skirt up showing her panties and Adam averted his eyes and turned away, embarrassed for her.

She looked back to tell him what she could see and saw he was looking away. "What's up?"

"The wind lifted your skirt and I've always been told to look away."

"Ah, that's so kind of you! But I'm not worried, it happens and it's too warm to wear trousers so I don't really care. Anyway, we're sort of honorary family now, so not to worry. Now if I didn't have any knickers on that would be different! But I wouldn't do that, would I?"

"Guess not."

"You wouldn't go out without your pants on would you?"

"Course not!"

"There you are then. Anyway, looks like apart from bits of the roof, there's nothing been left inside the front room."

"So can we go then?"

Jocelyn seemed to pause for a moment, lost in thought, then seemed to come back to her normal self.

"Oh Adam, you are so boring! Let's go round the back."

Reluctantly he followed her as she walked round the side of the cottage only to find a dilapidated wooden fence which she tested to see how sturdy it really was. Something kept urging her on and, satisfied it was safe, Jocelyn climbed up and over the fence as Adam just shook his head and obediently followed her lead.

There was a back door partially hanging off it's rusty hinges and she poked her head inside. "Can't see anything as it's so dark inside."

She pushed past the door as Adam watched, wondering what they might find.

Suddenly, "Well? Are you coming in or what?" Jocelyn called out from inside. Adam took a deep breath and slipped past the door and into the gloom where it took a few seconds for his eyes to adjust.

"BOO!" Jocelyn shouted as Adam jumped out of his skin, grabbed at the wall and accidentally pulled some of the deteriorating plaster off and onto the floor.

"That wasn't nice!" he managed to say as he caught his breath and stared at her with daggers.

"Scaredy cat, scaredy cat!"

But Adam's attention had been drawn to the other side of the room as his nose began to pick up on the awful musty smell. There was something there, or rather …

… someone lying face down on the floor with very dirty and scruffy looking clothes.

Dead.

Jocelyn turned and as her eyes adapted to the gloom she screamed and ran out, pushing at the door so it finally came away from its hinges.

Adam dodged past it as it clattered to the floor and was hot on her heels as they both raced back to the farmhouse shouting for Uncle Gary and Aunty Karen.

Gary was not happy at being disturbed, it was only early afternoon so there was still plenty more sport to watch, but as the two began to settle down and catch their breaths he managed to get out of them what had spooked them so much.

"The cottage? What the run down one at the edge of Ashton copse?"

Neither of them knew its name but Jocelyn ran outside and pointed roughly in the direction and Gary nodded.

"Karen, I'd best go and see. If it's what I suspect then I'll come back for the car and will have to go into Scrawford to the telephone box and call for the police and ambulance," he turned to the kids. "You two stay here and don't go anywhere for the time being. Play games or whatever but for today, no more roaming, alright?"

In unison, "Yes Uncle."

Half an hour later he was back, grim faced, had a few words with Karen then took their car and left. In the meantime, Karen convinced them to sit and watch Grandstand, but did allow Adam to have his book as he kept losing interest.

"Kids, I'm going to do a salad for tonight as I don't know how long your uncle is going to be away for. Adam, there's a new series started a few weeks ago on a Saturday that I think you might like, something called Star Trek, so if Uncle Gary isn't back by then, I'll let you watch TV and have your salad early.

Adam's eyes went wide with excitement. "Star Trek? Sounds like space?"

"Here's what it says in the Radio Times: 'A Taste of Armageddon'. Conflicts between peoples must be settled by diplomacy if they are not to be settled by war. Which is why the Enterprise carries an ambassador from earth to establish diplomatic relations with a distant planet. However, they are already at war with their neighbour, and have been for 500 years.'

Oh, I'm not sure that's suitable for someone like you but, well, I gather it is aimed more for the younger generation and it's on before the news so perhaps we can watch it. If I think it isn't suitable then I will switch it off. Understood?"

"Yes Aunty."

"Aunty?"

"Yes Jocelyn?"

"Do I have to watch it?"

"Be a good girl and watch it with Adam, it might help take your mind off what you found this afternoon. Then I'll see if I can find something you might like for another day."

"Alright. I hope I don't fall asleep with boredom!"

"Sometimes you just have to give something a try and you never know, you might like it."

After an hour of trying to watch Grandstand,

both Adam and Jocelyn were getting bored so Jocelyn went out of the room and came back shortly afterwards with the game of Frustration.

Karen let them play as they laughed and then moaned as each had good falls of the dice as they pressed the central pop-o-matic dice thrower.

Then the end titles of Grandstand came on and the announcer told them what would be on later in the evening, something called 'Dee Time', 'Comedy Choice: Further Adventures of Lucky Jim: Home, James', then later, the 'Roy Castle Show' but what caught their attention was the announcement of the Tom and Jerry cartoon straight after the news.

Then, as if it came from Adam's wildest dreams, the opening titles of 'Star Trek' began as the majestic starship raced towards, then away, from the screen then orbited a strange but wonderful planet, Adam was immediately hooked.

Jocelyn sat patiently, not being into machines as such, but as views of the bridge of the Enterprise was shown, there was a stunning woman, Uhura, who seemed to be just as important as the rest of the crew and Jocelyn was drawn into this strange new world.

Aunty Karen watched carefully but gradually relaxed as it seemed harmless enough, noting how Jocelyn was now just as captivated as Adam. She suggested that she should turn it off, but both kids implored her not to and Karen knew she'd found something to keep them quiet for the coming Saturdays.

Jocelyn wasn't sure of the person with pointed ears but had already fallen for the captain of the ship, whilst Adam was mesmerised by the majestic starship. It finished and it was clear Adam was completely bowled over. Jocelyn smiled at him as he tried to mimic the opening titles music as he sat there with a big grin on his face, but then the news and weather came on.

Thoughts turned to Uncle Gary who had not got back yet, but then as the weatherman finished, Tom and Jerry came on with an episode entitled 'Life with Tom' and both of them sat laughing their socks off at the antics of Tom the cat as Jerry the mouse always got the better of him.

Aunty Karen called them into the dining room when it finished and they took their places to start on the salads she had prepared. Every so often they glanced at his empty seat at the table; Gary was noticeable by his absence.

Evening meal finished, Aunty Karen let them watch some more television in the living room, until the 'Roy Castle show' finished at just after eight pm and still no sign of Uncle Gary.

Aunty Karen kept looking out of the living room window for a car's lights as she convinced them to play MouseTrap, until finally at eight forty five pm, a car pulled into the front yard, parked up and Uncle Gary entered taking his light jacket off and embracing Karen. Jocelyn and Adam rushed into the hallway and gave him a hug.

"What's happened Uncle Gary?" Jocelyn asked and he led them into the living room.

"Kids, it is one of those unfortunate things where sometimes things happen and you have no control over the outcome. A few weeks ago I had spotted a rough looking person loitering in Ashton Wood near to the cottage and I had approached him, asking him to be gone.

He did apologise and mumbled about just passing through the area and I didn't see him again. I don't need to go to the cottage as there's nothing there to salvage and it could do with being pulled down, but it looks like the tramp must have taken up residence and sadly passed away.

The police have found some identification as he did have a small wallet with no money, but a few scraps of paper and some photos of what they think may have been either a wife or girlfriend so they are going to try to find them to inform them.

The ambulance crew reckon he'd been dead for several days, maybe up to five days, so there is nothing any of us could have done. They think it was a heart attack. You did the right thing in telling me and they've now taken the body away and the police will keep me informed as to what they find out."

"You're not in trouble are you Gary?" Karen looked concerned at him and he shook his head.

"Oh, of course not. There's no suggestion of suspicious circumstances. The ambulance man said to me, it looked like it was quick and he just collapsed on the spot. He would have been there ages if it wasn't for you two going off and exploring the cottage. Mind you, it isn't really safe to go inside, the roof has partially collapsed and the wooden stairs inside are mostly filled with woodworm so you can't walk up them. So from now on, promise me you won't go into it again?"

"Promise."

"I promise as well," added Adam.

"Good, anyway, I'm tired and very hungry ..." he glanced at Karen.

"Good thing I have a Cornish pasty in the oven keeping warm then, I figured a salad would be no good for you," Karen then turned to the two kids, "Now, we can relax knowing Uncle is back where he belongs, but it is time for bed so you two go up and get yourselves ready and I'll be up in ten minutes to check on you, OK?"

In unison, "Yes, Aunty."

CHAPTER 7: THE LONG WALK
Monday, August 4th

"Looks like a good couple of days, kids, so I'd go outside and enjoy the weather before it's supposed to change towards the end of the week if I were you."

Karen called out in the hope they'd heard her. Gary was down in the south field of the farm with the cattle and was planing to be out all day checking on fencing in different fields of the farm, so she'd packed him his lunch and a flask and hoped that the kids would go out too, so she could get on with some ironing and general household cleaning she'd been putting off.

Jocelyn had surprised Adam by getting up early when he awoke to find her gone. He was taken aback that she had not woken him, so he quickly dressed and went to the bathroom, then made his way downstairs to find Aunty Karen clearing away what he assumed was Jocelyn's breakfast bowl and cup.

"Morning sleepyhead. It was a nice bright sunny morning, so Jocelyn woke up and wanted to enjoy as much of it as she could. She's out on the swing, so it's up to you if you go out to her or stay indoors reading. But it is a nice day and it would be a shame to be stuck indoors, don't you think?"

"I guess so."

"The table is laid and waiting for you, cereal for today and I've done a couple of rounds of thick toast and a hard boiled egg so I hope you are hungry!"

Adam smiled and nodded eagerly, heading into the dining room for breakfast.

#

Jocelyn was still on the swing when Adam walked out of the back door to find her. She was swinging quite high and memories of their first encounter came back to haunt him.

As she swung back, then forward, she launched herself off and landed on both feet like an acrobat and made a bow.

"Good morning my lord Adam, and pray tell, how are you this fine day?"

"Sorry?"

"T'is a fine day for exploring would you not agree? Perhaps your lordship would care to go on an adventure with me today?"

"Are you feeling alright?" he eyed her warily.

"Oh come on, play along please!" Jocelyn put her hands on her hips as she'd seen Aunty Karen do on occasions and shook her head at his lack of imagination.

"Mi'lady, you sound like Penelope from Thunderbirds, you do."

Jocelyn laughed and began to imitate being a marionette, walking jerkily towards him.

"Parker, fetch FAB 1, we have a mission for Mr

Tracy, the boys are out rescuing people so can't help."

Adam's eyes lit up. "You watch Thunderbirds?" he asked incredulously.

"Yes, now come along Parker, are you game to join in?"

Adam began to act like he was being controlled by strings. "Yus, Milady," they both fell about laughing.

"Seriously Adam, I was wondering if you and I could see how far we can get along a footpath that goes to Scrawford. When I was here two years ago, I found the path but it passes partially into a wood and it scared me so I never got through it. But with you, I think we can get further, maybe even to the village. Do you think Parker would help Lady Penelope succeed?"

"OK."

Jocelyn's eyes lit up and she gave him a quick hug which he grunted and tried to wriggle out of, succeeding in the process.

"There are some boggy patches according to Aunty Karen, especially after the recent rain so we'd best have our wellies on, but it is quite warm so I think you'd best have your shorts on, I'm alright as I have my skirt and blouse so I won't get too hot."

With that she pointed to the farmhouse and Adam dutifully ran off back into it to change, amazed that Jocelyn seemed to like one of his favourite shows.

#

With a home made rucksack, courtesy of Aunty Karen and a packed lunch with a sheet they could use to put on the ground, they walked up to the back gate, something that Adam had not done yet, so this was new to him. Jocelyn had a map that Aunty Karen had hand drawn showing roughly where they should go.

As she held the map against the gate Adam looked at it and noted the stream and wood as well as the rough indication of where the path should be.

They looked up over the gate and Adam pointed to a faint path that seemed to wander across the grassy field towards the distant wood.

"Is that the same wood that starts near the old cottage?" he said as he looked around and past the farmhouse. The outbuildings hid the thinner part of the wood so they couldn't see where the cottage was.

"Yes, it starts off quite thin near the cottage, but gets quite thick in the direction of the village and stops short of it. The path goes into it way over there and if I remember right, it goes quite a way in then follows the stream which also wanders in a squiggly way before leaving the wood. I only got so far into the wood before, well, I was only ten and it frightened me, it was quite dark in there and there are lots of sounds too that are scary."

Adam was taking all this in and wondering why he had agreed to this 'adventure'. Then he remembered.

"Mi'lady, I reckon FAB 1 will get stuck so we should go on foot."

"Quite so, Parker, a good observation. Let us continue for we mustn't let Jeff Tracy down or indeed the good name of International Rescue."

With that Jocelyn opened the gate and they marched through together, then Adam closed the gate behind them, remembering what Uncle Gary had drilled into them.

'Always close any gate you open in case sheep or cattle get out and stray.'

They walked for a while, both surprisingly quiet for a change, seemingly deep in their own thoughts. They crossed the field and saw there was no fencing, just the start of a few trees gradually getting denser as they peered into the wood.

Adam saw the look of trepidation on Jocelyn's face and broke the brooding silence. "I've got your back Mi'lady!"

She turned to him with a big grin. "Yes, indeed Parker, shall we continue?"

Adam nodded and they followed the thin path as it entered the wood. A few pinkish flowers were scattered here and there and Jocelyn smiled. "That's herb robert, aren't they pretty?" Adam just nodded as he spotted something with what appeared to be green and purple bell like flowers. He was about to pick one when Jocelyn almost screamed at him.

"NO ADAM! That's deadly nightshade, it's poisonous."

"Oh, you didn't tell me Mi'lady this mission was dangerous!" he tried to keep in character as Jocelyn laughed, but pushed him away from the clump of deadly flowers.

They carried on and then spotted the stream getting closer to the path.

"Have you noticed it's getting a bit boggy now?" Jocelyn observed.

"Yeah, the ground is beginning to squelch under my feet with each step. You sure we're safe doing this?"

"Yes, why else would there be a path?"

"Animals?"

"Oh, true, but I'm sure it must be okay otherwise Aunty Karen wouldn't have drawn us a map!"

"Yus Mi'lady!" they looked at each other and again began laughing. Adam surprised Jocelyn by reaching out and holding her hand before leading the way. Something he wouldn't have done just a week earlier, Jocelyn thought as she felt a warm feeling come over her.

The path began to follow the stream then seemed to disappear until Jocelyn pointed to the other side and it was clear that path crossed the stream at that point.

Adam saw several thick overhanging branches and jumped up, grabbed one and swung himself across, expecting Jocelyn to follow suite. Instead she waded into the stream then let out a yelp.

"ADAM!"

She'd sunk into the stream bed which wasn't too wide, maybe four feet at most. It had looked quite solid with lots of fine but varied sized stones of all sorts of colours littering the stream bed. But now she was stuck with the water just an inch or so below the top of her wellingtons and for once Jocelyn actually looked scared.

"ADAM!" she called again and now looked quite distraught.

"This is a job for International Rescue!" he cried out and before he could explain what he was thinking she put her hands on her hips and looked angrily at him.

"This isn't a time for games, I'm STUCK!"

"Trust me, Mi'lady!" Adam had spotted what he needed and quickly dragged the thick branch which had to be at least eight inches in width. He pushed it out to Jocelyn and laid it across the stream then used the overhanging branches to allow him to step on the branch whilst he held onto the overhanging branches for stability. He made his way across to her which admittedly wasn't far and motioned for her to grab hold of him and use him to climb up to grasp the overhanging branches.

"What about my wellies?" cried Jocelyn.

"Leave them for now mi'lady, I'll get them when you are rescued!"

Jocelyn looked at Adam in a new light and did as she were told, she grabbed his waist then managed to grab the overhanging branch before hauling herself out of her wellies, which on reflection did look funny being left there stuck in the stream. She climbed onto the overhanging branch and followed Adam back to the other side where he'd put the sheet from the rucksack down on the ground so she could step onto it instead of the damp ground.

She looked back forlornly at her stranded wellies but Adam was already in action and managed to balance on the thick branch he'd put across the stream. It took several tugs and pulls but he succeeded in pulling the wellingtons out of the stream bed, noting the grey clay deposits on them.

He dropped them next to Jocelyn who quickly put them on and stood up.

"There must be a layer of clay under the sand and stones we see on the bottom of the stream. Looks solid but easy to get stuck in. Lucky you are not heavy!" Adam observed.

Jocelyn looked at him then flung her arms around his neck and gave him a peck on his cheek, something usually only Aunty Karen and any of his mother's lady friends did when they saw him. He squirmed but for once it made him feel good.

"Parker, you have my thanks."

"Yus, Mi'lady. Shall we go on Mi'lady?"

"Yes Parker, we go on. Although to be honest Adam I'll be glad to get out of this wood!"

They scooped up the sheet and Adam stuffed it back into the rucksack after giving it a good shake and brush down. The path continued to meander away to the north of the stream and a little deeper into the wood but as it looked like Jocelyn was getting close to abandoning their quest, Adam gently held her hand reassuringly as they continued.

Up ahead, the shade of the trees began to lighten and soon they walked out of the wood. In the distance they could see a few rooftops and one or two large houses nestled in the shallow valley.

They stopped to survey the scene just before they reached what looked to be boggy ground as there were plenty of rushes scattered along a rough line following the sides of the valley.

"We'll have our picnic here if you like Adam?"

"Stay in character! Yus Mi'lady!"

Jocelyn smiled, but secretly was beginning to tire of it. She sighed whilst Adam was not paying attention, she'd continue for a little while yet with the charade.

For almost an hour they sat, munched their sandwiches and the slabs of chocolate cake Aunty Karen had baked the previous day. They chatted about school life, what each of their schools were like along with comments about friends or bullies each had encountered.

Fully rested, Adam had to admit he too was tiring of play acting Parker; he much preferred Scott or Virgil Tracy although he did like Thunderbird 3 and Alan.

They cleared everything away and, on checking the map, they worked out a rough route through the boggy ground as they followed what they hoped was the footpath.

Together they reached a slightly higher grassy hill and stopped to survey the scene. Scrawford was much closer now and as they debated whether to carry on down into the village, in the distance a church clock chimed three times.

For a moment it didn't quite sink in, then Jocelyn looked at Adam in alarm. "That was three o'clock! Didn't we set out at nearly ten?"

"Er, yes, I think so. Why?"

"Adam, we've been gone for five hours already! Take off the time for lunch and say a hour for when I was stuck, we'll still not get back in time for dinner! Aunty Karen and Uncle Gary will be worried about us!"

"Oh heck, Mi'lady, time to get back, pity we don't have FAB 1!"

Jocelyn looked at him, but had to chuckle and they about turned and set off trying to be careful as they navigated the boggy patch. Until Adam ran into a very soggy patch and one of his wellies came off, stuck in the mud as he went sprawling headfirst into the rushes.

He stood up and hopped over to his stricken wellington and pulled it out with a loud *swock*, then put it on as Jocelyn tried hard not to laugh at him covered head to toe in mud and dirty water.

"Hey, I didn't laugh at you did I?" he retorted as they both worked their way up and out of the boggy area and headed back towards the wood.

"Sorry, but you do look funny. Actually, you know Uncle Gary thinks you are too much of a bookworm and a sciency type, after this he'll probably like you more!"

It was a challenge but somehow they managed to navigate through the wood, across the stream without either of them getting stuck and finally emerged on the other side of the wood to hear distance cries of their names being called out.

In the distance just past the gate which was wide open, there stood Aunty Karen. She spotted them and put her hands on her hips as they ran as fast as they could to her.

She flung her arms around them both and gathered them in.

"Oh, for heaven's sake, where have you been? You've never been away this long and even your uncle is getting worried. He's headed off to the cottage to see if you'd got stuck in there as we weren't sure if you'd found the other path that skirts the north edge of the wood and round to the cottage. Look at the state you're in Adam, really, what am I to do with you both!"

They walked back and as they entered the farmhouse, Uncle Gary was coming in through the front door and the look of relief on his face said it all.

For once, as dinner was now late, Uncle Gary let them talk about their day exploring as they began to eat their meal and Karen just sat and smiled at how things had changed since the kids had joined them for the summer. Especially Adam, who was so animated as he tried to explain what Jocelyn looked like whilst she was stuck in the stream much to her annoyance, then laughter as they explained they were Lady Penelope and Parker.

Luckily, Uncle and Aunt knew exactly who they were talking about. Meanwhile, Karen couldn't help but think that both of them would sleep like logs that night!

CHAPTER 8: THE LEMONADE FIASCO
Wednesday and Thursday August 6th/7th

Over the rest of the week and into their second week being at the farm, Jocelyn had managed to entice Adam to explore some of the farm outbuildings, taking care not to get in the way of Uncle Gary. He didn't find it particularly exciting if he told the truth, but Adam was realising it was best not to show disappointment when Jocelyn was trying her best to get him out of the farmhouse.

Particularly when her favourite reply was *'we're supposed to be having fun!'*

After their adventure trying to get to the nearest village, even Jocelyn was happy for a time to play with the board games and stay indoors when the weather turned showery. Amazingly, Aunty Karen produced a girl's annual for her to read when Adam became fed up with the games and wanted to read his book.

Mid-week and although the weather was initially warm, there was a chill wind in the air due to a low pressure system drawing down air from the arctic, despite it being summer. Whenever the weatherman mentioned the arctic, Adam's thoughts turned to his parents as he wondered how they were getting on.

In the meantime, scattered showers ran

down the east coast and drifted further inland, scuppering any further exploration of the nearby countryside much to Jocelyn's chagrin.

Late afternoon on the Wednesday, the low pressure moved out towards Scandinavia and Denmark allowing a warm front to move in from the southwest as high pressure began to build again, so Aunty Karen brought out the home made lemonade for them to enjoy. Luckily she had plenty ready made as Adam in particular was quite thirsty.

Aunty Karen also had a surprise for Jocelyn when she noted in the Radio Times that they were showing 'The White Horses' at 5:15pm before teatime, so despite the subtitles and the foreign language she happily sat down to watch it even though she had seen it several times in the last couple of years. She did comment that it never seemed to be off the TV, but loved the lead character of Julia and of course the horses. That did lead Adam to consider an interesting question.

"Aunty Karen, if this is a farm, why don't you have horses or dogs?" Adam wondered as Jocelyn frowned, trying to concentrate on the TV.

Karen took Adam out of the room, down the hallway and they stepped out into the front yard. As they walked down the yard Adam was puzzled, surely Jocelyn would also be interested in the answer? Aunty Karen anticipated this.

"Remember, Jocelyn has been here twice

before so already knows what I'm going to show you. There, see, at the end of the far outbuilding. Jocelyn didn't show you that part did she? There are four stables as, in the olden days, horses were indeed part of the farm, used for ploughing the fields and transport to, well anywhere you wanted really."

"So, why don't you have any now?"

"Your grandparents on Uncle Gary's side modernised the farm, bought a couple of tractors, a combine harvester and much more. They had a car so didn't need the horses anymore although they looked after them until each finally passed away. I have to say that as a kid when I used to come up here for my holidays, it was a lovely sight seeing the horses in the fields and feeding them hay and carrots. They'd run up and down the field many a time but I never saw anyone try to ride them."

"But what about a dog? Uncle Gary said you have sheep and I always thought that meant you had to have a sheep dog to round them up?"

"My, young man, some deep questions today eh? It's an interesting thing but not many people know that Uncle Gary is allergic to dogs, but oddly not cats. They found out the hard way when he was little, half your age in fact. He was suffering from various skin rashes and for a while they couldn't figure out what was causing it. Then his parents sheepdog, 'Gilly' died of old age, at that time they'd stopped having sheep and were concentrating on just cattle, so they decided not to get another. His rashes faded away as his mother, Mollie, gradually cleaned the house from top to bottom and they realised Gary had to be allergic to dog hair.

Even now, he has to be careful so tries to avoid contact when he's out in town or sees someone coming toward him with a dog.

Uncle Gary is not so affected by cats and we occasionally have strays wander across from the other farm or even we think from Scrawford and occasionally he has to deal with a litter of kittens, but that's life. The cats that stay here are quite shy, but we do find they keep the mice and rats at bay so that's a good thing.

Look out for a ginger cat and a black and white tabby but we tend to find they keep to themselves as they're quite wild, so I wouldn't touch them."

They turned round and walked back into the farmhouse just as the end credits of 'White Horses' were rolling and Jocelyn came out wondering where they were.

"Aunty, there's a new series just starting called The Railway Children, can I watch it before dinner?"

"That sounds like a good idea, what about you Adam?"

"Huh? Oh, guess it might be alright if it has trains in it!' he followed Jocelyn into the living room as they could hear something that had to be the opening credits, so Karen left them to it and busied herself in the kitchen.

She knew Gary was expecting to be late in from the fields. After the programme, that pleasingly both Jocelyn and Adam seemed to enjoy, they tucked into a salad with most of the ingredients coming from the walled garden, along with several thick slices of cured ham. Boiled eggs, home made chutney and pickled onions added to the feast. Once again as it had turned warmer, more lemonade was brought to the table to quench their thirst.

Karen decided the kids had had enough television for the day, so suggested they have a play outside before they had to go to bed. Jocelyn suggested the swing and Adam gave her a look as much to say, no way, but she whispered in his ear and so he reluctantly followed her outside.

It transpired Jocelyn had promised to only push him gently and not repeat their first encounter with the swing. Almost eighty minutes later they came indoors tired out which pleased Karen. She was likely to have a peaceful night if they dropped off into a deep sleep. Both were heading upstairs when Uncle Gary walked in through the front door and they wished him goodnight before disappearing upstairs.

"Have they been good today?"

"Yes, good as gold, you know those two seem to be becoming close friends. Who'd have thought it when they first met!"

"I admit I was doubtful, but looking over the last couple of weeks, I reckon Jocelyn has done what Adam's parents have failed to do, make him enjoy the outdoors!"

"Well, to be fair, I have been using a little bribery on both of them to get them to see each other's point of view. Even Jocelyn now reads more than she used to when she came here in the past and, amazingly she's really into that space fiction programme on Saturdays which also seems to bring them together."

"That's why I love you, you should be an overseas negotiator if you ask me. Anyhow, I'm starving, what is there?"

"We had salad but you hunk of a man need feeding up so I've baked a beef pasty, potatoes, carrots, broccoli, cauliflower and a nice jug of gravy for you. Go clean up and it'll be on the table shortly."

Gary licked his lips as he headed into the kitchen and washed his hands as Karen duly served up his meal.

#

Jocelyn wasn't sure why she had slowly awoken but she lay there on her left side facing towards the window which seemed to be lit up. She frowned and reached carefully for her clock, 2:14 am! It was quite warm in the room but she was still puzzled about how light it was.

She thought back to her other holidays on the farm, then realised she was in a different room and knew the curtains in the room with the leaky roof were quite thick; they blacked out the room really well. This room had thinner curtains but even so, it should still have been reasonably dark.

She turned over and peered over the 'wall' they had been calling the barrier between them and put her hand to her mouth.

Adam was facing away from her but had thrown his bed sheet off and was obviously hot as he no longer wore his pyjamas. She stifled a giggle at seeing his exposed bottom but then turned back to the light coming through the window. She carefully slid out of the bed and walked quietly up to the window and drew one of the curtains to one side.

There, low down, was a slim crescent moon and to its upper right was a small smattering of close knit stars. A little further to their right lay another, above a hexagonal grouping of fainter stars and way down to the left of the moon, lay a bright star, just rising. Directly below the moon there seemed to be an orange or reddish star twinkling merrily away with what seemed like a '>' formation of stars associated with it.

It was a gorgeous sight and the night sky seemed serene and at peace with the world. A thought flickered through her consciousness; she had an inkling of why Adam was so into space, the stars and space exploration. She wondered what the recent moon mission must have been like for the astronauts up there in space.

Suddenly she became aware of a scuffling sound and turned round to see Adam quickly pulling on his pyjama bottoms, turning and scowling at her.

Jocelyn was about to say she was enjoying the night sky, although the view earlier of his bottom did remind her somewhat of the moon, but Adam's face was telling a different story as he began to hold his crotch.

"I need a wee!" he whispered, "but I don't want to wake Uncle Gary, otherwise he'll be mad at me. I don't like going out to the privy either!"

"Don't worry," whispered Jocelyn, "I'll come down with you and stay outside whilst you go."

"But I don't want you hearing me wee either!"

"Oh, don't be such a baby, I thought you were better than that. Do you need to go or not?"

Adam nodded affirmative.

"Quick, best put our socks on as the slippers may make a noise going down the stairs and remember, the third step up from the bottom squeaks! And put your pyjama top on too or you'll be cold."

They quickly found their socks, Jocelyn grabbed her small torch and carefully opened the bedroom door and peered out. All clear, so they made their way downstairs and along the hallway to the front door.

Jocelyn opened it and they slipped outside and round to where the outside privy was located. She shivered a little as it was night and outside was somewhat colder than indoors. There was a long concreted yard and at the other end they could see where the kitchen windows were. Indeed the small, thin upper window was slightly open.

Adam didn't care as he pulled open the privy door and looked inside. He turned to Jocelyn, "Gimme the torch!" She shook her head and handed it to him and he went inside but instead of closing the door he peered into the toilet seat opening, screwing his face up.

"It's just a metal bucket, it'll make a racket!" he backed out and quickly looked round, then spotted the kitchen drain so rushed over to it. Before Jocelyn could say anything Adam turned his back on her and she saw a stream burst forth into the drain.

"OH! Really Adam?"

She turned away, somewhat disgusted but the sound suddenly brought on her own urge so she stepped into the privy and closed the door plunging her into darkness. She fumbled for the bolt then managed to find the rather cold wooden seat. "Yuk!"

Meanwhile Adam finished off, shook, then turned to hear the metal bucket ringing to the sound of a mini waterfall and he giggled as he realised where Jocelyn was. He walked up to the door and waited until the sound died down.

"You finished?"

"Oh, you'll listen to me but didn't want me to hear you! I'm done but can't see anything as it's really dark in here. Can you pass the torch under the door?"

He turned it on and did as he was told. There was a sigh of relief and then the bolt sounded as if it was being released. The door swung open then Jocelyn put her hands in the bowl of icy water as Adam stepped in and did the same, grimacing at how cold the water was. They grabbed the towel hanging on the back of the door and each took an end and dried their hands before Jocelyn hooked it back up on the door.

Adam took a deep breath and let it out, "I really did need to go!"

"So did I and I didn't know it until you tried to fill the drain!"

They burst out laughing then went quiet lest they woke up Uncle Gary. With the torch in one hand they held hands as they walked back round to the front door.

Which had locked shut …

Both stared in horror as Jocelyn, then Adam, tried to open the door but the night latch was in the locked position and they didn't have a key.

"What … what do we do now?" asked Adam as he began to tremble as the cold night air began to seep into his bones.

Jocelyn shrugged, looked around, spotting something and had a thought. "Kitchen upper window!"

They raced over and stood under the kitchen window and sure enough the top window which was slim and horizontal in shape was slightly open. .

Jocelyn studied it and the larger window below it which was closed. "If we can reach in and unlatch the bottom window we can climb into the kitchen and onto the draining board top."

Adam looked at her then seemed to be in deep thought.

"I'm lighter than you so what if you kneel down and I climb onto your back and reach in?"

Jocelyn wasn't sure if she should be flattered or annoyed but she knelt down and formed a bridge as Adam carefully climbed onto her back.

She winced. "Thought you were light?"

"I, I can't reach down far enough to get to the latch!"

He got off her back, much to her relief as she straightened up and shook her head. "What do we do? We can't wake Uncle Gary as he'll be angry with us, he'll be getting up in under two hours. We can't stay out here that long as we'll catch colds!"

"I just need to be a bit higher then I might be able to reach down and unlatch the main window. We need something larger to stand on!"

Adam suggested and they both looked around but there was nothing.

Jocelyn suddenly had a thought. "There's an old water trough that's not used. I think it was from the time they had horses here. It's just outside the stables so if we could get it here it might be enough!"

Adam didn't argue as he was shivering and knew they had to do something. They walked round the farmhouse and to the stables and sure enough there was the water trough.

It was a struggle as it was heavy but between the two of them they managed to carry it in stages until it was placed upside down under the kitchen window.

Jocelyn helped Adam step up onto it although there was a slight wobble and he looked at her in terror, wondering if he would fall off.

He reached in and down but still couldn't quite reach the latch and shook his head in despair.

"What're we going to do, I'm freezing now!"

"So am I!"

"I'm sorry!"

"What?"

"Sorry I needed the loo!"

"Hey, Adam?"

"What?"

"I didn't want to admit it inside but so did I!"

"We're silly really. All because we didn't want to wake Uncle Gary!"

"Hairy Uncle Gary!"

"Uncle Gary's a hairy ape!"

They both giggled but then reality reminded them of their dilemma as they both shivered.

"What about …"

"Eh?"

Adam was thinking, 'what would the astronauts do?'

Something came over him and he suddenly had an idea and ran off back round the other side of the farmhouse. When he returned he had the remains of a wire coat hanger he'd spotted a few days earlier that had been left on the washing line. He quickly climbed up onto the trough and reached in and down with the coat hanger and hooked the latch.

It pulled up and the window opened. He quickly pulled it fully open and then climbed in and onto the sink.

Unfortunately they hadn't spotted the plate and dish from uncle Gary's meal earlier and the plate went crashing to the floor, miraculously not smashing into millions of pieces but bouncing across the floor. Adam jumped down inside and Jocelyn quickly followed him.

They stood there rooted to the spot on hearing a commotion from upstairs and then loud footsteps pounding down the stairs. The kitchen light suddenly came on, blinding them and as their eyes adapted there was Uncle Gary in the door way as he shouted, "I'm armed with a shotgun so get on your knees and beg for your lives …"

Terrified, Adam and Jocelyn fell to the floor crying as Gary stood looking at them completely perplexed as to what was going on.

"DON'T SHOOT UNCLE GARY, DON'T SHOOT US! We needed the toilet and didn't want to wake you but we got locked outside and couldn't get back in until Adam had his idea."

Gary looked at the sorry pair shivering away in terror in dirty socks and no slippers and quite cold by now. He burst out laughing as he uncocked his shotgun and put it on the kitchen top.

"You two! You are a right pair aren't you!" he closed both kitchen windows making sure they were properly latched, leaning into the window he spotted the upturned water trough and had to smile to himself at their ingenuity then indicated to them to come to him for a hug.

"Right. No harm done and from now on, if you do need to go in the night, then use the upstairs bathroom, just don't pull the chain. Alright?"

In unison: "Yes Uncle Gary."

"Right, let's have a bit of fun as Aunty Karen is wondering what's going on so let me march you two into our bedroom to surrender to her, got it?"

They nodded and he grabbed the gun at which point both kids flinched but Gary opened it up and showed them there were actually no cartridges loaded! They marched up stairs as Uncle Gary kept saying in a loud voice that he'd captured the intruders, then they entered the bedroom and Aunty Karen let out a sigh of relief.

"We had too much lemonade Aunty Karen and we both needed the toilet and didn't want to wake you!" Jocelyn explained then shivered.

"Oh you poor bairns, you look frozen stiff. No more lemonade just before bedtime from now on. Right, Jocelyn, get in my side and Adam you get in with Uncle Gary. It'll help you warm up as our bed is nice and cosy. Best get those dirty socks off mind! Then you can go back to your room when he has to get up."

They did as they were told, glad of the warmth of the bed as Uncle Gary shook his head.

"Why didn't you use the outside key?"

"Eh?" came from both as they snuggled down under the sheets.

"There's a spare key slotted in a small gap under the front window just in case either your Aunty or I get locked out. Didn't we tell you?"

"Come to think of it Gary, I forgot and it has been a couple of years since you were last here Jocelyn so I guess you did to!"

There was a muffled groan from under the sheets from Adam as Gary switched his side light off. He looked at his alarm clock and sighed, 3:20am. He'd have to get up soon so closed his eyes and tried to get to sleep. It seemed to him no sooner as his eyes closed when indeed the alarm sounded and he switched it off. Karen was instantly awake as it was their normal morning get up routine but the two sleepy heads didn't stir. Carefully both adults managed to climb out of bed without disturbing them and they stood at the bottom of it and just smiled.

"They'd have slept through the Blitz!" Karen whispered to Gary and he nodded and whispered back.

"Grab your things and we'd best get dressed in their room for now."

They did so and crept out of the room. A short while later they slipped back in and surveyed the situation.

"What do we do? Leave them there for now?" wondered Karen and Gary shrugged.

"Pointless waking them up and sending them to a cold bed in the other room. Look, I know I was against them sharing but in the end they're, well, they're not err, how do I say ..."

"Exactly, too young and they've been as good as gold. Become firm friends but I've seen no sign of anything untoward. I think my little barrier down the middle of the bed has worked. Let's leave them for now and I'll check back after you've had breakfast."

With that they headed off downstairs as quietly as they could. Three quarters of an hour later Karen looked in on them only to find Adam missing. She quickly crossed the hallway and found him tucked up in the other bed, fast asleep and Karen quietly chuckled at the thought he must have been horrified to find himself sleeping right next to Jocelyn.

#

At the breakfast table Jocelyn was tucking into her cereal when Adam wandered in and sat down.

"I wasn't dreaming was I, that there was a key?"

"No you weren't dreaming and yes there was a key!" she replied as Karen entered with several thick slices of toast for them.

"Good to see you've managed to get up then Adam, sleep well?"

Jocelyn jumped in before he could reply. "I think that's a trick question Adam!"

"Uncle Gary snores!" Adam said instead and Jocelyn nearly spat out her cereal. Aunty Karen tilted her head at Adam. "Don't you mean 'Hairy Uncle Gary snores ...'"

Jocelyn and Adam stared at her wide eyed and looked at each other in horror.

"It's alright you two. He's not here and I agree, he is hairy and he does snore! I heard you both the other week. But despite his faults, I love him! However, NEVER say it to him or that he snores, OK?"

"What, that you love him?" asked Jocelyn, puzzled.

"No, that you also say Uncle Gary is a hairy ape. Now that one is a bit naughty don't you think?"

In unison with their heads bowed ... "Yes Aunty Karen."

"Good, now finish up quickly Adam. So have you two got anything planned for today, it's not a bad day for getting outside again."

Both looked at each other and shrugged. Karen had to smile at how they seemed to be more and more in sync with each other and she felt good at how things were turning out.

"If you don't mind, I'd prefer you to stay out of the farmhouse for most of today so with that in mind, I've already packed up a few sandwiches, cake and two bottles of lemonade, that last thing not to be drunk too quickly! I have a lot of cleaning to do today, then a pile of ironing so it's better for me if you go off outside. BUT no getting into trouble. Uncle Gary really did think we had intruders early this morning and I'm sure it scared you when he came downstairs with his shotgun!"

They both nodded as Adam finished off his toast and drank his tea, rather quickly, but it was soon gone as Karen handed them the rucksack with the food and drink stashed away in it.

So, to stay out of Aunty Karen's way, they wandered out to the wood again, had a picnic and generally played games; tag and I-spy were popular until they were tired out and headed back ready for their dinner.

CHAPTER 9: SPACE EXPLORATION ON FOOT!
Friday August 8th

"It's a nice day, what have you two got planned for it then?" Karen looked at them hoping Adam would again go out exploring with Jocelyn so she could get her chores done for the day.

Adam was just finishing off his toast and marmalade and shrugged. Jocelyn smiled. "How about going on the swing for a bit?" Adam screwed his face up, there was only so many times he'd go on it before getting bored.

"I'd like to read my Astronomy and Space book if I can?"

"Boring!" Jocelyn said out loud what she felt about that. "Tomorrow that spacey TV show is on isn't it Aunty Karen?" Karen looked at her a little puzzled but picked up her Radio Times and flicked through to Saturday and smiled.

"Yes, Star Trek, an episode called 'Mudds Women', not sure if I can let you watch that one. But then it is before teatime so can't be that bad."

"Well Adam. Think of it like this, what would that really nice gorgeous Captain say and do if he didn't go exploring space? He'd be boring wouldn't he!" teased Jocelyn as Adam's brain began to work on what she'd said.

"Oh, alright then but not the swing!" He looked at Aunty Karen and sighed but didn't want to be in her way. Jocelyn inwardly smiled as she loved getting her way and walked out into the hallway to get her coat and shoes. "Coming then Captain?" she teased.

Adam followed her out as Karen smiled at him and winked, pleased that at least he'd be out in the fresh air.

#

They walked out into the courtyard as Adam kicked at a few loose stones watching them bounce against the walls of the outbuildings. "Where are we going then?" he asked as Jocelyn seemed to be leading the way.

"Don't know. We've done the wood and stream towards that village, Scrawford, and we've gone through the field where the old cottage is. Both of those have been in the north, east and west of the farmland, so what about the lower fields?"

"Are they the ones with the cattle in?"

"One of them is, the other has sheep."

"Sheep field then!"

"Not so *sheepish* now are you!"

"Funny girl. You'll have to be the navigator so I command you to put in a course for the sheep field and take us there!"

"Yes Captain, what speed: run or walk factor?"

Adam snorted and looked at her, amused she

was playing along. "Walk factor two!"

"So, normal then, my pace. This way!" Jocelyn walked out of the courtyard and then turned left to stand next to a stile. "Ahh, I forgot, we have to go through the cattle field to get to the sheep field. I just need to check something with Aunty Karen, be back in a mo," with that she ran back into the farmhouse but was only gone a few moments.

"Good news, there's no bull! Permission to continue mission Captain?"

"Permission is given, onwards and over the stile."

They did so and tramped through the field, avoiding the cow pats as they followed what looked to be an animal track, probably a badger or fox, mused Jocelyn.

As they did so Adam was taking note of the landscape and something was piquing his interest. "Hey up Jocelyn, have you noticed that there seem to be several hollows and depressions here and over in the other field across the stream?"

"Haven't noticed, where?"

Adam stood next to her and pointed out three prominent ones where there was a raised rim and rougher grass growing along with nettles and what looked like the rosebay willowherb plants they'd seen on the edge of the wood on their long walk.

"Oh yeah, look odd don't they?"

"Thought you'd explored the farmland before when you were here?"

"Not all of it, last time I was only ten!"

"I'm nine, actually nine and a quarter so I'll be exploring the fields earlier than you when you were here."

"Harumph! Are we going to explore or what, *Captain?*"

"I have an idea. What if we go to each in turn as if they are a planet and we take it in turns to come up with a story that we have to investigate?"

Jocelyn raised her eyebrows trying to imitate Mr Spock. "Interesting. I like it. Nice one, see, you're not bad for a boy!"

"Cheeky! As I am such a good person and captain, you can have the first turn."

"That one over there in this field but near the hedge is closest, so let's go to that one Captain."

"Set course then!"

"Aye aye Captain. Onwards at walk factor *three!*"

She set off at a fast walking pace that caught Adam by surprise so he briefly ran to catch up and fell in time with her pace.

"Jocelyn?"

"Yes?"

"If you could be someone from star trek, who would you be?"

"I've always liked helping mum, dad and friends and I feel I want to be either a nurse or even a doctor when I grow up, so I think either Nurse Chapel or Doctor McCoy, I guess. You?"

"The Captain, of course but Spock and Scotty would be my other choices."

"I fancy the captain, he's bold, daring and always in charge of things. I would be Mrs Captain Kirk!"

Adam screwed his face up at the thought there may be a hint there from Jocleyn as he liked play acting as the captain but said no more.

They reached the first 'planet' which was a circular hollow at least twenty feet wide and three feet deep. The floor was stony as if they had been dropped there deliberately and it had hardly any vegetation at the centre where the most stones were concentrated.

"Orbiting the planet, Captain, and it appears to have no life but is very rocky."

"Sounds like a boring place, we'd …"

"Captain, the rocks, they're ALIVE and they're launching towards us," Jocelyn picked up some very small stones and chucked them into the air. She was clever in that they were so small they didn't hurt as they landed on them. Adam still ducked and gave her a scowl.

"Get us out of here then!"

"Sir, the bombardment has stopped, they, they're talking to us!"

'Charming' thought Adam, "Talking stones?" he said as he decided to humour her.

"I am receiving a message from their stony

leader. They thought we were dangerous but they've realised we're just a boy and a girl! They usually like to roll and so are officially called the 'Rolling Stones'," Jocelyn couldn't stop herself laughing as she said it and fell to the ground in a fit of giggles.

"Silly girl!" but Adam did chuckle to himself and held out a hand for her to get up with.

"Take us away from this planet of rocks and on to our next mission," he commanded and Jocelyn gave him a quick salute then pointed at Adam.

"What?" he looked around wondering what she meant.

"Where *IS* the next hollow? It's your turn to choose a mission."

"Oh, we'd best carry on into the sheep's field as I spotted one over there."

Jocelyn looked around then spied the gate to the next field and they walked towards it. "Do you think there will ever be something like Star Trek?"

"Could be, I hope so, but think it is a long way in the future."

"Captain, the sensor thingys show a dangerous barrier ahead called a gate, do we turn back?"

"No, this is a great ship and will survive as we go through it! Onwards!"

They reached the gate but it was padlocked so couldn't be opened. Adam climbed up and over, then Jocelyn did the same but on reaching the top she performed an amazing acrobatic flip and landed on her feet like they did in the Olympics. She brushed down her skirt and shrugged.

"That was ... wow!" uttered Adam, impressed.

"I'm pretty good at gymnastics. I'm in the team to represent the school sometime next year at an interschool event for the county."

Adam's estimation of Jocelyn had gone up several notches. He was nowhere near as agile as she was, certainly when it came to gymnastics.

He spotted the next 'hollow' and pointed to it as he marched off in that direction. "My turn this time. When we get to it, you be an alien spaceship that wants to attack me and we start off either side of the hollow from each other. Then we can try to catch the other, but we can't go into or cut across the hollow, got it?"

"Yes Captain! So it's like 'tag' then?"

He shrugged. "Guess so." They reached the hollow and it looked remarkably similar to the first one which made Adam think about asking Uncle Gary or Aunty Karen about them when they got back.

They took up positions facing each other across the hollow and each watched warily what the other was doing. Adam moved to his left then dashed back to his right. Jocelyn stayed still then feigned to run to her right so Adam ran further round to his right but wasn't paying close enough attention before realising she'd doubled back and was rushing towards him.

She didn't stop but tapped him on his shoulder. "Plaser hit, you're it and damaged!"

He spun round and gave chase but she was much faster than him and he had to stop for a rest as she gleefully stared back at him, once again opposite but also catching her breath.

"It's phaser, not plaser!"

Jocelyn stuck her tongue out at him so he retaliated in kind and they laughed at how silly each looked to the other. She sat down as if taunting him and he began to creep round the hollow but then she stood up and run round to try to catch him again. Adam however did something she hadn't thought of. He ran away for several yards from the hollow and sat down on the grass.

She was his side of the hollow now and she couldn't see how he could get back to the 'planet' without her getting another hit on him.

Jocelyn became wary as she approached and just as she lunged for him he rolled to one side, jumped up tapping her on her leg, ran back and around the hollow laughing as he did so. "Gottcha!"

Jocelyn narrowed her eyes and closed in on the hollow then began to run as fast as she could round it as Adam tried to run around it's perimeter but she was too quick.

She caught him and they both fell to the ground as she began to tickle him on his ribs and he was left gasping and crying out for her to stop because he couldn't catch his breath between laughs.

"I have destroyed you and taken you and your crew slaves to do all of my biding from now on!"

They lay there panting and he rolled over and looked her in the eyes. "That, that was fun. Clever thing you did."

"If you were older it would be harder to catch you. You're quite good but I've got longer legs."

Adam casually looked at her bare legs with the skirt partly pulled up above her knees but he went red in the face and turned away.

She stood up and straightened the skirt. "You can look at my legs, we all have them you know!"

"Yes, but. I've always been taught not to stare at girls as it's rude."

"That's good, but us girls wear skirts and you can't help but see our legs and there's nothing wrong with that. You're wearing shorts and I can see your legs so what's the difference?"

Adam shrugged and had to admit she was right. Her logic was flawless and he mentally pictured her with pointed ears and grinned. He decided not to tell her he liked her legs which was why he'd gone red faced.

"Where to now?" he asked as he scanned around the horizon.

"Is it me but if you take a line from the first one to this and carry it on down the slope of the hill, past the stream in the valley bottom, there looks like there are two close to each other. Look through the wire fencing into the next field."

He followed the line of sight and indeed there was a pattern, or rather a line but the last two did seem closer together but at an angle to the line.

Jocelyn had already decided and was walking off towards the far gate where it led into the next field. He caught up with her and they found the gate could be opened and passed through, making sure they closed it behind them. Jocelyn noticed a well made wooden bridge that crossed the stream just a few yards further along the field, so headed for it, crossing as Adam caught up with her.

As they approached the pair of hollows Jocelyn had come up with a story. "Right, this is my turn and so Captain, we're approaching a double planet that has alien space horses on it." Adam rolled his eyes but was slightly behind her so she didn't see.

"Captain, the space horses are known to migrate from one planet to the other but something is wrong, they are veering off course. If we don't do something they will die if they are lost in space."

"So?" wondered Adam. Jocelyn looked at him, annoyed.

"This was your idea of a game and it's my

turn so ... what are we to do *Captain?*"

"Erm, science station, what can be causing them to veer off in that way?" Adam put on his captain's voice.

"Scans seem to show there is a strange space rock that is pulling them off course. It is small so we might be able to destroy it." Adam pointed to a small rock only a foot or so across that lay on the surface between the two hollows and smiled.

"They're called asteroids, so, aim weapons at the asteroid and fire everything we have at it!" he shouted and he and Jocelyn rushed up to the rock and began kicking at it.

Naturally it was tough and they quickly stopped lest they broke their toes, but Jocelyn exclaimed loudly, "We've done it Captain, we've destroyed the rock, err, asteroid, and the space horses have been saved! They are sending us a message."

"Uhura, what does it say?"

"Thank you for saving our kind. On our planet, we have a sacred custom that their saviours must get married."

"Huh? What?" Adam was caught by surprise.

"Oh, it's the space horses custom so we have to get married, otherwise they are offended."

"Ewww, no way, marry a girl!"

"What do you think happens between a girl and a boy?"

"No! It's silly, it's just a game. I'm not doing that."

131

"But Adam, that's the point, it is only a game, we'd not really be married."

Adam was walking away, heading back the way they came so he could go back to the farmhouse and back to his books. No marriage nonsense!

"No. I don't want to play anymore, you've spoiled it!" he crossed the bridge over the stream in a mardy mood now.

"Harumph! Boys!" Jocelyn started walking back and caught up to him but he wouldn't look at her, just stared ahead looking where he was going. "Spoilsport. And I thought your were a nice boy too!"

"I AM!"

"Then prove it. It's only a game and I thought we were becoming good friends."

Adam slowed a little but didn't stop as he took this revelation in. *She'd said he was a nice boy! They were becoming friends ...*

"Adam, please?"

He grumbled something but she didn't quite catch what he said.

"So?" she asked quietly.

"Oh, go on then. But if Aunty Karen has finished what she was going to do then she should do it. Perhaps in the memorial garden."

Jocelyn's eyes widened with glee and they continued back up the fields.

#

"You want to do *what?*"

Karen looked at them both and wanted to laugh out loud considering how they had first started off.

"It's only make believe Aunty."

"I know Adam, it's just quite funny you agreeing to it. Oh well, come on, let's go to the bench."

Jocelyn raced out into the front courtyard and disappeared as Adam and Karen walked through the farmhouse to the back door and then into the walled garden to stand near the memorial bench.

"You know Adam, this is quite a mature thing to do, I can see you don't want to do it really but you're putting that aside for Jocelyn."

He had his head down looking at the wooden feet of the bench.

"She said something that, I don't know, affected me in a strange way."

"What did she say?"

"She thought we were becoming good friends, said I was a nice boy. She's right about her being my friend, even if she is a girl."

"Friendship takes many forms and doesn't have to be only between boys and boys or girls and girls, it can include both. Otherwise when you get older there wouldn't be any more Adams or Jocelyns now would there?"

"I'm glad it's just make believe though!"

Jocelyn came skipping into view and had something in her hand which turned out to be a buttercup posy. She stopped in front of them and put it around her neck.

"Ready!"

Adam turned away and rolled his eyes but Karen gave him a look and he turned back and smiled.

Jocelyn took Adam by his hands, again much to his dismay but he continued to force a smile. Aunty Karen cleared her throat.

"Dearly beloved space crew, do you Captain, er, what are you called again?"

"Adamski!" replied Adam mischievously.

"Do you Captain Adamski take …?"

"Jocelynski!" Jocelyn looked Adam in the eye as if to say two can play at that game.

"… take Jocelynski to be your wife, to have and to hold from this day forwards for ever and ever amen."

"N–yes." Adam knew he had to say it.

"Yes, I do" Jocelyn said gleefully.

"Then I confirm you are man and wife, live long and whatever it is they say on that programme and be good to each other for the rest of the holiday!" Aunty Karen winked at them both as she added in her own clause.

"Isn't there something else we should do Aunty Karen?" Jocelyn again had a mischievous look about her.

"Oh, well, not sure if this is wise young lady

but, you may now kiss."

The look of horror was something to behold on Adam's face as Jocelyn caught him by surprise and laid a smacker on his lips.

He recoiled backwards in shock. and began to spit to one side and wipe his mouth. "Hey, I didn't agree to …" he caught the look on Aunty Karen's face and turned back to Jocelyn who looked like she was about to burst into tears. "You took me by surprise. That's all."

He gave her a hug and then looked from one to the other. "Can I go now?"

"Yes dear. I think you were very good and perhaps both of you should go into acting when you are older!"

Adam didn't wait and was off running back into the farmhouse. They couldn't see him race upstairs to the bathroom and thoroughly wash his face then dry it vigorously.

In the meantime Jocelyn smiled at Karen then headed towards the farmhouse skipping and saying '*Adam is married to Jocelyn, Adam is married to Jocelyn*!'

Karen just hoped it wasn't going to cause trouble between them after all the good that seemed to have happened between them.

\#

Jocelyn remembered what they were going to ask Uncle Gary when they saw him. Now the news had finished and they'd left the dinner table to sit in the living room, now was the time to ask. "Uncle Gary, we went over the stile, and noticed some strange hollows in the field and into the next two which seem a bit odd."

"Oh, that's what you were doing. I saw you from the top field but it looked confusing. I dare not ask as at one point you looked to be chasing each other round one of the pits!"

"We were playing our version of Star Trek where each of the hollows was a planet and we took it in turns to make up a story at each one," added Adam.

"That explains that I guess. Oh, yes, the pits or hollows as you call them. Well in the war one of our Lancaster bombers was in trouble and still had a few bombs left so they couldn't land. They were flying around and managed to drop the bombs as they flew over here and all of them blew up forming the hollows you see now."

"Did they make it back?"

"Almost, it crashed just past RAF Grasceby and there was only one survivor although some witnesses said two people managed to jump out. That second person was never found so I guess they were mistaken."

"That's sad," Jocelyn looked puzzled by something else, "the first hollow, in the cattle field, it had lots of stones in it which seems odd."

Adam smiled, "We called it the rocky planet and the rocks turned out to be alive!"

"Oh, I know the one you mean. We have a lot of stones, mainly flint and some iron nodules, there's clay and sandstone underneath and so I have to occasionally go over the fields and remove the larger stones on the fields I plough and that's where I put them."

"Oh, the clay, Jocelyn, I bet that's what you got stuck in, in the stream in the woods the other week."

"Sounds about right Adam. Can be quite deep so it sounds like you were lucky. It's why we have quite a few bogy patches dotted around the farmland. Something to do with the boundary between the sandstone and the clay layer."

"You really know a lot Uncle Gary!" gushed Jocelyn.

"Nah, we've been farming this land now for a couple of hundred years so we get to know the nooks and crannies so to speak."

"Plus he has a friend who teaches geography which helps educate him!" added Aunty Karen and Gary screwed his face up at her.

"I'm quite a learned man, I'll have you know."

"We believe you Uncle!" Jocelyn looked swiftly at Adam who hesitated then understood.

"Yes, we do."

"Thanks kids, glad someone does!"

CHAPTER 10: THE TUNNEL
Sunday August 10th

Sunday morning and Jocelyn convinced Adam it was time to go out exploring again. Aunty Karen had had a quiet word with her about chanting that she and Adam were married and Jocelyn reluctantly agreed not to say anymore, lest Adam got upset.

Jocelyn once again insisted on having the rucksack Aunty Karen had made up for them. *'I'm older, taller and stronger than you, Adam'* was her only comment. Adam just nodded, glad he didn't have to carry it.

They stood in the yard as Adam looked around then at Jocelyn. "So? Where do we go? Not to that old cottage, we almost reached the village the other way but I'm not sure I want to go that way again."

"If we go down the farm track for about a mile or so, just past that turning for the old cottage, but this time we go a bit further as I'm sure a couple of years ago there was another pathway going off north-ish from the main farm track. I think there are some fields and animal tracks we could wander along?"

"OK, lead on then as I'm already getting bored!"

"Typical bookworm, want to go back indoors and annoy Aunty Karen do we?"

He stuck his tongue out at her but she just stuck hers out too and then giggled and they set off.

They reached the first rough track that led up to the old run down cottage which they could just see in the distance as they peered over the gate.

Adam sighed. "Looks sad and lonely."

"Yeah, I feel scrry for that poor man dying there. A lonely thing to pass away like that."

"But we're not going there, right?"

"Oh no, over there, this road slopes down and the track I think we want is just over the brow of the hill. See the field to the left, it's got sheep on it."

"What? Those dots are sheep?" Adam peered at the tiny dots and shook his head.

"They're a long way off silly!"

She shook her head at him then set off again making Adam have to run to catch up. Just then a man in causal clothing on a bicycle approached as they were talking about the fact that Uncle Gary had not had time to repair the roof over the other bedroom. Discussing that they were sharing a room and bed and wondering how long for. The person overheard some of the conversation as he stopped in front of them.

"Excuse me, I'm looking for Ashton Wood Farm, is it down this track?"

"Yes, Uncle Gary and Aunty Karen own it. We're staying for the summer holiday but having to share a room as the other bedroom has a leaky roof!" answered Jocelyn without thinking.

"Oh, sorry to hear that. I had a parcel delivered to me by mistake, so I'm dropping it round to them. It's so good to see a brother and sister getting on so well."

"We're not brother and sister!" blurted out Adam indignantly as he scowled at the thought that Jocelyn was his sister.

"We're married though!" threw in Jocelyn mischievously, without thinking.

The man looked at them puzzled and shook his head, thanked them and cycled off down the track.

They walked along until they reached another rough dirt road branching off at a slight angle and, to the side of the gate, there was a stile. Jocelyn easily clambered over it; Adam duly followed, again, glad he didn't have the rucksack.

They followed the dirt track until on the north side they came to an interesting feature. A dip that both looked like a ditch, but didn't look like one. It was a puzzle. It was quite wide with an embankment and lots of wild shrubs and bushes along with a few quite small trees growing sporadically along it.

"I never got this far, what do you think?"

Adam was studying the ground after climbing nimbly over the wooden fence. "This is like rough stones under my feet. It doesn't feel right but reminds me of something."

It looked as if various animals were using it as a route. Adam looked about, then spotted a broken smallish branch that he figured would do the trick. He beat back the nettles along with several quite tall pyramid type plants which he knew weren't foxgloves.

Jocelyn watched him studying the plant then had a brainwave. "You know what we should have brought, Aunt Karen's 'Observers book of British Wild Flowers'!"

"I could run back and get it, as we're supposed to be out all day, then we could use it to find out what we're looking at. It won't take me long if I run!"

"Oh, OK, that's great. Tell you what, see if she has something for bushes and grasses too. And, go up to our room and in the side cabinet I have a small torch in case it gets a bit dull further in that ditch."

Adam set off at a fast pace, leaving Jocelyn to wonder just how much energy he had, knowing he'd probably be shattered when he got back. She had an idea and climbed over the fence and cleared a spot ready for them. Meanwhile, bicycle man rode back past Adam and cheerfully waved before disappearing over the brow of the hill.

#

Adam was out of breath when he reached the farm and surprised Aunty Karen when he came in through the front door.

"Oh no! What's happened? Where's Jocelyn? Is she hurt?" Karen was expecting the worst.

"No, no," he took a deep breath, "we're OK. Jocelyn sent me back as you have something called 'Observers Guide to Flowers'?"

"Oh, that's a relief. Yes, that's a good idea, see how many different types of plant life you can identify. I should have thought of that the other week. Let me see." She went into the dining room and looked along the bookcase there. "Here you go, one about wild flowers, one on grasses, here's one on trees and shrubs, another on birds, oh and one on butterflies."

Adam looked at the five books and was glad they were small.

Thanking Aunt Karen, he rushed upstairs, much to her surprise then a short while later came down quickly, said bye bye then was out the door and away. Karen scratched her head than looked at the washing basket and took it upstairs for the next set of washing to be collected and cleaned.

Panting at all the running, Adam reached the spot along the lane to find that, over the fence, Jocelyn had laid out the table cloth Aunty Karen had put in the rucksack and with paper plates she had their sandwiches and cake laid out with two plastic mugs ready for the lemonade to be poured.

"Lemonade, Parker?" she asked.

"Yus, Mi'lady!" He climbed over the fence and dropped the small bag down on the grass next to them and spilled out its five books and the torch.

"I thought Aunty would have lots of books for us. Let's eat, then we can pack away and start to identify those red plants. As they ate they kept looking round and pointing out a flower or grass and begun by identifying rosebay willowherb as the pinkish red pyramidal tall flower, then white and red campion in clumps and crested dog's-tail grass.

Adam spotted a clump of bright yellow flowers with lots of insects and several blue and brown butterflys of various sizes fluttering about and landing on them. "What about that one?" he pointed at it and walked over as Jocelyn flicked though the pages then startled him when she shouted.

"NO! That one is called ragwort and is poisonous!"

Adam halted and put his hands on his hips as he looked at it carefully and took note of the butterflies. He had the butterfly book in his pocket so pulled it out and leafed through.

"That blue one is a common blue, oh, I think that brown one is a female - hah! Funny that, the boy is bright blue when the girl is brown yet still called a common Blue! That larger one is a meadow brown and that really dark one looks like a ringlet with its spots."

"That's pretty good for one plant, isn't it?"

"Yes, there's also an ants nest at the base of the plant so I'm moving!"

Jocelyn had packed away the small bags with the crusts of the sandwiches, she hated the crusts but Adam had devoured every last bit of the sandwiches he'd had. She handed him a plastic cup and filled her own and his with lemonade which they quickly downed. Finally with everything back in the rucksack, Adam looked a little shy.

"What's up?"

"I need a wee!"

"So? You always seem to want one at the oddest times! You're alright you boys, you can hang it out anywhere, as long as it's not in front of me! Go behind that shrub there, I won't look but make sure there's no nettles or ragwort!"

"Yus, Mi'lady!" Adam wandered a little further back up the track to a patch of shrubs that looked like rhododendrons according to the Observers Book Jocelyn was quickly looking through. Trouble was Adam mentioning it meant she now needed to go.

"Adam, don't come back down this way until I call you as I need to go now and I haven't got a tiddler like you, so can't go just anywhere!" She heard a snort come from Adam's direction.

"Tiddler!" he laughed, "Dad calls mine my 'little dangler'!"

Jocelyn shook her head at that wonderful bit of information she didn't really need to know.

She walked a bit further up the unusual shrub filled ditch muttering away to herself, "As if I needed to know that!" she then found a suitable spot, looking about to make sure Adam hadn't walked back.

A few minutes later she wandered back out. "OK Adam, where are you?" she spotted him bent over looking at the ants scurrying around a small anthill and he stood up. "What now Mi'lady?"

"This ditch and the track we followed looks a bit like an old railway track. Uncle Gary said something a couple of years back that there used to be a railway that went from Bardney to Louth and passed by somewhere near to the farm. I wonder if this is it?" She peered deeper into the ditch that appeared to head off into the low slope of the hillside.

She nodded in that direction and they began to walk along, Adam occasionally beating down any nettles that might sting them. He was warm but wondering if instead of shorts, he should have worn trousers. He mentioned this to Jocelyn and she laughed.

"Think about me! I'm in a skirt so can easily get stung, you keep sorting out the nettles!"

They continued on and found a wider patch with what looked like concrete slabs for a couple of yards either side of where they figured the track must have been. Jocelyn put the rucksack down, walked back a few paces then performed a couple of cartwheels much to the surprise of

Adam who was a bit taken aback at seeing her pink flowery knickers!

"What's up? You see more on the beach!" she retorted and did another couple of cartwheels back the other way towards him.

"Do you?" Adam said a little on the quiet side.

"Eh?"

"See more on the beach?"

"I don't understand?"

"I've, I've never been to a beach, so I don't know what you mean about seeing girls knickers on the beach?"

"Err, for one, you've never been to a beach? And two, I mean everyone wears something like shorts for boys and a skimpy bathing suit for girls. It's like the ice skating on TV when Uncle Gary watches that programme, Grandstand. They wear almost nothing and people don't say anything!"

Adam was looking at her in shock with his mouth wide open.

"And close your mouth," she did a handstand and amazingly stayed upside down for almost a minute, not bothered about her skirt draped about her head and her knickers showing. She did a little acrobatic jump and landed on her feet.

"Close your mouth Adam, you'll catch flies! You really mean to say you've not seen girls knickers before or a girl doing a handstand or cartwheel?"

He shook his head and suddenly Jocelyn was

sorry for him. "I'm sorry. I didn't know. I didn't think it was a big deal. It's not like you can see anything! At least I'm wearing some!"

Adam began to walk ahead, lost in his own thoughts as Jocelyn tried to grasp how sheltered his life must be back at home.

They walked a little further until the end came into sight, a railway tunnel that had been filled in with soil and with what looked like the broken remains of some of the original sleepers the tracks must have been laid on.

"Dead end but definitely an old railway tunnel," Jocelyn said out loud, not really bothered that they could go no further. Adam had other ideas.

He walked up to the blocked up entrance and noticed that the sleepers had been put across the entrance then the compacted soil pushed up against them. However, some of the soil had been washed away. They must have only had a few sleepers left as there was a hole where something else had been put in place but had rotted away.

"Hang on. Pass us your torch Jocelyn."

She did so, her curiosity peeked by what he was doing. He shone it in the gap. "I can see the rest seems to be clear," he scrabbled away at the rotten section and it pulled away leaving a gap large enough for them to squeeze through. Jocelyn was shaking her head.

"I don't know about this. What if we got in

and the tunnel collapses?"

"It can't be that bad, the engineers who built tunnels like this made sure they were pretty solid. The field this goes under looked like it is often ploughed so if a tractor can go over the top then I reckon it's probably alright for us."

"Honestly Adam, I'm not sure about this, it feels, I don't know, odd, spooky even." She briefly shivered, almost like the saying that someone had just walked over her grave.

Adam looked at her incredulously. "Who's the one always telling me to be adventurous? Go outside and have an adventure, go exploring you say when I prefer to read. Yet now, just when I actually want to explore this tunnel you go all soft and girly on me!"

"HEY! I'm a tom boy and I'm tougher than you, so watch it boy!"

He grinned. "That's the Jocelyn I have come to know and love … I mean like, like, that's what I mean, like!"

She scowled and moved past him as she grabbed the torch and peered in. Without another word, she crawled through the hole as Adam politely looked the other way, then when she hissed at him as to why he wasn't following, he pushed into and through the hole to join her.

\#

Eddie, Phil and Stu were ambling across the fields

on the other side of the valley and generally getting up to no good when Eddie suddenly stopped. The twins abruptly came to a halt, almost walking into him.

"What's up Ed?"

"The sky you dollup! Pass me your telescope Stu."

Stuart reached into his bag and brought out his pride and joy. His grandfather's telescopic telescope. One he'd apparently used in the war and it was always by his side. Rest in peace Grandad, he thought as he handed it over.

Eddie homed in on what had caught his attention. They were across the shallow valley and he's spotted someone or something near to the old rail tunnel entrance.

"That's interesting, it looks like a boy and a girl are somehow pushing their way into the old tunnel across the valley. Let's go see!"

The twins never argued with Eddie. He was their leader, even though he could be a bit rough at times and certainly didn't seem to have any consideration for others. He also had a reputation at school for being a bully.

They marched along following the old animal trails, jumping over the small stream then up the other side to join the dirt track. He knew he shouldn't be on farmer Gary's land as his own father and farmer Gary didn't get on, but he couldn't see farmer Gary and was prepared to take the risk, seeing these two strangers doing something they shouldn't be doing.

It took them almost fifteen minutes to get there and Eddie peered in with an evil look about him and motioned to the twins as he told them what they were going to do.

#

"Blooming heck Jossy, let me have some light!"

"DON'T call me that! You know full well I hate it!"

She lowered the light to the ground so he could see his feet. It was wet and dank inside the tunnel as well as being quite cool.

"How far do you think it goes on for?" Adam was now going off the idea, but just then Jocelyn screamed then brushed something off her hair.

"SPIDERS!" she exclaimed.

"Well, what do you expect coming in here. It must have been sealed up for years!"

"Harumph!"

"And to you too!"

"Hope we don't catch anything being in here."

"And again I say, who's the adventurer now?"

They continued further into the tunnel but the torch could only illuminate a short distance. It wasn't very bright but they could at least see the ground. Looking back, the light streaming through the hole they'd made at the entrance at least made Jocelyn feel a bit better.

They didn't pay much attention to the time until the torchlight illuminated the other end showing it was blocked by rubble, wood and soil suggesting they'd reached the other entrance.

"Well that's it!" she said. Adam went up to the rubble with the torch flashing it around but realising it was much more solid and compacted than at the other end.

Looks like we'll have to go back. Jocelyn, I said we will have to g …"

She shushed him to be quiet as she stared back down the deeply black tunnel. All the while as they had made progress, the light from the hole they'd made at the entrance reassured her they could get out.

"Adam, why is the light at the other end flickering?"

They watched horrified as the far end light flickered out …

\#

"That's it, that'll do lads. That'll teach the nosey buggers, whoever it is, to go into dangerous tunnels like this. They'll struggle to get out, that's for sure. Glad you found those large slabs of concrete for us to wedge up against the hole Stu."

"I really don't like this Eddie, it's wrong. They won't be able to get out, we'd be classed as murderers!" whined Phil as Stu also looked worried about their actions.

"Quit yer whining. I'm sure they'll get out but it'll teach 'em a lesson!"

"Wonder who they are?" Stu shook his head, "I have a bad feeling about this."

"Don't know, don't care. Let's get off and back to dad's farm and we all agree we didn't come this way, did we?" Eddie asked with an air of menace in his tone.

"If that's what you say Eddie," muttered Phil reluctantly.

The trio walked back, climbed the fence then headed back down and across the valley, little knowing someone had spotted them from afar.

#

"Adam, the end of the tunnel. The light's gone out. Even if it had gone cloudy there would still be some light. I think someone's trapped us in here!"

They started to quickly walk back, having to take care not to run and fall in the dark. Jocelyn, and indeed Adam, was now beginning to genuinely feel scared and had to make sure they missed the few bricks that had fallen from the tunnel roof after all these years. After what felt like forever, they reached the other end but were in for a shock. Adam went up to where he'd made the original hole and started clawing away but there was what felt like a solid slab pushed against the entrance. Jocelyn joined him but they couldn't budge it. Desperately they tried digging away at another section of the entrance but to no avail.

Breathing heavily now with sheer fright Jocelyn held the torch up to their faces and it was clear they were both shaking with the realisation they were trapped. To cap it all, nobody knew where they were.

Adam took a deep breath and again marshaled his thoughts. "What would the astronauts do?" he said echoing them out loud.

"What?"

"I know. I think I saw something metallic up one side of the tunnel roughly half way along. They sometimes built ventilation shafts and emergency exits. It might be one."

"How do you know?"

"I'm not just into space. I love anything like planes, spaceships, steam trains and cars. I just didn't think to check up if there was a railway in these parts."

He took her by the hand. "I won't let anything happen to us, to you. There is always a way. I'm sure of it!"

With that he started walking back down the tunnel making sure there was enough light for both of them to see the ground. Something seemed to urge them on, both felt as if they were being guided, but shrugged off the feeling and put it down to being in the cold, damp tunnel.

They didn't know how long it took but eventually they found the metal ladder and they shone the torch up it. It disappeared into a vertical shaft and a look of hope lit up their eyes.

Adam clambered up first, quickly followed by Jocelyn and he reached what seemed like a metal covering. He pushed at it as he wedged himself against the shaft wall but it only gave a little.

"I can't budge it!" Next thing he knew, Jocelyn squeezed up next to him and wedged herself tight. Together they pushed and it gave a bit more but it was exhausting and despite several attempts, they could only push it so far up as whatever had grown over it was keeping it in place. Tired out they tried to rest to gain strength to have another go when suddenly the cover was ripped away and they were dazzled by the bright light shining in and heard a voice cry out …

"Bloody hellfire! How did you two get in there?"

#

Gary was checking the hedges of several of his fields as there were signs that some of the hedging was dying off. He'd have to re grow some sections before plashing it down to form a new hedgerow.

Off in the distance, across the valley he spotted trouble. A well known mischievous gang of three boys around fourteen or fifteen years of age, the eldest, the son of a neighbouring and troublesome farmer with whom he'd had the occasional run in.

He shook his head and carried on his work as he neared the field edge. It lay over the old railway tunnel from the now defunct Bardney to Louth railway. Something seemed to nudge him from behind but he put it down to a gust of wind, but what caught his attention were the large tufts of grass and a patch of rushes that for some reason kept moving of their own accord. He blinked several times thinking he was seeing things.

He knew of the rumours that the tunnel was haunted which was plainly ridiculous as there had never been any incident or accident in the tunnel. As far as he was aware no one had wandered into the tunnel and been killed. The grass and rushes again moved up and down slightly, swaying as they did so and he shook his head in wonderment, this is taking the biscuit he thought to himself.

Reaching it he heard faint voices and stepped back.

"Bloody hell! It *IS* haunted!" But then his practical nature kicked in and he looked at where the grass was moving noting it was almost circular.

"Good god, the old vent shaft. He rushed back to his tractor and grabbed the shovel he always kept with him, on getting back, he wedged it under the rim and heaved it up.

Two familiar but dirty faces looked up at him whilst trying to shield their eyes.

"Bloody hellfire! How did you two get in there?" he was almost lost for words as he hauled Jocelyn and Adam out and they lay on the ground crying with relief.

#

"We thought we'd die down there and no one would ever find us!" wailed Adam as he and Jocelyn held on to Uncle Gary tightly, not wanting to ever let their hero go.

"Now now, it's alright now, you're safe but how on earth did you get in there? It was sealed up almost a decade ago!"

"We found a ditch that looked strange and went into the hill side," Jocelyn began as she calmed down, "There was a small hole and we were wrong but we made it big enough to go inside to explore. We got to the other end but it was sealed tight, then as we turned to head back, we saw the light from our hole flicker as if someone or something was there. Then it went dark and we used the torch to show us where to tread to miss the puddles and dead things, but when we got back to our entrance, it was blocked and we couldn't move what looked and felt like concrete."

"Hmm," Gary's thoughts turned back to the sight of the three lads running across the valley, directly away from the tunnel entrance that lay on his land. "Come with me you two, let's check out what's been done to the entrance, I used loads of earth and some of the remaining debris from when they took up the track when I blocked up the entrance on my section of land."

He put the vent lid back in place and moved some of the grass back onto it to once again hide the location of the ventilation shaft.

It only took a few minutes, maybe five or six, thought Adam, before they followed the slope of the hill down and there, running diagonally to their direction, was a sudden drop. They skirted round until they were at the fencing Jocelyn and Adam had had to climb over when they had first noticed what they thought of as a ditch.

"We had our sandwiches there then explored the ditch as Adam thought it looked like a railway line. Oh!"

They stopped and stared at the two patches of bare ground where Jocelyn had been doing cartwheels on the concrete slabs just a few hours earlier.

There were two patches of disturbed earth where they should have been and scrape marks leading off towards the tunnel entrance in the distance.

As they followed the marks, it became clear why Jocelyn and Adam had not been able to get out or push whatever it was aside.

Both slabs had been pulled up and laid over the spot where Adam had managed to make a hole to get through.

"So there you are. I think I know who did this to you but we have a problem. I can't report it as a byelaw was passed a few years back prohibiting anyone entering the tunnels due to safety issues. So if I say anything to the authorities then you'd be in trouble, so would I as they could argue I didn't seal this end up properly.

It really scared you both didn't it?"

They nodded and hung their heads in shame.

"Look, we'll have to tell Aunty about this but not a word to either of your parents. Right?"

In unison, "Yes, Uncle."

"Good. Let's head back up the hill and you can help me check on the state of the hedges and fencing, how's that for you? I think it will cheer Aunty Karen up that you have helped me today, yes?"

He needn't have asked, they were just so grateful they'd been found by him and saved.

The bonus was getting the early ride home on the tractor and trailer. Jocelyn managed to squeeze into the tractor standing behind Uncle Gary and holding onto his waist whilst Adam was happier in the trailer holding on and watching the fields roll by, even if it was a bit bumpy.

On explaining their adventure to Aunty

Karen she was not pleased with the situation, but Gary laid her fears to rest and pointed out the kids had used common sense and had worked out the right way to escape. They didn't know the grass had grown over the ventilation shaft lid, but they had shown initiative.

Naturally Karen had to point out the obvious to him when the kids had gone to bed.

"And what would have happened if you hadn't been in that field today?"

Gary had to admit that it was pure luck …

CHAPTER 11: BEACH TIME
August 11th to 12th

"That blooming sister of mine! Never been taken to a beach? That's outrageous!"

Gary looked across the dinner table at Karen and shook his head. So much for not talking at the table, he thought.

"That's what Jocelyn told me whilst Adam was in the trailer, isn't that right Jocelyn?" he said as he looked at Jocelyn for support.

Adam was looking from one to the other and then in horror at Jocelyn for spilling the beans.

"It's true isn't it Adam? You weren't having me on?" Jocelyn looked at him with her soft, deep brown eyes and a look as if to say *let's go to the beach, let's go to the beach, let's go to the beach* ...

Adam felt a little trapped, but nodded.

"You've never been to a beach?" reiterated Karen, shocked.

"No Aunty, I haven't, unless I was so small I can't remember."

"Well, we'll have to change that then won't we!" Karen was in a defiant mood and Gary knew she was not going to let it go. He decided to take the initiative.

"Right. OK, I can see where this is going. SO! This is what we'll do. I can get done by ten in the morning tomorrow as I'm ahead of things at the moment. How about Skeggy?"

"No, Gary, it's August and the place will be teeming with tourists and day trippers from the midlands."

"Ingoldmells?"

"The same. And Chapel St Leonards too."

"It's that time of year. How about Anderby Creek? Probably quite busy as a lot of folks come across from Nottinghamshire, but it's got everything, great beach, fish and chip shop, Harrisons and Roses stores, parking. What about it Karen?"

She looked at him and nodded thoughtfully. "'bout an hours drive I seem to remember. How's that sound kids?"

Jocelyn was almost ecstatic whilst Adam wasn't sure, looking around at their faces however, it looked like he had no choice, so he nodded.

"Will I have to go in the sea?" he asked reticently as Karen smiled at him.

"Not if you don't want to Adam, what did your parents pack for you?"

"I have a pair of shorts and a couple of summer shirts."

"That's what I figured. Marion never was one for the beach and would never even think to pack swimming trunks or something like a T-shirt. In her eyes, you were coming to a farm and she always thought we never went anywhere else. I'll have a look at your shorts and I'm sure we can find something at one of the shops for you so you change into them when we're there."

"Are there changing rooms then?" he asked.

"Erm, we'll sort out something once we're there, don't worry Adam. It's a day out for me too!" offered Gary and smiled at him, then grimaced as the news finished, he'd missed it with all the talking but the weather did look good for the next day with mostly sunny skies and a light onshore breeze.

That late evening, when they were supposed to be asleep an over-excited Jocelyn turned on her small light, slipped out of bed and rummaged through the sets of drawers pulling out various items of clothing looking for her swimsuit.

"Yes!" she exclaimed and disappeared below the bed her side as if she was lying on the floor. Adam dare not look as he heard her scuffling about on the floor then a few minutes later she jumped up.

"Ta da!" she stood there in her swimsuit but Adam was turned away. "Well look you dummy!"

He turned and shook his head. "What're you like?"

Jocelyn did a pirouette then curtsied but Adam wasn't impressed.

"Go to sleep, I'm not looking forward to tomorrow as it is!"

Deflated Jocelyn turned the light off, stripped off now that Adam had turned away and buried himself under the sheets as she put on her nightdress.

It was to be a sleepless night.

For Adam, he was too nervous, for Jocelyn, too excited, yet now tempered with an annoyance at Adam's reaction which she didn't understand

#

Morning.

It was an hour's drive, a little slower than Gary had hoped considering it was Friday morning and most traffic was to the south of them going along the A158 from Lincoln to Skegness. On their route, Alford was quite busy, then for a short while heading on the A1111 before turning onto a smaller road at Bilsby, where they made better progress.

Jocelyn and Adam were in the back seat of the Austin Countryman, Gary's pride and joy. Adam was quiet for the whole journey but Jocelyn seemed to have ants in her pants according to Aunty Karen, as Jocelyn remembered the route from her last time staying with them a couple of years earlier.

Her excitement reached fever pitch as the road twisted and turned into Anderby Creek itself and they drove to the end into the crowded car park and stopped in one of the few remaining places.

"OK, everybody out. Toilets are over there so go now or forever hold your peace!" Gary shouted.

They all got out as Karen laughed, "Who's getting married then?"

Adam and Jocelyn exchanged mystified glances but, seeing a sign, they raced off to the toilets.

"So what's the plan then Gary?"

"When those two come back, as it's almost half past eleven, how about getting fish 'n' chips first and having them outside, then when we're done, see what space there is on the beach as it does look busy!"

And so they did just that.

#

Lunch finished Karen ushered the kids to follow her down the main road to the stores whilst Gary scouted out the beachfront.

In Harrisons they were milling around when the store lady came up to Karen.

"Looking for anything in particular, dear?"

"Oh, actually yes, we don't have any swimming trunks for my nephew, he's with us for the summer but my sister didn't pack anything like that for him. I'm not even sure what size but I'm guessing something similar to the shorts he's got on. Hey, Adam, over here please."

Adam dutifully walked round and found Aunty Karen with a nice lady. She sized him up and smiled. "I have just the thing. We have almost everything here and often find people come out missing something or other. What about sandals as he doesn't want to be walking on the beach with those shoes on, they'll get ruined."

"Good point, those too, oh and some for Jocelyn."

The lady held the trunks against Adam's shorts and nodded. "Yes. Should be alright and keep everything ship shape and tidy. Don't want anything dropping out now do we?"

Adam looked a little alarmed at her but Karen just smiled as Jocelyn skipped round the aisle with a bucket and spade set as she looked pleadingly at Karen.

"Oh alright then. Oh this is Jocelyn …"

"I'm his sister!" Jocelyn blurted out as Adam stared in horror at her.

"Yes, I can see the resemblance and many a boy and girl that come here can't stand each other which I can see in your eyes both of you."

Karen scowled at Jocelyn as Adam was still dumbfounded at the sheer gall of Jocelyn. Sister indeed! He was about to launch into a rebuttal when Karen indicated for them both to go outside whilst she paid for the goods.

"She's actually my goddaughter of my best friend, but on holiday with us too. They actually get on quite well but she does like to tease him a little."

"Girls will be girls and boys will be boys. He seems a quiet one."

"Prefers reading and staying indoors, so we're hoping this brings him out of his shell if you know what I mean."

"Yes. We see lots during the summer, all sorts pass through here, we get 'em all. Have a good time and if you have a problem with the trunks or sandals then I'll be here for you."

Karen paid up and walked outside to find Adam and Jocelyn facing away from each other.

"Right you two. We're here today on a glorious day at the beach so let's have none of this malarkey, understood?"

They both turned and looked at her with their heads hung low.

In unison: "Yes, Aunty."

"Right, I've got sandals for you both so take your shoes and socks off and put these on," they quickly did as they were told and Karen inspected them, "Good, I'm glad they fit, I always was a good judge on peoples feet!"

They behaved themselves as they walked back up the street, put the shoes and socks in the car then up the slope and down onto the beach. Gary had been right, lots of people were there. Jocelyn's eyes lit up as she spotted the donkey rides as she excitedly pointed to them.

"All in good time, all in good time. Anyone see Uncle Gary?"

They scanned the beach then spotted his

head and an arm waving at them from further up the beach. It was a good few minutes walk in the warm sand and Adam was now pleased he'd got the sandals on and did enjoy the feel of the warm sand beneath his feet.

They reached Uncle Gary who had erected a windshield that also provided some privacy for changing behind. As they reached him he stepped out showing off his quite small and tight fitting trunks.

"Now I remember why I married you!" quipped Karen as Jocelyn and Adam exchanged bemused glances.

"Right, who's changing next?" Gary barely got the words out before Jocelyn grabbed her bag and rushed inside. A few moments later she emerged in her swimming suit and her sandals and walked past Adam grinning.

"Right, you next Adam. Hurry up as we've not got all day!" barked Gary and Adam did as he was told. He was quick and emerged still fully dressed.

"Aunty Karen I have a question."

"*Okay ...*"

Adam leaned in and whispered into her ear and she stifled a laugh. "You take them off as well and only wear the trunks."

"Oh," Adam disappeared behind the screen and emerged a few minutes later in just his trunks and sandals.

Gary reached into the large bag he'd brought

and out came a lightweight beach ball which he threw towards Adam who deftly caught it, leading Gary and Jocelyn to clap in appreciation. With them distracted, Karen quickly changed and came out from behind the windbreak to a wolf whistle from an appreciative Gary.

"And now I remember why I married you too!" he said as they embraced, much to the disgust of Jocelyn and Adam who rushed away from the adults to play with the ball. Gary had done well, they were well along the beach and away from the majority of the others enjoying the nice day.

After a while, Adam tired of chasing after the ball as Jocelyn always waited until the last minute then kicked it away. He flopped down onto the soft sand and Jocelyn ran up and plopped down right next to him.

"I was really enjoying that. What next?"

Adam wasn't paying much attention to her as he'd spotted a shell and was now examining it. She pouted her lips and then took a closer look at it in his hands, getting quite close to Adam.

"So, whatcha got there then clever clogs?"

"I think it's a clam shell. Wish we had something to tell us."

They heard a shout and saw Uncle Gary had walked up to them. "I expect you two will want something like this as you've stopped running around like lunatics!" he dropped an 'Observers' book down as well as a large carry bag. Jocelyn snatched it up as Adam read the cover of the book. Uncle Gary smiled at them, then walked back to Aunty Karen who was lying out on a beach towel soaking up the sun.

"Wow, brilliant. It's the 'Observers Book of the Sea and Seashore'." He held up the shell he'd been looking at "This ones a cockle shell. Let's see what else we can find."

"Shells and nice pretty stones?"

"YES!" They looked excitedly into each others eyes and grinned as they stood up and began to walk along the beach with their eyes peeled to the ground.

Half hour, an hour, back and forth as they watched out for the tide but their timing was perfect as it was on the way out. They picked up so many items that they had to carry the bag between them as they walked back to their beach spot and plopped to the ground and lay out, shattered, next to Karen and Gary.

"Was that fun kids?" asked Aunty Karen. An emphatic 'yes' resounded from the pair. They all rested then Aunty Karen whispered something in Uncle Gary's ear and he sat up.

"You know you two. I'm going to use that spade your aunty bought and dig me a nice place to lie in as I'm sure the sand underneath will be much cooler," he winked at Karen who just smiled, knowing what he was up to.

With their help, Gary dug what seemed to be more akin to a shallow grave, then he lay down in it and closed his eyes.

"Ahh, yes, bliss," after a short while he pretended to snore as Aunty Karen then played her part. She beckoned to them and whispered, "Whilst he's asleep, why not bury him. Just leave his head clear OK?"

The grins on their faces said it all so carefully Adam began to sprinkle sand over Uncle Gary's hairy chest. Jocelyn started with his feet and worked her way up until she was covering his lower abdomen and made a face to Adam as she covered Uncle Gary's trunks as she tried to avert her eyes. Adam took over from her to save her any more embarrassment.

After a few minutes Gary was fully covered and still snoring away as Adam and Jocelyn giggled and Adam surprised Jocelyn.

"Bury me now if you like," he whispered and together they dug out a hollow for him to lie in and she began to fill the bucket and tip it over Adam. Chest, feet and legs then she carefully tipped several buckets over him until his trunks were covered, oddly enough she wasn't embarrassed this time. She finished with his chest and he smiled up at her.

Aunty Karen fished out two smaller towels.

"Best just put these over their heads otherwise they may get sunstroke." Jocelyn took them and covered Gary and Adam as she giggled then lay down, exhausted at the effort. At which point Aunty Karen threw her a towel to cover her head too.

"I should have got some hats for you whilst at the shop. Never mind."

They all lay out there, peaceful, although every so often Adam blew at the towel to push it off and eventually he managed to lift himself out of the sand and brush it all off. He looked at Jocelyn.

"Your turn now!"

She didn't object and they made the shallow pit longer as she was almost a foot taller than Adam, she lay down in it and Adam piled on the sand. She was fully covered when he did the unexpected and gave her a peck on the cheek then ran quickly behind Aunty Karen who'd set up a deck chair and was sitting in it reading a book.

Jocelyn just smiled meekly at him. "Adam, can you put the towel over my face so I don't get burnt?"

He did so, surprised she'd not told him off. He had no idea why he'd given her a kiss on the cheek but the whole day had been an amazing experience for him and part of that was down to the fun he'd had playing ball then beach combing with her.

Aunty Karen took note of everything and two words kept popping up in her mind …

Puppy love.

#

Jocelyn had fallen asleep; Adam got unduly worried and shook her gently.

"Jocelyn, Jocelyn, please wake up!"

She stirred and sat up pushing off the sand from her upper torso and saw that Adam was concerned.

"It's alright, I must have fallen asleep! I was so tired after last night as I couldn't get to sleep being so excited."

"Tell me about it. You kept me awake most of the night too!"

"Sorry."

"Hey, you two, we'll soon have to head home so why not go off paddling before the tide comes in whilst me and your uncle get changed?"

Jocelyn grinned. "Help me up?" she held out her hands and Adam grabbed them and hauled her out of the sand. Instinctively he began to help brush the sand off her until she grabbed his hand.

"I'LL do there thank you very much!"

"Oh, sorry, was just trying to help," he lowered his head and she just smiled.

"I know. But there are some places you just don't touch a girl, understand?"

"Yus Mi'lady!"

They burst out laughing and walked away towards the sea leaving Karen to pull Gary out of the sand and shake their heads at the pair receding into the distance.

Gary turned to Karen.

"You know, I take it back about me moaning for you saying yes to both of them staying just a few weeks back. We'd make great parents, don't you think?"

"Yeah, but we've tried and the doc said it might not happen."

"Seeing them two together and how they've become such firm friends, I think we should ignore the doc and have another try eh?"

Karen had tears in her eyes. "Yes, my love. Once these are back where they belong, in their own homes eh?"

He nodded as he watched Jocelyn trying to entice Adam to get in the sea.

#

"Are you sure about this?" Adam was not confident about going in the water.

"You can swim, can't you?"

"Yes, not very well, but yes."

"Then come in and join me. I promise I won't push you under!"

Adam stepped gingerly into the sea as it lapped back and forth over his feet. Initially it felt cool then as he got in up to his chest he started to enjoy it.

"That's it, you're getting used to it now," Jocelyn splashed away as she swam a few feet from Adam and turned, pushing down against the water to keep herself upright. Adam doggy paddled over to her but was gasping and spitting out the slightest trickle of sea water that had got in his mouth or nose.

She swam away, parallel to the beach as she'd been taught, all the while keeping an eye on how the tide was behaving. Adam splashed noisily towards her but slipped under the water and she ducked under and pulled him up, hanging on to him. He was shaking and it was clear he was no longer enjoying himself.

"Come on, back to the beach. Let's just walk along the edge of the water and paddle for a while," Jocelyn suggested and Adam was only to pleased to do as she suggested.

They got out and began to walk, the sun began to warm them both up and dry them off.

"Thank you sis!" he said quietly. Jocelyn stopped dead in her tracks. Then remembered.

"Hah! Well, I think we're better than brother and sister. We're friends."

He smiled at her then spotted Uncle Gary and Aunty Karen waving for them to come back. They ran all the way and stood next to the adults who were now fully clothed.

"Right you two, dry off and get dressed. If you're good, we'll have a second lot of fish and chips then head for home, what do you say?" They looked at Gary and both grinned. Adam nodded to Jocelyn, "You first."

"Thank you Parker."

"Yus Mi lady!"

Gary and Karen just exchanged glances and chuckled as Jocelyn disappeared behind the windbreak and changed, coming out and Adam going in and doing the same.

After the best fish and chips they'd ever had, probably because they were ravenous after such a great day at Anderby Creek, they piled into the Austin and headed for home. Adam and Jocelyn slumped together fast asleep, making it a wondrously quiet journey home for Gary and Karen, much to their relief.

CHAPTER 12: FIGHT!

The next few days were changeable as several weather fronts swept across the land and with frequent squally showers, Jocelyn and Adam found themselves either reading or playing the board games whist trying to stay out of Aunty Karen's hair.

Mousetrap tended to dominate, although for some reason Jocelyn always seemed to win the most times. Adam fared better at Frustration but his celebrations did tend to be a bit on the loud side which irritated Jocelyn.

A couple of times she did convince Uncle Gary to let her go out on the tractor with him as he checked on the sheep and cattle, which helped break the slowly mounting tension between the two kids. Adam was still happiest when he could be left alone to read his books and once Uncle Gary realised Adam had his copy of the Observers Book of Astronomy, he let him hold on to it to read up on the night sky.

But one evening, when they had gone up to their room, both seemed to be in bad moods and barely talking to each other which was completely out of character for them considering the last week or so.

Jocelyn grabbed her nightdress and went to the bathroom to change but did so quickly and without thinking she walked back and went straight into the room just as Adam was pulling up his pyjama bottoms and he angrily spun round.

"JOCELYN, NO! You should have knocked!" he glared at her as she walked round to her side of the bed.

"Doubt there's much to see anyway!"

"Nasty girl!"

"Prove it then! Don't forget we're married you know!"

"No way!"

"Chicken!"

Adam sat heavily on his side of the bed, looking purposefully away from her but didn't expect the attack.

Thwack. Jocelyn had grabbed her pillow and brought it down on his head catching him by surprise. He rolled on the bed, initially in shock as she quickly hit him again and he scrambled out of the way. He found his pillow and swung it high and brought it down but missed her and he fell on the bed. Jocelyn took advantage and struck once more with a direct hit and he slumped to the floor as she began to laugh.

Soon Adam scrambled round the bed on all fours and caught her by surprise hitting her on her left arm with his pillow before she could turn and defend herself. He followed up with several quick blows as she fell back onto the bed and rolled off, but by now both were beginning to giggle as they tried to avoid being hit.

Jocelyn struck out with all her might and, in slow motion, brought her pillow down on Adam's head then watched with horror as the eiderdown burst out covering them both in feathers.

Just as Karen and Gary ran into the room wondering what all the noise was about. Adam and Jocelyn were now standing facing each other in fits of giggles at the state Adam was in, but then they saw the looks on the adult's faces.

"WHAT THE BLOODY HELL DO YOU THINK YOU ARE DOING?" bellowed Uncle Gary as Aunty Karen looked as if she too was about to explode.

The kids looked down and Jocelyn spoke quietly. "We're really sorry. We didn't mean to get into a fight."

Adam was nodding and trying to look as sorry as he could, whilst covered in eiderdown.

"Right. I don't care who started it or why, but you'll clean this all up and for the next week you'll do all the washing up and any chores Aunty Karen asks you to do!"

Aunty Karen nodded, agreeing and walked out to fetch her dustpan and brush as well as her Hoover junior vacuum cleaner.

On returning she watched over them as they thoroughly cleaned up the feathers and tidied the room before allowing them to finally go to bed.

Lights out and they lay there in the dark.

"Sorry Adam ..."

Silence, then he started gigging again.

"Uncle Gary's face!"

"Aunty Karen's, I thought she was going to explode!"

"Why did we fight?"

"I, err, entered the room before you had finished getting changed. You've got a nice bum!"

Adam pulled the bed sheets over his head, "Eww! Noooo! Go to sleep!"

"Yus Mi'lord!"

Adam could be heard guffawing under the bed clothes but he stayed under so she didn't see his red face ...

They were as good as gold the next day. In the meantime, although they knew Uncle Gary had spent some time on the roof, it came as a bit of a shock when Aunty Karen and Uncle Gary wanted to talk to them. It felt ominous as they sat together on the settee and Gary cleared his throat.

"Now, we both understand that the last few weeks since you arrived have not been easy and that you've had to share a bed and room which has not been ideal. Especially as you are, well, err boy and girl."

Karen rolled her eyes and jumped in. "What Uncle Gary is trying to say is that he's fixed the leaking roof as far as he can tell and so the other bedroom has been tidied up, bedding dried out and replaced and one of you can now move into it to give each other privacy. Who wants the other room?"

Surprisingly, Adam and Jocelyn just looked at each other, dismayed, which in turn took the two adults by surprise.

"Well, it was a choice up until now but one of you is moving into it, so, Adam, it's you," Gary decided not to beat about the bush and pointed at him.

"I, I guess that's the best thing but I have to admit it'll feel strange for the rest of the holiday," Jocelyn looked at Adam for support, but he looked a little lost.

"You're still in the same house, Adam, it's not like we're sending you away!" Aunty Karen said, noting how sad they both looked.

Adam just nodded quietly. "I'll go upstairs and get my things," he got up and without waiting, left the room as Karen quickly followed him and together they went upstairs.

Jocelyn sat in silence. She thought she would have been happy but somehow it felt awful, as if they were being punished. Which to a certain extent, they were.

"Uncle Gary, is this because of us fighting last night?"

"Not exactly Jocelyn. I mean, if the other room had been OK then you'd both have had separate rooms from the start so, we're finally able to do that."

"Oh, alright. It'll be strange."

Just then Karen entered the living room

minus Adam.

"He's moved his stuff, not much, he only had one suitcase and a few books. He's decided to go to bed early."

Jocelyn looked at the clock on the mantelpiece, only half past eight.

"Is it OK for me to wish him goodnight?"

"Yes dear, but be good and knock on the door first."

Jocelyn nodded and left them, quickly running up the stairs.

She knocked and heard Adam gruffly say 'come in'.

He was sat up in bed looking sadly at her. "I didn't expect this, did you?"

"No. Are you going to be okay?"

"Guess so."

Jocelyn sat next to him and gave him a gentle hug then got up and walked to the door, "You know where I am ..."

Adam just nodded as he began to slide under the bed sheets. "Night night, sis!"

"Nighty night, bro."

She heard him chuckle then left him to go to what was now her room.

#

It felt very odd to each of them suddenly finding they didn't have someone to talk to late at night if they awoke, but life settled down as the weather improved. Jocelyn and Adam took it in turns to check the other was up and ready for breakfast each morning and it became the new norm much to Uncle Gary and Aunty Karen's relief.

CHAPTER 13: OF DOLLS AND LEGO

With mixed showers and sunny intervals forecast, it was back to board games, reading and general silliness that Aunty Karen sometimes called their antics. Adam was downstairs in the front room reading once again and as Jocelyn was bored she wandered back upstairs to her own room, dropped onto the bed and grimaced.

Her eyes wandered round the room. Although she'd been there almost three weeks now, she'd never really explored the bedroom cabinets. All she'd done was use the lower two drawers in the bedroom chest cabinet next to her bed for her clothes and the nearest of the wardrobe cabinets for hanging dresses. Dresses which her mother had insisted she bring even though she was on a farm.

Adam's shirts and trousers had been hung up in the same wardrobe as hers although he didn't have many clothes and they were now in his room. His mother didn't seem to have been as organised as her own, mused Jocelyn.

She spied two more wardrobe cabinets and wondered about them. She felt compelled to look, guided even, as if by an unseen hand.

The largest had two doors and was locked; the one next to the right hand wall was split into a large door on the right and a smaller door above a set of three drawers on the left. Inquisitively she wandered over to it and tried the doors. They were unlocked and she gasped in wonderment at what she found in the smaller compartment above the drawers.

Three old fashioned wooden dolls of varying sizes, a large one to two much smaller ones, one of them being a marionette. For a split second it reminded her of the Thunderbirds puppets, but to be fair none of the dolls were as glamorous as Lady Penelope.

They were all clearly very old and she slowly and methodically examined each one, fascinated by the intricate detail of the old fashioned clothing that they were wearing. The paintwork forming eyes, fingers and toes was fading and one of the dolls, the medium sized one seemed to suggest it was once representative of a dark skinned person. She immediately though of Uhura from Star Trek and smiled.

The largest doll didn't have painted on eyes, but a clever system of white balls with an inset for the iris and pupil that looked uncannily life like and the 'eye's could move slightly depending on how you held the doll.

For a good two hours Jocelyn played and imagined stories involving the dolls before she suddenly wondered what was behind the larger of the two doors of the wardrobe and so she opened it.

An intricately designed dolls house! Jocelyn

was in her element. Taking it out and placing it on the bed, it opened out to show all the rooms on three floors, intricately carved furniture, miniature paintings on the walls in some rooms, tiny utensils in the kitchen, the attention to detail was amazing.

She couldn't help wonder why Aunty Karen had not shown her them before. In past holidays she'd always had the other bedroom, the one that Adam now had and she had looked in all the unlocked wardrobes and drawers, but there was nothing like this.

Intrigued, she was about to go downstairs when curiosity made her look in the drawers.

Brand new boxes of Lego, four of them still sealed, various sorts including a large box for building a small town with a parking lot, houses and much more. Three other boxes with spare bricks and an assortment of different shapes and sizes. Adam would kill to play with this lot she thought and picked the largest box up and rushed downstairs to find him.

Still in the living room, Adam looked up as Jocelyn rushed in. "Look what I found in our old room in one of the wardrobes!"

His eyes widened with glee as he took the box from her and started to open it.

"Mum and Dad won't get me this as they prefer me to have Meccano and I can't stand the stuff! Too fiddly with nuts and bolts! This is great!" he surprised Jocelyn with a light peck on the cheek then set about sorting through the contents.

"There's more upstairs, I'll fetch them down," she bolted out of the room and dashed back upstairs, returning quickly, followed by an intrigued Aunty Karen who was wondering what all the noise was about. Her eyes also widened but for a different reason.

"Where, where did you get those from?" she stuttered in shock, although she already knew the answer as her heart sank.

Jocelyn looked at her puzzled. "In my bedroom in the right hand wardrobe, there's also dolls in there that look really old and a brilliant dolls house."

Karen looked at her with a mixture of shock and annoyance.

"Damn! I forgot to move them!"

"Aunty! Rude word! Why?" Jocelyn was puzzled then it began to dawn on her the Lego was brand new and still sealed.

Or it had been until now as Adam was opening every box with utter delight.

"Too late, damage is done. The Lego was for Adam as his Christmas present. This also means …"

"The dolls house was for …"

"You, also for Christmas."

"Oh, Aunty Karen, I'm so sorry, I didn't mean to find them, it was by accident."

"I know love, I should have put them in my

room but we didn't have much space. I should have locked it. Well, too late now. Erm, about the dolls though, come with me up to the room."

They left Adam happily building something with the Lego and went upstairs in silence. In the room Karen saw the dolls on the bed and the dolls house now on the floor near the window with one of it's sections opened up.

"Jocelyn, the dolls are not actually play things and not meant for you, only the dolls house."

"Oh ..."

"All three dolls are heirlooms handed down from my great-grandmother and to me are priceless and have to be looked after carefully. So playing with them could damage them. I know it seems unfair now that you've seen them and by the looks of things begun to play with them, but understand that these are really precious to me. I had hoped that if Uncle Gary and I had been able to have children and one was a girl then she would inherit these dolls from me and carry on the tradition.

Do you understand?"

"I guess so. They are quite old, aren't they!"

"Yes, I'd forgotten they were in this room and every so often I do get them out and examine them, the craftsmanship and sheer detail is extraordinary. I don't know if there are any others like them, so they could be worth a bob or two which makes them an investment."

"I didn't play with them like my dolls at home as I saw they were old so I'm just like you, I looked at them carefully as I was amazed by them too. If, if you don't have a girl ..." she trailed off as she wondered if asking would be the right thing to do.

"You are our goddaughter so if I don't have a daughter of my own then I will make sure you inherit them."

Jocelyn gave Karen a tight hug. She helped Karen put the three back in the wardrobe and Karen reached up and felt along its top before smiling and bringing down a small key. She locked the small compartment but left the larger one unlocked.

"You can store the dolls house in there and take it out to play with whenever you like and when your parents pick you up you can take it with you. We'll sort something else out for Christmas, and for that matter for Adam too."

Karen left her playing with the dolls house and sighed but, on the other hand, both kids had something new to play with and keep them occupied and, with luck, out of trouble.

#

It was almost 9:43pm and although she'd not been in bed very long, Jocelyn had fallen quickly into a deep sleep. That is until she drifted up to consciousness aware of a light tapping at her door. She got up and crossed the floor knowing it had to be Adam but it wasn't fair for him to have disturbed her like this.

She opened the door and there he stood in his pyjamas but also looking somewhat annoyed.

"What's the matter? Monsters under the bed?" she hissed at him somewhat more harshly that she'd intended. Then she became aware of the faint but deep thrumming and Adam pointed down the stairs.

"They're playing music and I can't get to sleep!"

She walked with him to his room and they sat on the bed and listened intently. Now she knew what to listen for, Jocelyn could just hear the thrumming from downstairs.

"It's not as loud as I expected. But it isn't fair! Why not play music when we are awake and can enjoy it too!"

"Not sure I'd enjoy it."

"Oh Adam, you can sometimes be really boring. Tell you what, get dressed and meet me on the landing. We're going downstairs!"

Adam looked at her as if she'd spoken and alien language. "We are?" he asked a little surprised. He'd hoped he could simply move back into her room and get some sleep.

"We are! Get moving and I'll get dressed. See you in a minute!"

Jocelyn hurried out of the room into her own then hunted through her drawers to find something suitable, got dressed and walked out onto the landing.

Surprisingly, Adam was dressed and waiting with his hands on his hips looking serious. "You go first, it was your idea, but I think we'll be in trouble!"

"Not if I have my way, anyway, I can twist Uncle Gary round my little finger, come on," with that Jocelyn quickly walked down the stairs then waited for Adam to catch up before she carefully opened the door to the living room.

The good thing about having a living/dining room knocked into one was that everything could be moved into one room to make space for dancing. There they were, Aunty Karen and Uncle Gary gyrating away as Jocelyn gently pushed the door open then walked in and put her hands on her hips and looked as annoyed as she could.

Aunty Karen spotted her first and looked surprised just as Uncle Gary then realised they were no longer alone. Putting on her sternest voice, Jocelyn spoke before the adults had a chance to recover.

"You woke poor Adam up and even I could hear something was going on. Why can't we join in the fun and dance with you just for an hour or so?"

Adam was a little shocked, he had thought they were going down to ask them to keep quiet, he wasn't aware that Jocelyn wanted to join in the dancing!

"Oh, well, err, sorry Adam, we thought we'd got the record player on low so as not to disturb you," Uncle Gary looked at him and shrugged. Aunty Karen had lifted the stylus off the record and stopped it as she looked at them both.

"You two should still be in bed and it wasn't that loud. Still, now you are up, and dressed I see, oh well, there's no harm if you want to join in. But mind, we'll make it about an hour but we've been good and not played the records since you first arrived and we just wanted to have a dance."

She turned back to the collection of records and remembered something Jocelyn had said the previous week. She put the record on, turned the volume up and the look on Jocelyn's face was a picture as The Beatles single, 'Can't Buy Me Love' struck up and Uncle Gary grabbed her by the hand and they began to dance. Karen turned to Adam but he shrank back looking annoyed and hesitant at the same time.

"Come on Adam, a bit of fun and dancing won't hurt you," Aunty Karen said, but Adam backed out of the room and closed the door.

Jocelyn spotted this and scowled but Aunty Karen joined her and Uncle Gary as they danced and they tried to sing along to the single.

For Jocelyn it was heaven as she loved the Beatles, especially Paul, but deep down she was saddened that Adam didn't seem able to let himself enjoy popular music. The single ended and they clapped as Aunty Karen then looked through their record collection and put on 'Cinderella Rockefella', followed by 'I Heard It Through the Grapevine', then 'Ob-La-Di, Ob-La-Da' and 'Keep On Running'. As it finished Jocelyn had had enough of a certain person's absence and left the room.

She was surprised to find Adam sat on the third squeaky step with his head in his hands, instead of up in his room.

"What's wrong with you? Everyone loves music!"

"Not me!" There was something in his reply that caused Jocelyn to take stock and not answer harshly.

"What is it Adam, we're friends, you can tell me."

He shuffled to one side and she sat down next to him and waited. Unbeknownst to them Karen and Gary had opened the door slightly and were listening.

After a few minutes looking anguished, Adam spoke, "My Mum and Dad like those brass bands and going to events where they always seem to play such things and a few old fashioned dances. There are a couple of old aunts on Dad's side of the family who always grab me and make me dance with them and I hate it!

I like to be quiet and not be dragged around the floor with aunts who smell of drink, sweat and smoke. I just don't like it. There's nothing that I like. Except, well except that music they played for the astronauts when it was on the news."

He went quiet as Karen looked at Gary and screwed her face up as she whispered to him, "That bloody sister of mine, makes my blood boil how they are bringing him up without decent music! First no beach for him and now we find out he doesn't hear decent music. Let's see what we've got. I don't think we've got that music, what was it also sprach zara something but we must have something we can play for him."

They slipped back into the room as Jocelyn put her arms around Adam's waist.

"Your mom and dad, well they have what they grew up with, but there's lots of music and songs out there which I'm sure you'd enjoy if you'd give it a chance. I won't make you dance and I'm sure neither will Aunty and Uncle. They're not like that, so why not come back into the room and you can sit and watch us as we dance and you never know ..."

Just then the door opened fully and Uncle Gary came out to them.

"Hey Adam, we err overheard some of what you were saying to Jocelyn, and although we haven't got that Apollo music we do have a few instrumentals that are sort of space-y if you'd like to hear them?"

Adam's eyes widened with pleasure and a grin spread across his face then changed again. "I won't have to dance, will I?"

"Only if you feel like it, bear in mind we don't do formal dancing like your parents, we're free and easy and do whatever the music says to us," added Aunty Karen. Jocelyn looked at Adam with her soft brown eyes looking deep into his soul, urging him to rejoin them and Adam relented.

In the room Uncle Gary put on 'Telstar' and Adam stood transfixed as Gary, Karen and Jocelyn tried to dance to it. Adam found his right foot begin to tap the floor, he couldn't keep up with the music but it didn't matter to him. It finished but before he could say anything, Uncle Gary looked over at him, "This is from a TV show in the states, not quite spacey but I think it's great," he put on 'Peter Gunn' by Duane Eddy and as soon as it started Uncle Gary and Aunty Karen started off dancing apart but walking towards each other slowly in time to the beat moving their hips and arms from side to side.

Jocelyn watched for a few seconds then did the same, advancing towards Adam who grinned coyly then as she held out her hands towards him in time to the music, he did the same and they gyrated towards each other. Adam was mesmerised. Why didn't his parents listen to music like this, he kept wondering as he and Jocelyn danced slowly around each other trying to mimic Uncle and Aunt. It came to an end too soon, Jocelyn smiled and hugged him.

"Thank you, it's good to dance isn't it?"

"Yes, err, like this but not to what my parents like."

Another record was put on the turntable as Uncle Gary turned to Jocelyn, "One for you as we've done a couple that I thought Adam might enjoy. A TV theme you might recognise …"

'White Horses' came drifting across the room and Jocelyn jumped up and down, ecstatic. Not one to easily dance to, but Adam held her by the hands and they rocked from side to side as it played. He saw how happy it made her; for some reason it made him happy too, to see her having so much fun.

"OK, now let's get some vibrations going," as Uncle Gary next put on 'Good Vibrations' then 'Blackberry way', back to the Beatles with 'All you Need is Love' whereupon Jocelyn was singing along and Adam chimed in a few times.

"This is from the Rolling Stones," Uncle Gary and Aunty Karen began to sing along to 'I can't get No, Satisfaction'.

Adam leaned into Jocelyn and whispered in her ear, "Who comes up with these band names!"

"The bands themselves of course, silly!" she laughed just as it finished and another instrumental: 'Wipe Out', then back to the Beatles with 'Lady Madonna' much to her excitement.

The tempo slowed down with Scott McKenzie and 'San Francisco: Be Sure to Wear Flowers in Your Hair' then Uncle Gary announced it was almost time to stop but he was going to finish with three instrumentals: 'Nut Rocker' followed by 'Kon-Tiki', then he paused at the end of that one and said, "Last one, a nice soothing track that'll just be right for you to go back to sleep with," and he put on 'Albatross'.

When it finished Adam looked as if he was going to cry. Jocelyn held his hand and looked concerned as did Karen and Gary.

"What is it? Why so sad?" she asked and he looked down at the floor and wiped the tears from his eyes.

"Sorry, I just didn't want tonight to end. Music is so much more than brass bands and big bands like Mum and Dad listen too. I want music like this from now on."

"Good music will move you, great music will touch your soul. Their music does it for them, but some of us need something else and modern music really get's into you, heart and soul. We'll have a few more music nights before you both have to go home, don't worry about that," Gary said as he smiled at how Adam had embraced the music.

"OK, now you two, off to bed and I hope you sleep well and have good dreams."

With that the dynamic duo rushed upstairs, but at the top of them Adam held on to Jocelyn and she looked at him puzzled. Then he gave her a quick kiss on the cheek and rushed into his bedroom and closed the door.

She smiled, felt her cheek then walked into her own room with a big grin on her face.

CHAPTER 14: RIDING THE FIELDS AND A SURPRISE VISITOR
Friday August 15th

Friday lunchtime, around twelve thirty, Uncle Gary came in from the yard, took his work shoes off and wandered into the kitchen where he could hear someone making a noise.

Karen came out of the pantry that led off from the kitchen, it was always cool in there as it had thick walls and no windows so it was ideal for storing fresh produce, all kinds of food stuffs and some of her pots and pans. It was well used despite them investing in a new fangled refrigerator the previous year.

"You OK love?" she asked, wondering why he was not out in the fields as he normally was at this time of the year.

"Yes," he held her by her waist and gave her a kiss, making her a little suspicious.

"Alright, what do you want?"

"Eh? Nothing. I've done what I need to do, so if the dynamic duo are around then I thought this afternoon they might like to come out on the tractor and trailer again with me. Adam did seem to like it after their little tunnel escapade, so perhaps he might like to help out."

"Well, I know Jocelyn would jump at the chance and those two seem to have got much better now as friends, so Adam may just be swayed."

"Good, where are they?"

"Out back, the swing of all things. Seems Jocelyn is well and truly forgiven for their first encounter."

"Good job too. Would have been somewhat awkward over the last few weeks otherwise."

With that Gary headed for the back door to find them.

#

Not surprisingly, Jocelyn was full of enthusiasm and for once even Adam appeared to have lost his reticence at joining in.

They were now heading out along the farm track before stopping at the entrance to one of the fields they had not been in yet during their explorations. Gary opened the gate, got back on the tractor and they trundled in just far enough before stopping when he disembarked and closed the gate. Jocelyn was in the trailer this time with Adam but they weren't alone. There were loads of turnips, but Uncle Gary had not explained what they were going to do, so she was puzzled.

Further down the field they finally came to a halt as a group of sheep began to wander their way towards them.

"They know, you see!"

"What Uncle Gary?" Adam asked as he climbed down off the back of the tractor. Jocelyn was still in the trailer watching them, along with the approaching sheep.

"Have you noticed it's been quite dry for a few weeks with only a few minor showers and the grass is not at all happy. So," he unhitched the latches and let down the trailer back and pointed, "we're going to push some of these out onto the field. You watch as the sheep will start to follow us when they realise what we're doing. So, Adam get back in the trailer, hold on tight but kick the turnips out a few at a time as I drive away from those water troughs. As the sheep follow us, some will stop to munch away on the turnips that are on the grass.

Keep kicking them out, I mean carefully, not like in the world cup, you're not trying to score a goal and anyway it'll hurt your feet if you kick hard against them."

Adam climbed up and held onto the trailer side but close to some of the turnips. Jocelyn took up position on the other side.

The next half hour was spent trundling slowly around in arcs this way and that as the two kids emptied the trailer and the sheep obediently followed until they became too busy eating the precious food.

The trailer was somewhat dirty so naturally they also looked a little grubby, especially their hands where they'd picked up a few of the smaller turnips and threw them off to each side.

Finished with that job, Uncle Gary instructed them both to stay in the trailer as he fastened the back up and he then drove to the top of the field, opened another gate and went through, stopping to close it, then Jocelyn and Adam realised where they were roughly heading.

In the direction of the old abandoned cottage.

However they trundled past it as the land rose a little higher until they reached the brow of the hill where Gary stopped, put the brakes on and turned off the tractor.

Getting into the trailer they all stood and he directed their gaze around. The cottage and the start of Aston Wood lay off to the left slightly below them, in the south they could see the patchwork of fields, some with crops in them going down into the shallow valley, then up the other side. A distant farmhouse was almost just a speck as Gary pointed it out.

"That's Mr Edwards' farm, he has most of the other side of the valley whilst I own and farm everything this side and a bit beyond this hill too," he motioned for them to turn around. "That large thin mast is the Belmont television transmitter in the distance. Our TV channels are beamed out from there across the county. But as we have Anglia TV, it comes across the Wash from Norfolk and the signal gets weakened so," he rummaged in a bit of sacking that the kids had assumed was just rubbish, and he fished out an old pair of binoculars and handed them to Jocelyn as Adam looked a bit miffed.

"You'll get your turn in a moment young man. Right, Jocelyn, see there's a tower over there and some dishes next to it?"

"Yes."

"That's Stenigot, the dishes were used in the war. Now move slowly round and look out for a smaller tower against the horizon."

"Oh, got it, a bit small but I think there are dishes on it near the middle and top."

"Yes, that's the Winceby transmitter, some locals living near to it call it the Hameringham tower but the point is that it intercepts the TV signal from Norfolk, boosts it to Belmont which then can send out a strong signal all across the county and beyond. Let Adam have them now."

She did so and Gary ran through the same sequence again as Adam scanned along the horizon.

"Now, Adam, look roughly southwards, can you see a small solid looking thin tower sticking up, almost as if it's in the sea?"

"Ahh, got it."

"That's Boston Stump, the big church and tower at Boston. Some say it's the tallest church tower in England. Not everybody mind, but in our county we like to think it and Belmont are the tallest of their kind in the land. Keep looking to the left and you can see a shimmering ground, slightly bluish silver. That's the sea."

Adam handed the binoculars to Jocelyn who looked in the direction he was pointing in and she spotted it. Then she wandered round towards the west.

"Oh, there's a group of similar towers on a ridge!"

"Mighty Lincoln Cathedral. It's a fine structure and along with Boston Stump, was used by our airmen in the war for navigation."

Adam took the binoculars as Jocelyn offered them to him and he viewed it too and was suitably impressed.

"I was always told by Mum and Dad that Lincolnshire was flat but we're in hills with valleys and lots of different fields."

"That's typical of those outside our county. In the south of the county and coastal parts, yes it is fairly flat but here, we're in the Lincolnshire Wolds and Lincoln itself stands on the Lincoln edge. One day, perhaps we should go into Lincoln and make your parents climb up Steep Hill, it's not named that for nothing!"

They stayed for another hour or so as Uncle Gary pointed out several kestrels, a few hares and rabbits, the sheep milling about in the field they had been in earlier and watched the mostly blue sky with a few fleeting clouds scuttling by.

They also spotted the hollows in the fields in the distance and it was even clearer from this vantage point that they formed a shallow arc. Cattle were in the field nearest the farm as they enjoyed using the binoculars to explore the landscape taking it in turns whilst Uncle Gary just smiled, pleased they were enjoying themselves.

#

Karen heard a knocking on the door and headed to it from the kitchen, drying her hands on her apron. She was surprised to find a rather stern looking woman, very slim, perhaps around her fifties with a small black briefcase in one hand and a clipboard in the other, standing there.

"Can I help you?"

"That depends. This is Ashton Wood Farm?"

"Yes, my husband and I own the farm. What's this about?"

"I'm from the local authority and it has been reported to us that you have two young children who are not your own that are living," she paused as she referred to her clipboard notes, "living in the same bedroom and indeed bed and *are married*? I have been charged with investigating the matter and interviewing any and all persons involved to ascertain the truth of the matter and to ascertain if an offence has been committed that may require the children to be taken into care. Is your husband here and the children?"

Karen was still reeling from what the woman

had said. "Err, no, the kids are out exploring our farmland and my husband is out in the fields."

"For now then, may I come in and ask you some questions and I hope in the meantime they return soon."

"I, I guess so. I'm sorry but who's been putting about this awful rumour?"

"That is not for me to discuss but as you can imagine we have to investigate every case where children may be being mistreated or raised in an inappropriate way."

"But I don't understand, they have separate rooms and are on holiday here with their parents' blessings."

"That is for me to ascertain, can I enter or are you going to deny me entry?"

Karen stepped to one side. "Come in, we don't have anything to hide but I think you'll find my husband will be furious at the slur on our good name."

"My dear, we take everything seriously and if there is nothing untoward, then I don't see you having a problem. However, if there is anything then, well, I have to make my report and recommendations, you understand, it's not personal."

"No, but it feels like it," Karen showed her into the living room then had a thought, "You haven't given me a name or anything to prove who you are and if you really are from the local authority?"

"Sorry, my mistake. Miss Bowder is my name, here are my credentials," she handed over a letter which did indeed confirm what she'd been asked to do and Karen noted that a concerned, but unnamed individual had raised the matter.

"Very well, we have nothing to hide as the kids are here on holiday. Would you like a cup of tea then I'll answer as best I can although I think you'll find there's nothing to the assertions."

"Tea would be fine, thank you, no sugar and a little drop of milk if I may."

Miss Bowder sat down in the living room and opened her notebook ready to take down anything that might be useful. She looked around the living room noting it was clean and tidy and placed a tick in a checkbox near the end of her official set of notes that had a variety of questions and checkboxes. A tick was good and a cross was poor but for now, things had started on a positive note.

Karen returned with a tray and two cups, indicating which one was for Miss Bowder. Karen then went to the sideboard, opened up a drawer and fished out two letters and handed them to her. "These are two confirmation letters from both Jocelyn and Adam's parents showing that they are here for the summer holidays."

"Thank you, that is very helpful and was a good thought of their parents." Miss Bowder read the letter from Jocelyn's parents first and raised an eyebrow.

"It's not quite in my remit to comment on the parents reasons but 'going on a Caribbean cruise' for the whole summer?"

"Quite. They actually won the cruise and as they usually can't afford a holiday, let alone go abroad, they wanted to take full advantage, They never had a honeymoon so this was their chance but they found they couldn't add a child to the itinerary. Jocelyn usually spends a couple of weeks in the summer here with us anyway as Gary, that's my husband, and I are her godparents. Her family live in a council terrace and since she was eight, Jocelyn has come up here for the fresh air and open countryside.

She couldn't come to us last year as she was poorly, I think it was chicken pox. She'd been looking forward to this summer since then."

Miss Bowder looked at the official headed letter from Adam's parents and seemed impressed.

"Government funded work in the arctic in northern Norway. Impressive, I can understand their reasons and that again children would not be included as they would need caring for whilst up there which would detract from their duties."

"Yes, both are highly thought of in their fields and I gather didn't have much of a choice about it. However this is Adam's first visit and he's a bit of a bookworm, if you know what I mean, so it's taken him a week or so to come out of his shell. In fact it's been Jocelyn who has done what we didn't expect to achieve and they've become good friends.

Mind you, as far as boys and girls are concerned, they still get into minor disagreements, you'd think they were brother and sister! That's why they are out now exploring some part of the farm, but we have gone to great pains to point out the dangers and as Jocelyn is already aware of them she's been a great guide for Adam."

"This sounds all well and good but I do need to confirm or disprove the allegation that they are sleeping in, not just the same bedroom, but also the same bed as this would not be considered normal practise unless they were brother and sister in real life."

"Of course, neither would we condone them being together. Shall we go up to their rooms?"

"Yes please."

They got up and Karen led her upstairs, first into the right hand front bedroom where Jocelyn had left out the dolls house near the window. Miss Bowder opened a few drawers, finding plenty of girls clothes along with a girls annual casually left on the solitary wooden chair by the door.

"Quite tidy, isn't she?"

Karen smiled. "Yes, that's reminded me I haven't checked on Adam's room and I know he's nothing like as tidy as Jocelyn!"

They crossed the landing to the other front

bedroom and opened the door. Not surprisingly, Adam's room was quite a mess with Lego strewn across the floor, bedclothes thrown open with the bed unmade, a pair of underpants lying by the bed and several astronomy books on the dresser.

Miss Bowder chuckled. "I had a younger brother and our mother despaired as his room was much like this. I'm satisfied with the sleeping arrangements. I just need to check on something as we always do our research before undertaking an interview.

I gather from Louth County Hospital that the boy, Adam, had an accident, let's see, on July 26th, can you just run through what happened?"

"Oh that was the day Jocelyn arrived. Adam arrived the day before and I had forgotten Jocelyn was also coming for the summer. When she and Adam first met she was quite upset as she thought she had the summer here to herself. She had been before so went out to the swing out back and Adam followed her. It seemed she was quite upset and when he took his turn on the swing, she started to push him but was in a world of her own and pushed too hard. Poor Adam fell off the swing and we heard the shout so we went out and felt it best to take him to the hospital just as a precaution. Naturally Jocelyn had to come with us and she was utterly distraught and so apologetic to Adam.

I think that's why they've become close as

she is three years older than him and seems to have taken on the task of looking after him and helping and encouraging him to get out more. He in turn seems to have forgiven her and they've found quite a few things in common which has really helped. I sometimes catch them playing Thunderbirds, you know, Lady Penelope and Parker and it's quite funny to hear them play acting.

I think that's what's calmed things down and they both seem to be really enjoying the summer now."

"I see, a final thing, *marriage*?"

Karen laughed and shook her head. "They were playing a game and one of the tasks meant they had to play act at getting married. You ought to have seen Adam's horrified face. However I performed the so called ceremony and they ended up laughing it off. Jocelyn does occasionally tease Adam that they're married so I had to knock that on the head as it was beginning to upset him, but they're OK now."

Miss Bowder smiled and chuckled. "Well Mrs Ashton, I've seen enough and I can assure you this won't be going any further. The accuser clearly misunderstood them and they were probably jesting between themselves and he misheard them. I'm sorry to have disturbed you and as far as I'm concerned it looks like they're in a good place."

"It is better for you to do your job as we know

there are children out there not as fortunate as Jocelyn and Adam."

"Quite. I'll bid you farewell."

They walked downstairs and Miss Bowder collected her coat, stepping out to her car just as Adam and Jocelyn walked into view.

Karen's heart jumped into her mouth … All it would take now would be for one or both of them to let slip what it was like before they were separated.

Miss Bowder smiled at them.

"Hello, you must be Jocelyn and Adam? Tell me, what's it like sharing a room and a bed with each other?"

Karen's heart sank.

Adam though, screwed up his face. "Eww, no way, share a bed with a girl? I'd rather be sick!"

Jocelyn had also spotted Aunty Karen's face, fortunately Miss Bowder was facing the kids and not Karen at the time.

"I don't mind playing with him but sharing a room, that's gross no thank you!"

Both carried on past Miss Bowder and went into the farmhouse as the lady turned to Karen.

"Sorry, I had to ask, just on the off chance, you might say. Sounds like you have your work cut out and I bet you're glad when they do go outside to play?"

"Tell me about it. Is that all now Miss Bowder?"

"Yes. No change to my assessment and I wish

you good luck. Having one or the other here over the summer sounds like fun but both at the same time? That makes you a hero in my book!"

With that Miss Bowder got in her car and drove off.

Karen went inside to find the kids kneeling on the settee looking out and watching the car disappear behind the outbuildings. She let out a big sigh.

"You two have no idea how close we all came to being in serious trouble."

"Why's that Aunty?" wondered Jocelyn as Adam looked worried too.

"Someone must have overheard you talking about sharing a bedroom and bed and reported us to the authorities. I suspect I know who too, as you haven't had much contact with anyone else whilst here. That chap who brought round the parcel that was delivered to the wrong address. Did you happen to say anything to him by accident?"

"Oh, I think I was saying something like wanting my own bed and bedroom when he cycled up to us and asked where the farm was. We let slip we weren't related as he thought we were brother and sister and that we were married. I'm sorry Aunty," Jocelyn looked upset and Karen held her gently.

"How were you to know he's the sort to cause trouble. Luckily she didn't come to us a week or so ago, otherwise things might have been different."

"But, but you haven't done anything wrong really?"

"Look at it like this, if you were really brother and sister then there wouldn't be a problem as many siblings often sleep in one room as lots of parents can't afford a big house.

But as you are not related to each other then that complicates things. But that's in the past and done with, you've both been good so no harm's been done in the end. As they say, if no one knows, then no one cares. I've just got to tell Uncle Gary tonight so he is forewarned. I suspect he will remind me it was my idea."

Later that evening, she was right of course.

CHAPTER 15: A TREE-MENDOUS ACHIEVEMENT

Saturday August 16th

The weekend saw a favourable change in the weather. On the Saturday, a spell of sunshine and light clouds encouraged Adam to go out exploring with Jocelyn and she insisted they go back to the wood they'd partially explored when they tried to get to the village.

Jocelyn skipped along the animal path as it entered the wood as Adam examined the plant life, remembering to avoid the poisonous ones. Deeper into the woods, they diverged from the original path before they reached the stream where Jocelyn had become stuck. A smaller animal track intrigued them and for a while the trees became quite dense, but thinned out when they came across a natural clearing with a stunning ash tree standing proud just off centre.

"Wow, that's a big un!" Adam ran up to the trunk which was wide and knobbly, suggesting it had to be quite old. There were also a few small niches cut into it, suggesting someone may have climbed it regularly and had made hand and footholds. He took hold and began to climb up to the first low hanging thick branch and crawled along it.

Jocelyn was looking around taking in the size of the tree and suddenly came against the upside-down giggling face of Adam. He'd hooked his legs around the branch and was hanging there watching her get closer.

"Silly boy!"

"You're upside down!'

"How daft are you? You're the one hanging upside-down. Mind you don't fall off and bang your head. Hah! Might knock some sense into you."

"Cheeky! Join me?"

"What! If I hang like that, I'll show my knickers!"

"You did that when you did the cartwheels and handstands when we explored the entrance to the tunnel last week! So I've seen yer knickers!"

Jocelyn had to laugh at his logic. "You know, for a boy, sometimes you do make sense!"

Her sense of adventure took hold as she found the hand holds and climbed up, then shuffled along side saddle on the branch before carefully positioning herself next to Adam then hooking her legs tight to the branch and flopped down. Naturally she was right and her short summer dress flopped down almost to her chin and both of them had to stifle laughing in case they fell off.

"I like those, they've got little yellow butterflies on!"

"Hang on, you've never seen them before!"

"I found them the other week when I accidentally looked in one of the drawers, sorry!"

"At least mine are clean, bet yours aren't!"

"They are that!"

"Not according to Aunty Karen. She says you're a mucky little pup and only change every few days or so!"

"Huh! Thank you Aunty! Mine are clean today."

"Don't believe you, prove it!" she answered mischievously.

"Huh! Cheeky!" he changed subject, "Fancy seeing how high we can climb? The blood's going to my head so I'm getting back up," Adam scrambled and managed to pull himself up to sit on the branch as Jocelyn did the same, mainly to stop him getting a better view.

"It does look like someone's been here before and made sure there are hand and footholds going up the trunk. Must be someone local. I'm game if you are, but if it gets too difficult or I feel unsafe then I'm going back down."

"OK, you first."

"No chance buster, if I wore trousers then yes, but I'm not having you enjoy the view, naughty boy Adam!"

Adam shrugged and they gradually climbed higher until the branches became thinner and they reached a point where they could see above the rest of the woods out into the distance before the branches became too weak to hold them. Belmont TV transmitter could be seen one way, although only the top half, the other way they could see across the valley and just make out the other farm, but Aunty and Uncles farmhouse was hidden by the wood.

It felt like a serene view and they enjoyed a few moments looking around to see what else they could spot, but Jocelyn tired of it and suggested to Adam they go down.

"Time to go down but we'll have to be very careful, climbing up is one thing but it's always harder going back down."

Adam looked down. "We did get quite high, didn't we?"

"Err, yes, but slow and careful, got it?"

He nodded and gradually they found their way down, mainly reversing their route and using the various hand and foot holds, although twice, Adam slipped making Jocelyn's heart jump into her mouth, but he clung on and eventually they reached the ground.

"Crikey, not sure I want to do that again in a hurry! It felt odd but when I slipped a couple of times I felt like someone held me!" Adam said as he looked up into the canopy.

"Too true, although at least I can say that I've climbed it! I think you climbed too high and the altitude affected you. Someone holding you, Hah!

Anyway, right, now show em!"

"Eh? What?"

"You've seen mine, now I see yours!"

"No way!" Adam began to run away but

caught his foot on a root and tumbled over as Jocelyn pounced on him, pinning him down. "Fair's fair, let me see!"

"NO! gerroff!"

She held him tighter. "Either you do it or I pull your shorts down. You're not getting away with seeing mine and me not seeing yours! I MEAN IT!"

Adam was stunned at how strong Jocelyn was but knew he owed her.

"Let me up then," he grumbled reluctantly. He stood in front of her and unzipped his fly and partially opened the shorts to reveal his white underpants. He was about to take the shorts down when Jocelyn stopped him.

"That's alright Adam, we're even now."

Surprised and relieved, he zipped up his shorts and watched her begin to walk away.

"Thank you," he said quietly with a dawning appreciation of his friend, she wasn't that bad really, as girls went, he realised. They made their way back through the wood and Adam began to mess about, jumping up and swinging on low hanging branches, then running ahead and climbed a little higher. Suddenly a branch snapped and he fell down against a thin branch, tearing through his shorts and he began to scream in agony.

Jocelyn raced over to him terrified as to what he'd done.

Adam's face was contorted as she realised the

stick had pushed up the front and side of his leg into the shorts and had twisted Adam's under pants in a type of tourniquet. There was no wonder he was screaming.

He was panting heavily and was red faced, with his face screwed up in pain. She sat next to him and held him as gently as she could.

"Adam, I, I'm going to have to look as I don't know what damage has been done. I need to loosen your shorts and try to get the stick out. Is that OK?"

"Y, yes, yes, just do it, it really hurts down there," he gasped in fits and starts.

She held him and unzipped the shorts and managed to pull the stick carefully out as Adam then rolled over on the ground, crying and holding his crotch and whimpering about 'them' burning.

She held him again, not sure what to do.

"I don't want to, but I think I need to look to see how bad it is ..."

"Just do it! They hurt like mad!" he cried.

Jocelyn shook her head and carefully pulled his pants away and down trying not to cause any more pain although Adam winced and screwed his face up again. She didn't know if it was through pain or embarrassment, probably both she figured.

"Alright, they're quite red, but I reckon that's to be expected."

He was still gasping, "They're so hot, I can't

stand it."

"I've had an idea," she opened their rucksack and pulled out the glass bottle which only had a little lemonade left in the bottom. "Drink this up and I'll go to the stream and fill it with cold stream water."

He did as he was told and Jocelyn rushed off to the stream. Racing back, she hesitated.

"Adam, I, I have to do this, trust me please."

She noted the large red bruise running up his leg and ending at the top of his hip and felt sorry for him. Carefully she again peeled down his underpants and positioned the cool glass bottle so that it was resting gently on the affected area. He continued to sob but sighed with relief.

"Oh, that's better, sooo cool," he continued to pant but slowly his normal breathing returned as Jocelyn sat next to him and held his hand. She fished out her handkerchief and gave it to him to wipe away his tears.

"I'm sorry, I had to do something, I, I had to look to see what I could do. Sorry."

Adam let out a long sigh. "If it had been another boy with me I reckon they would have panicked. I'm, I'm glad it's you. I think you might make a great nurse as you were so careful and worked out what to do."

Jocelyn smiled and gave him a quick peck on the cheek, "We need to get back, can you stand and walk?"

"Ye- yes, I think so. Help me up."

They took the bottle out and stowed it in the rucksack, although Jocleyn couldn't help think that it would have to be thoroughly cleaned before she touched that bottle again! Adam struggled as he held on to Jocelyn's arm but he stood up and wavered a little as with Jocelyn's help he carefully pulled up his pants, very gingerly then pulled up what remained of his shorts. He looked like he'd wet himself too when it had happened, but Jocelyn hadn't said anything to save his embarrassment; they began to walk back somewhat slowly and awkwardly.

They'd not quite reached the entrance to the walled garden when Jocelyn called out for Aunty Karen. She suddenly appeared, spotted them and rushed to meet them exclaiming as she asked what had happened.

Jocelyn explained as quickly as she could as Karen helped Adam into the farmhouse, then the front room and onto the settee. She was about to take down his shorts and pants when she realised something.

"Jocelyn, out!"

"Err, but I've already se …"

"OUT!'

#

"Is he alright Aunty?"

"Yes love, He's going to be quite bruised, so is his ego after you pulled his pants down and put an ice cold bottle next to his testicles."

"I had to do something, he was screaming out that they were burning so what could I do!"

"I guess you did the right thing under the circumstances. He understands and says that he wishes he'd not seen your knickers. Care to explain, young lady?"

"We climbed the big ash tree and at first hung upside down on the bottom branch. He's seen them before when I did cartwheels so it didn't bother me."

"JOCELYN! A lady doesn't do such things like that!"

Jocelyn laughed. "That's not what Uncle Gary told me about you when you were both kids!"

Karen winked at her. "Touché. Anyway, he'll be a bit bruised and will walk a bit funny for a few days, but he's pretty lucky. From what I gather, those bits down there are quite tough!"

"Is he covered up so I can go in and see him?"

"Yes love, he's got a blanket over his lap but nothing else under it so don't be a tease!"

Jocelyn went into the front room, Adam looked shyly at her as he watched her come up to him. She dragged one of the wooden chairs across from the dinning table from the far end of the room and sat next to him.

They held hands and didn't talk for a while.

Finally, "Do they still hurt?"

"Yes."

"If you need anything just ask."

"Do you think Aunty Karen will let me have some lemonade?"

"I'll go and ask her, I'm sure she will. I'd say don't move, but you already know that!"

She popped out and a short while later came back with a small glass. "Aunty Karen says don't drink too much otherwise you'll need the loo, it might be painful to pee for a while and the nearest is the outside privy!"

"Oh, good point. I'll only sip."

Aunty Karen came in with the torn shorts. "You've done a good job wrecking these, young man. I forget, did your mum pack a couple of pairs?"

"No, I just have two pairs of trousers and a pair of shorts. I don't think Mum thought I'd be outside exploring!"

"No shorts now though Adam," quipped Jocelyn trying to bring a smile to his face.

"Exactly, you've plenty of underpants so they're not a problem but I have to go to Louth tomorrow anyway, so I'll have a look round and get you some new shorts. How do you feel now?"

"A bit better than before, cooler there if you know what I mean. Can I put something on now?"

"Well, that depends on how delicate you are feeling there."

"I can try."

Without being asked, Jocelyn went out of the room and they heard her bound up the stairs and, as Adam's room was directly above the living room, they heard her run across the room and rummage in one of the drawers.

A few minutes later she rushed downstairs and presented him with a clean pair of underpants and his trousers.

He looked at her, unsure of how to react, but he shyly took them and said, "thank you, sis."

Karen glanced at each of them in turn and shook her head. "We'll leave you to get dressed unless you need me?"

Adam's face took on a look of horror, despite the fact that Aunty Karen had helped him out of his shorts and pants, but that was when he was still in agony and didn't care.

Now, it was different.

"I'll do it. Thank you."

They left him to it.

Ten minutes later after hearing him struggle and Karen holding Jocelyn back from going in to help, he emerged and walked gingerly to the stairs. "Is it OK for me to go up and lie down?"

"Of course you can. Jocelyn, follow him up to make sure he doesn't fall down the stairs."

Adam wrinkled his nose at the thought he needed a bodyguard, but relented and slowly made his way painfully up the stairs. He went through into his room and Jocelyn stopped at the door.

"Whatcha going to do?"

"Take them off and lie here as I'm sore."

"Alright. I'll go then."

She took him by surprise again by giving him a peck on the cheek. "Apart from your accident, I enjoyed climbing the tree with you," she hesitated, "I owe you now."

She winked at him and didn't wait for an answer or retort, closing the door as she left.

#

They sat at the dinner table as the news finished and the weather forecaster indicated a hot spell might be on the way. Uncle Gary had kept quiet until it finished.

"So, meat and two veg OK now?"

Both Karen and Jocelyn almost spat out their tea as Adam sat looking sheepish.

"Yes Uncle."

"Teach you a lesson, never take nature for granted. Mind you, you almost got to the top of that old ash tree? I'm impressed."

"There were hand and footholds which really helped," Jocelyn noted.

"And guess who carved them all the way up, eh, Jocelyn?"

Both Adam and Jocelyn looked with wide eyes at him as Karen chuckled.

"Remember, who owned the farmhouse before us?" she asked. Gary smiled at the kids.

"I was a boy here once, you two. Took blooming ages to cut all those very helpful notches up the trunk. Some of the thicker branches were good too so I hope you used them as well?"

Adam nodded. "Yes, we did."

"Now tell them the full story!" suggested Karen and they looked at him and her, puzzled.

"I got almost to the top like you two. On the way down I fell off and broke my arm! My parents were furious."

"Yeah, and you never climbed it again after all that effort!" quipped Karen.

"Now you know why it took so long to fix the leaking roof. I'm sorry to admit, it left me afraid of heights!"

"Cluck, cluck, cluck!" Karen was enjoying his discomfort.

"BUT. Let's not forget that these two climbed a dangerous tree and could have been killed!" Gary changed tack and stared from one to the other making them squirm.

"But we didn't, did we Adam? Fall from it!"

"It was worth it for the view!"

"Exactly!" Jocelyn concurred with a nod of her head.

"I have to say I am actually pretty proud of you both and I do remember the view, although mine was spoiled as it was quite a cloudy day. In fact, it was a little foggy and I think that's why I fell as the lower branches were a bit slippery."

"How high was you when you fell, uncle?" Adam was intrigued.

"Oh at least thirty feet up!"

"Liar! You told me it was ten feet! Otherwise you'd have been killed!"

"Well, it felt like thirty foot! Could have been forty even!"

The kids couldn't stop laughing although Adam winced every so often, but at least it cheered him up for the rest of the evening.

CHAPTER 16:
NIGHTWATCHING WITH GARY
Monday August 18th

Monday evening, after dinner, Uncle Gary disappeared upstairs for a while leaving Karen and the kids to clear the dishes and wash and dry them before Jocelyn and Adam had a few games of Frustration. Adam was making a good recovery and not walking awkwardly any more and he'd privately confirmed to Aunty Karen that his testicles no longer hurt or were red, so he was pretty relieved no damage had been done.

It was nearly twenty past eight and the sun was setting as the kids expected to be told to head upstairs to bed, but tonight would be different.

Uncle Gary had gone out to the car a few times then came indoors just as Karen was about to tell Jocelyn and Adam to go get ready for bed.

"Right, change of plan for this evening. How do you kids fancy staying up late with me to watch the stars, planets and the moon and listen for night time wildlife?"

Even Adam's eyes went wide with excitement at this prospect.

Aunty Karen frowned. "How late?"

"They're on holiday and we'll be back between ten and eleven. It'll be good for them as it's a lovely clear night and I have a surprise for them when we get up to the top of the fields."

"Oh alright then, I'll stay here as I want to watch' Boy Meets Girl: Across the Frontier' on BBC2 at five past nine, but if they start to get sleepy then you bring them straight back, OK?"

"Yes dear. Don't worry. I think they'll enjoy it. Now, you two, get your coats on as it will still get a bit chilly and where we're going is the same spot we went to the other day on the brow of the hill so there may be a bit of a chilly breeze.

Meet me at the car in a few minutes. Well? What are you waiting for?"

They dashed out and could be heard excitedly putting on their coats and shoes. Gary did the same and together they walked out to the Austin Countryman and got in; the kids didn't see what was hidden by a blanket in the back.

In the gathering dusk, Gary drove them up the track, then opened the gate and drove through before closing it again and very soon they were at the brow of the hill and he ushered them out of the car. He handed Adam the binoculars and told him to share with Jocelyn as he had something to set up. It was eight fifty and Adam spotted a slim crescent moon hanging just above the southwestern horizon and gasped at the sight in the binoculars. He urged Jocelyn to look and she also gasped, jiggled up and down with excitement, then moved her view to the right of the moon.

"There's a faint star to its right, just about

visible and it twinkles a lot. She moved further to the right and suddenly went 'Wow!'

She handed the binoculars to Adam again and he started from the moon and found the smaller star then moved a little further on and gasped.

"There's a bright star like thing but there's something either side of it!"

"Sounds like you've spotted Jupiter then," Uncle Gary said as he placed his old but trusty refracting telescope down and roughly lined it up on the moon. He motioned for Adam to look in the eyepiece and as Adam did so he couldn't contain his excitement.

"Uncle Gary, Uncle Gary, I can see craters! There's a big dark oval patch close to the edge."

"Ahh, that'll be Mare Crisium, the Sea of Crises. Quite prominent at this phase. The moon is roughly half way between new and the first quarter. Let Jocelyn look quickly because we need to look at Jupiter before it sets."

Jocelyn took hold of the eyepiece but brought the telescope to line up with her rather than keeping it on the moon. Uncle Gary gently showed her how to use the small finderscope to line up on the moon, then look through the main eyepiece without moving the telescope up to her eye and she too was taken with the view. Gary gave the binoculars to Adam and pointed roughly lower and to the right of Jupiter.

"Do you see another star Adam?"

"Yes, yes I can."

"That's the innermost planet, Mercury. Jocelyn, can you see where Adam is looking with the binoculars? Point the telescope in that direction and see if you ca …

"GOT IT!" she exclaimed with triumph. "It's just a bright star but seems to be fading in and out."

"Ahh, there's some slight haze bands low down causing it to dim then brighten again."

She let Adam have a look but both agreed they couldn't see anything more than a star like object.

"That's because it is a small planet, not as small as distant Pluto, but still it's the next smallest of the planets in our solar system. Now, Adam, put it on Jupiter, the bright star to the right of the moon.'

Adam did as he was told and quickly learned how to use the finderscope to spot the planet then look through the main telescope before inhaling sharply. He pulled away and let Jocelyn take a look. She was suitable impressed too.

Adam was shaking his head and almost overcome with the excitement. "There, there were three dots to one side and a single dot on the other and the star was actually a small disk with two dark bands across it!"

"Well done that young man. What about you Jocelyn?"

"Yes, I can see them and the bands. That's

amazing, what are they?"

"Well, I don't know anything too fancy as I'm not an Einstein, but I do know that Jupiter has two main bands and four moons that this telescope can show, so I reckon that's what you are seeing. Let me have a quick look."

Adam gave Jocelyn the binoculars as Uncle Gary lined up on the planet and smiled.

"Yes, looks like I'm right. Something you didn't know about me and I don't normally shout out about, but I am a member of Lincoln Astronomical Society and so know a few things about what can be seen in the night sky. It's the club's tenth anniversary this year, not bad eh?

So, so far you have seen Mercury, Jupiter and the moon. That star just to the right of the moon and a bit higher is Spica in Virgo ..."

"That's a constellation, isn't it?" butted in Adam.

"Yes. OK, so Jocelyn, as you have the binoculars, look in a similar distance as Jupiter to the moon, but the other way and a bit further. Can you see a reddish star visible to the naked eye?"

"Yes."

"Put it in the binoculars but slightly to the left of centre, what do you see?"

"Ohh, there's a fainter orange star to its lower right!"

"Good, the bright one we can see with our eyes is the planet Mars and in binoculars you can also see the red orange star called Antares in Scorpius. In fact I can now see it with the naked eye as the sky gets darker. See that Adam?"

Adam nodded as he'd taken over the telescope and was moving back and forth from Mars to Antares. "It's brighter than Antares but I can't see much of a disk on the planet!"

"No, you won't. It's a small planet so although it is well placed at the moment this telescope is only a basic one so can't show its disk very well. If I put a higher magnification eyepiece in, then it'll be harder to keep it in the view and it'll still look like a bright dot. Even so, you've now seen four planets."

"Four? Mercury, Jupiter and Mars ..." Adam was thinking it over when Jocelyn suddenly shouted out.

"EARTH!"

Gary laughed. Good girl. Yes, we can still see our planet as we're on it!"

They looked back towards where Mercury had been but it had already set and both the moon and Jupiter were now low in a deep ruddy red sunset sky.

Uncle Gary fetched a sheet for them to sit on and lean against the car then he covered them with a blanket as they sat down. He began to point out the stars and constellations as the sky grew darker and more popped into view. He took out a torch but when he turned it on, it was red!

"Red light doesn't spoil your vision at night

so amateur astronomers use them to look at charts to find objects to view with their telescopes."

He produced a book and opened it. "This is my Nortons sky atlas and it's one of the best out there. Now it's getting darker, can you see the milky band going up from the south to the left of Mars and arcing right across the sky overhead and behind us?"

In unison and quite quietly as they were in awe, "Yes, Uncle."

"That band is our Milky Way galaxy and we are in it. All the stars you see are in our galaxy. Isn't that amazing …"

Adam suddenly shouted and pointed upwards.

"A shooting star, make a wish," he closed his eyes and grinned. Jocelyn almost had tears in her eyes.

"This is magical Uncle Gary. I didn't know you were interested in this!"

"I didn't either. I thought you didn't like anything spacey!" added Adam.

"Now kids, what's the saying, never judge a book by its cover. I'm usually too busy or wrapped up in farm work, but occasionally I come up here and just look at the stars. If you live in or near the cities, it's too light from them so you don't get to see this view. Yet I have it all the time when the skies are clear. I wouldn't swap my life with a city dweller, not and lose this."

Gary continued to guide them round the sky pointing out a few things with the telescope, when he could find them in the finderscope that is. A globular cluster called M13, the star clouds along the Milky Way, coloured stars and much more.

Then he spied something that he was sure would blow their minds. "Adam, aim the binoculars in that direction and carefully wander round that part of the sky and tell me if you spot a fuzzy blob."

As Adam did as he was told, Gary aimed the telescope and just at the same time as Adam spotted the target. Jocelyn was looking through the telescope at it.

"It looks all fuzzy, a glow in this!"

"Same here but there are a few stars nearby in the binoculars."

"Don't blink."

In unison: "Eh?"

"The light from that object has travelled just over a million or more years to get to your eyes so, don't blink!"

"Wow, what is it?" Jocelyn beat Adam to the question.

"The Andromeda galaxy, it's another galaxy like our Milky Way. But it's light takes that long to reach us so if you blink, some of that light is wasted!"

They silently let that sink in with awe as they gazed in wonderment. Gary used the red torch to look at his watch. It was nearly twenty to eleven as he was thinking of them heading back when he noticed two objects he knew the kids would love.

He got up and aimed the telescope at a star low down in the east and called for them to take a look. Adam was first and couldn't contain himself.

"Oh my god, oh my god, that's SATURN! I can see the rings even with this!!!" Jocelyn took a look and was mesmerised by the small but clearly oval object with two darker gaps between the edges of the rings and the planet. She also spotted something else.

"There's a dot to the upper right of it, quite close."

Gary took a look then indicated to Adam to take a look too.

"That was well spotted Jocelyn, that's Saturn's largest moon, Titan. Good spot indeed. Can you see it Adam?"

Adam was speechless but nodded that he could. He stepped back and was clearly at a loss for words, so overwhelmed with what he'd seen that night.

Gary noticed something else just rising off to Saturn's left. Jocelyn had the binoculars and he roughly pointed in the direction as she followed and gasped. Adam had the telescope and scanned along from Saturn with the finder, then stopped suddenly. Gary could tell that both of them had found the object he wanted them to see.

"It's, it's a sparkly group of stars! I, I saw that early in the morning the other week from the bedroom window!" uttered Jocelyn as Adam took in the view. Gary smiled at them but they were too mesmerised to see.

It's called a star cluster by the name of the Pleiades or Messier 45 or the Seven Sisters star cluster. It's just rising and if you look with your eyes, you can just make it out."

The kids stood open mouthed as they spotted it and swapped instruments to look at it again.

Gary suddenly whispered to them to keep dead still and quiet but to look slowly to their left.

At first they couldn't see anything except a dim view of the field sloping away from them and the starry night. Then they spotted them.

A group of four badgers were crossing the field near to their position and had stopped, sniffing the air. Their white stripes just about stood out in the light summer night sky, then they seemed to decide all was well and they carried on past the enthralled threesome and disappeared down the hill out of sight.

"So there you are, you've even had badgers. Did you hear the hoot in the distance, somewhere down across the valley?"

"Yes," they replied quietly.

"A barn owl calling out to its mate. Well,

sorry to say but we'd best get heading home otherwise Aunty Karen will scalp me for keeping you out so late. But it was worth it, wasn't it?"

Both nodded vigorously as Uncle Gary packed away the telescope, blanket and sheet and they drove back to the farmhouse to an anxious Aunty Karen who just shook her head but smiled at how excited Jocelyn and Adam were. The kids raced up to their bedrooms as Karen went up to Gary and held him by the waist.

"Good as you thought it would be?"

"Better, even owls and badgers so I couldn't have asked for more."

"Well, I for one, don't expect them to sleep much as they're buzzing like bees around a hive. I hope they do sleep, but reckon tomorrow night might be a quiet day if they're still sleepy!

"Reckon you're right. I might even have a lie in tomorrow as it really felt good and they were as good as gold tonight."

With that Karen headed into the kitchen to make them hot cocoas before heading to bed.

CHAPTER 17: NIGHT CAPERS
Early hours of August 19th

Jocelyn awoke and used her torch to look at her clock. She got out of bed and wandered over to the window and parted the curtains. The sky was crystal clear and ablaze with stars, "That's it. I'm going to sneak outside and enjoy the sky for a while longer. You with me?"

Silence, then she remembered they were no longer sharing a room. She sighed, then as carefully as she could, she opened her bedroom door and crept across the landing to Adam's room and opened his door, slipped in and closed it behind her. "Are you asleep Adam?"

"No. Can't. I'm too excited with what we saw earlier!" he replied as he sat up wondering why she had come into his room.

She crept back to her room and, grabbing her clothes, she tip toed back. "It's just gone twenty minutes past midnight and I know Aunty Karen and Uncle Gary have gone to bed. If we're quiet, we can get dressed and go downstairs, now we know there is a key to get back indoors when we're finished. What do you say, want to see more of the night sky?"

He couldn't resist and as it was dark, they turned their backs to each other and got dressed quickly.

Jocelyn carefully opened the door whilst

trying to shield her torchlight so it wasn't too bright and they slipped out and closed the door, cringing when it did a light click. They paused, awaiting sounds from Aunty and Uncle's bedroom.

Nothing. Sighing with relief, they tip toed down the stairs remembering to avoid the squeaky one, unhooked their coats and as quietly as they could, put on their shoes.

Adam had a brainwave and quietly went into the front living room and looked along the bookcase.

"Got it!" he whispered to himself as he picked the small book off the shelf and put it in his pocket. He rejoined Jocelyn who was getting a little impatient.

They reached the door, the moment of truth as each remembered the last time they'd snuck out and accidentally became locked out.

"You just stay holding the door open and I'll check the key is still out here where they said," Jocelyn shone the torch to the small spot under the windowsill and there was the key and she grinned. "It's there, you can come out now Adam."

He joined her and they slowly closed the door making sure the Yale lock didn't make too much noise as it locked shut.

"Now what?" wondered Adam, but Jocelyn pointed the torch and he nodded and followed her lead. They entered the walled garden and made their way to the memorial bench and sat down. The farmhouse before them was dark, a black silhouette with a slightly lighter backdrop of the hill and dark woods leading up to the horizon.

The sky was filled with stars and Adam sighed with delight and fished the book out. 'The Observers book of Astronomy' by someone called Patrick Moore.

They didn't have a red torch so Jocelyn again shielded as much light as she could with her fingers and they leafed through it gradually as they began to work out what constellations they could see.

The bench faced north with east to their right and west to the left so together they stood and looked around towards the south. Adam pointed out three bright stars and looked in the book.

"I think they're called the summer triangle, top left is Deneb, that's in Cygnus, it's a swan. To its right is a slightly brighter one, Vega, in Lyra, it says it's a lyre but it looks like a harp if you ask me."

"What's the bottom one then?"

"I'm just finding that one. Ahh, Altair, in Aquila the eagle. Don't think it looks like an eagle!"

"Oh, I don't know, off to the sides is like the wings and the star lower down is its head."

"This says that's its tail but there are no stars

for the head. What were they thinking?"

"Who?"

"The Greeks and Romans. They named them a long time ago. Cygnus does look right but the bright star at top is actually its bum!"

"Really?"

"Not quite, it's the tail end again. The main stars look like a cross and it's sometimes called 'The Northern Cross' but the faint star at the end pointing down is the beak."

"I'd be cross too if I were flying downwards like that. It could crash!"

"Silly, but it'd be funny if it did! The Milky Way passes through it all."

"Why Milky Way?"

"They thought it looked like a milky river in the sky."

"Looks a bit turbulent if you ask me!"

"I'm reading about it now. I'm glad you brought your torch. Found the page. It's because there are patches of dust that block or dim the stars behind it."

"Aunty Karen wouldn't stand for that much dust! She'd soon have it cleaned up!" she suddenly jumped up, excited and pointing. "Shooting star, make a wish!"

Adam recovered from being startled and did so. They sat down as Jocelyn began to trace one of the northern constellations with her finger. Adam looked in that direction and smiled.

"The Great Bear, Ursa Major."

"Looks like a saucepan to me. Aunty Karen has used it to hit uncle Gary over the head when he's been naughty as the handle is a bit bent."

They giggled at that, neither realising they were both imagining the same scenes from a Tom and Jerry cartoon they'd seen recently.

Adam pointed to the bright right hand two stars as they pointed up.

"They're the pointer stars, they point the way up to the north star. See it?"

Jocelyn looked and nodded. "Is it me or are there some faint car headlights pointing up through the tail?"

Adam peered at the tail of the Great Bear and could just make out some faint beams fading in and out and then they were gone. "I saw something, perhaps there was a car the other side of the hill, there is a road off in that direction, you know, passing that big transmitter tower so might have been that."

"Adam, look, that cluster and Saturn are higher now."

He looked as Jocelyn leaned into him to get a better view. He wasn't sure what to think, normally he'd run a million miles if a girl sat next to him like that, but this summer holiday had changed him in ways he didn't understand. All he knew was that he no longer minded Jocelyn being so close and he looked at her and smiled.

"Look at us two, when we first met you tried to kill me with the swing!"

"Glad I didn't succeed!"

Adam lay his head against her shoulder and she tilted her head and rested lightly on his as they looked out at the starry heavens and gently held hands.

#

"Hello you two. It's a good spot for a bench, isn't it?"

Adam and Jocelyn came awake and stared at the lady who was then joined by a man. The lady indicated for them to shuffle up into the middle and then they sat down either side of them.

Both kids stared and didn't know what to do or say as it dawned on them that they could just see through the newcomers.

"Now little ones, don't be frightened, we're Gary's parents, Mollie and Geoffrey."

Both kids stayed quiet as mice, not knowing what to say and frozen to the spot.

"It's alright, we understand. We sometimes drift here and reminisce about old times and remember Gary playing here and growing up on the farm. It was very nice of them to put up a memorial bench to us."

Adam found his tongue, "Isn't it for Aunty Karen's parents too?"

"Yes, but we lived here a very long time, whilst Karen's parents, your grandparents Adam, only visited a few times. So we're the ones who spend our time here."

"So, you are ghosts then?" Jocelyn had to ask.

"Oh, yes, we don't seem to, well how can I put this, we're on or in another plane of existence for want of a better term. We come and go but don't have much control over it. We were drawn here and can only assume it is because you two are enjoying the same things as we did when we were alive."

"It's very peaceful here isn't it Jocelyn?" asked Geoffrey.

"Yes, yes it is. Do you miss being alive?" she blurted out and both ghosts chuckled.

"I guess that has to be a yes. We didn't expect to be killed you know," sighed Mollie.

"But in some ways, it was better we both passed whilst together," Geoffrey smiled at Mollie and she nodded.

"And we can see how well Gary and Karen are doing with the farm," added Mollie.

"Just remember, we're not really here and you should always try to enjoy your life as much as possible so, we'll leave you now and you can wake up …"

\#

Jocelyn bolted upright as she came awake, in doing so she jostled Adam who awoke too then they each looked at each other and looked around at the dimly lit scene.

"Did we ..?" she stuttered.

"I don't know, we must have been asleep."

"Mollie and Geoffrey ..."

"Yes, but how did you know what I dreamt?"

"I, I don't know ..."

"I'm getting cold, we ought to go in now, I'm not keen on staying out here any longer."

They stood up and walked quickly along the path and back to the front door of the farmhouse, little realising they'd been watched for the last ten minutes from a window.

This time the front door was no problem and they entered, locked it up, took off their coats and hung them up then removed their shoes, before carefully creeping up the stairs to their rooms.

Jocelyn realised Adam was shivering quite badly.

"You OK?" she asked quietly.

"N, n, no, I'm really cold and can't seem to get warmed up." he stuttered.

"Same here. Adam?"

"What?"

"Come into my bed, we have to get warm or we'll end up with colds."

"But, but we'll get in trouble?"

"No, we won't."

"You sure you want me in there?" he said as they entered her room.

"Adam?"

"Y, yes ..?"

"You talk too much, go get into your pyjamas

and come back OK?"

He was soon back and stood wondering where to lie down when Jocelyn opened her side of the bed and indicated for him to get in.

He did so and snuggled in as she put her arm around him and whispered, "I heard somewhere that this is what the Russians do to keep warm."

"I still don't know where Russia is!"

"Somewhere off Norfolk I gather."

"Oh, that's a bit close isn't it?"

"Adam?"

"Yes?"

"NEVER say a word about this, got it?"

"OK."

They snuggled down and pretty soon fell deep asleep.

#

They'd heard them come back in after watching them from the landing window, but let them think they'd got in unnoticed and went back to bed.

Gary's alarm rang for 4am but he turned over and stopped it then reset it for 6am. "I can spare a few hours today."

Karen however got out of bed and went over to the door. "I'll just check on them, normally they're fast asleep and I reckon after all the excitement last night they'll be spark out!"

She tip toed along the landing and opened

the door quietly to Adam's room. The bed clothes were thrown open and no one was present. She grimaced then walked back out across the landing and opened Jocelyn's door, then stood there taking in the situation. She tip toed back to her bedroom and shook Gary who moaned and opened his eyes.

"What?" he croaked.

"You gotta see this for yourself," she carefully made her way back along the landing and quietly opened the bedroom door as Gary caught up with her.

Peeking in he took stock and they closed the door and went back to their room.

"So?" he asked sarcastically.

"They're snuggled up to each other!"

"And who's fault could that be I wonder?"

"But, but they've been so good for the last few weeks."

"Yes, but did you see how they were snuggled up to each other? He has his back to her. If you ask me, and I know what it's like out at the dead of night even in summer, it's bloody cold, I can tell you. So my guess is they were cold and did the natural thing. Look Karen, he's nine and she's twelve, not exactly raging teenagers are they! I doubt Adam has any feelings yet, or dare I say it, fully evolved equipment to do any damage!

They've had their fair share of arguments in the last few weeks so I doubt even Jocelyn is daft enough to risk doing something as stupid as, well, you know what."

"We started out like that! We argued then came together and look what happened!"

"For a start, we were in our late teens, I was a working lad and you had your head screwed on right. Secondly, well, we turned out alright didn't we? And we didn't 'do it' until you were eighteen!"

"True. They've gotten closer in the last week or so and that's why I'm worrying now. At least that Miss Bowder can't see this!"

"Karen, we've done the best we can and if you ask me they are good 'uns. Perhaps we shall see something blossom over the next few years when they come back for their summer holidays."

"Hark at you changing your tune. So you think they'll want to come back each year?"

"It'll be down to their parents but if I'm honest, I thought they'd be a pain staying with us, but I'm actually glad now you said yes."

"You big ol' softie. Get back in bed, time for me to ravage you!"

"Promises, promises." and he winked at her and began to strip off as they reached their own room.

#

Jocelyn slowly opened her eyes and daren't breathe. Adam was still fast asleep but she

249

unwrapped her arm from around his waist and wondered what to do. Aunty Karen would kill them if she found them lying together but just as she was about to try and wake up Adam, he stirred.

He tried to turn over then realised with horror he was lying next to Jocelyn and froze.

"Adam? You awake now?"

"Yes."

"You'd best get back to your room before Aunty Karen looks in on us. We'll be in deep trouble otherwise."

He managed to wriggle round and looked at her in the face.

"I'm sorry, I didn't mean to stay all night."

"You wally, it's just been a few hours, but we don't do it again, understood?"

"Yus Mi'lady."

A sudden gentle tapping at the door then Aunty Karen entered, not knowing what to expect.

"Wakey, wakey, rise and shine!"

They rapidly sat up in bed wiping the sleep from their eyes and looked at her.

"Oh, same bed now, are we?"

Jocelyn and Adam looked quickly at each other mouths open in shock and not knowing what to say.

Aunty Karen sat at the end of the bed, eyeing them up. "So, sneaking out to look at the stars, eh?"

The kids performed a double take and looked terrified.

"No need to worry. We heard you both try to go downstairs quietly but we're wise to you now. Saw you from the landing window and watched you go to the memorial bench and look round at the sky. You stayed out a while and even fell asleep on the bench. What made you both wake up at the same time and look round as if you were looking for someone?"

"Err, we didn't, I think I woke up because I'd got cold and didn't know I was leaning against Jocelyn, so woke her up at the same time when I moved," suggested Adam. Jocelyn was impressed at his cover up and taking the blame.

"And when I looked in on you around six am to see you both snuggled up here in Jocelyn's bed?"

"Adam was still very cold, so I didn't want him to catch a cold. We didn't do anything, promise!" both kids looked like they were about to burst into tears.

"I understand. I know you are both young but I'm sure you realise there is a reason why there are boys and girls, men and women. I do have hot water bottles to warm you up. Understand?"

They nodded vigorously.

"Now, it's almost eight so get yerselves up and I'll see you downstairs for breakfast. How about a nice cooked one as you've had a busy night?"

The looks on their faces showed such keenness and, as Aunty Karen left the room, Jocelyn got out of bed, grabbed her clothes and raced out of the room to claim dib's on the bathroom.

CHAPTER 18: DISASTER

That afternoon the skies above Lincolnshire grew darker as a storm front moved in. It began raining at teatime and although the lights flickered a few times the power stayed on, but the rain grew heavier with each passing hour.

Unbothered by it all, Adam and Jocelyn took to their favourite board games of Frustration and Mousetrap and were even given permission to play up in Jocelyn's room so that they didn't disturb Uncle Gary after he came in a little late from working in the fields.

Despite the fun but noisy evening they did notice the wind was picking up and the rain lashing down on the window, but Aunty Karen came up with mugs of hot chocolate as it had turned a little chilly. They happily drank it once it was cool enough and took their mugs down to the kitchen and washed them up, leaving them on the draining board then trouped into the living room and said goodnight to Uncle Gary and Aunty Karen.

They scrambled upstairs, Adam just beating Jocelyn to the bathroom to do his teeth but she pushed in with him, reminding him neither needed to change in there now they had their own rooms. Finally, teeth brushed, they stood on the landing and listened to the storm rage away.

"You going to be alright?" asked Jocelyn.

Adam looked at her in bemused shock.

"Me? Are you going to be alright?" he threw back at her and she shook her head.

"Of course, I'm older and more mature than you are and don't get frightened easily by something as silly as a bit of wind and rain!"

"Hah! Neither am I!" the landing suddenly lit up with a bright flash and a sharp roll of thunder, startling both of them yet they tried to put on brave faces.

"That was really close!" mumbled Jocelyn just as Aunty Karen shouted up to them.

"You two okay up there?"

In unison: "Yes Aunty."

Jocelyn: "Adam was scared though!"

"No I wasn't, you jumped halfway across the landing!"

"No I didn't, you did!"

"Oi! You two, enough, bed, both of you! Now!"

They went their separate ways and settled down to sleep.

#

Well, they would have done but the storm raged on as heavy rain then hailstones crashed down on the roof.

Gary and Karen came up to bed and Karen popped her head round each door.

"Adam, you alright?"

A sleepy voice answered, "Yeah, it's loud isn't

it?"

"Yes love, can't last much longer so see you in the morning."

"Night Aunty."

"Night night Adam."

Next, Jocelyn's room.

"You asleep Jocelyn?"

A light snore came from her bed and Karen smiled, that girl could sleep through anything, Karen mused. As she went into their own room Karen saw Gary was in his pyjamas but didn't look happy.

"Can you hear a flapping?"

"No, why?"

"Must be me, could have sworn I heard something as we came up the stairs. I'll have to check the roof on the house and the outbuildings in the morning as this is pretty fierce."

"We've been here how many years now? Only had that one incident above Adam's room back in June."

"Yeah, and they said that was a once in a hundred years storm and listen to it outside ..."

"It'll be alright. Let's get some sleep. Up at the normal time?"

"Yes, alarm's set as usual."

They climbed into bed and despite the noise, were soon fast asleep.

Until just turned midnight when there was an almighty crash and then squeals from the room next door.

Adam's.

Instantly awake, they rushed out to find Jocelyn in hysteria standing in the open doorway to Adam's room.

Looking in, half the ceiling lay on the bed covering it with debris as the wind whistled round the room and the rain poured in.

Adam was buried under it.

"ADAM!" shouted Gary and Karen as Karen held on to Jocelyn who was shaking and crying, calling Adam's name. "Stay back, take Jocelyn downstairs for now and I'll find Adam."

"Stuff that!" cried Karen but motioned for Jocelyn to go downstairs. She didn't but retreated to her own room with the door open so she could watch as they searched for him.

Gary was tearing at the ceiling debris clearing it from the bed and could hear muffled sounds as if Adam was trying to call for help. Karen joined in as the rain continued to pour in and the wind whipped debris around the room. Adam's voice became a little louder and, as they removed the last pieces from the bed they stood back, shocked.

He wasn't in the bed.

Then they heard him again and Gary began to pull sections of the lath and plaster ceiling from the side of the bed to find Adam scrambling out from under it and running into Karen's arms sobbing.

They got out of the room and Gary closed the

door, fortunately it hadn't been damaged when the ceiling collapsed in and he turned to Karen and Adam as Jocelyn ran out of her room and wrapped her arms around Adam, crying.

"Let's get downstairs, it'll be safer although I think it's only Adam's room that's affected," Gary pointed to the stairs but Karen had another idea.

"Jocelyn, take him downstairs and Uncle Gary and I will fetch bedding for us all, we'll sleep on the floor in the living room until things calm down."

The kids did as they were told.

When Gary and Karen came downstairs they found them huddled together on the settee with Adam clinging on to Jocelyn and whimpering. She was quietly talking to him, trying to calm him down as Uncle Gary knelt down in front of them.

"Adam? Adam? It's alright now, you're safe. What happened?"

"I could hear it getting worse and something sounded as if it was breaking. Something semed to tell me to hide so I jumped out of bed and crawled underneath just in time. There was a loud crash and next thing I knew, I couldn't get out from under the bed. I could hear the wind and things flying round the room and I'm wet all on my back."

Jocelyn nodded. "It's okay, it's not blood, it's rainwater, I'm wet now but I don't care. I'm here for you Adam."

Karen shook her head but was touched by such a caring bond that had developed between them.

"Right, however we do need you to get out of the wet clothes, sounds like both of you now."

"I'll dash upstairs and see what I can find that's not wet of Adam's. Karen, can you get something for Jocelyn? When you come down, Jocelyn can get changed in the kitchen whilst Adam changes in here."

Very soon both children were dressed in their daytime clothing and were back on the settee cuddled up, although Adam was a bit brighter after being checked over by Gary.

"Well? Is he OK?" Karen was concerned.

"Yes love, not a scratch. he was very lucky and good for you for being so alert Adam, proud of you, young man."

Adam nodded. "Can I stay here with Jocelyn on the settee, uncle."

"Yes of course you can as long as Jocelyn doesn't mind. We'll be here on the floor and hopefully the storm is moving away as it seems a bit quieter now."

"Happy to stay on here with Adam. We're safe here."

Karen had by then managed to put down several layers of blankets and sheets, indicating they could get into the makeshift bed.

Gary walked over to the light switch and the room went dark. they heard him fumble his way onto the 'bed' with a grumble from Aunty Karen that he'd almost stepped on her, but eventually all went quiet and with a sigh of relief, they could tell the storm was indeed subsiding.

#

Daybreak. Without his alarm, you'd have thought Gary would have overslept under the circumstances but like clockwork, he awoke just after 4am, spotted the time on the goldstarburst wall clock over the fireplace and turned back over, snuggling into Karen as he promptly went back to sleep.

Something pinged his subconscious and he slowly came awake, as did Karen as they remembered they were sleeping on the floor. The room was bright and the wall clock said eight twenty five as he turned to see no one on the settee. A sound from above and voices told him the kids were upstairs and he bolted upright, bringing Karen fully awake.

"Was-a-time is it?" she mumbled.

"Eight twenty six. I think the kids are upstairs above us in Adam's room."

"What the 'eck do they think they're doing?"

They grabbed their dressing gowns; rushed upstairs to find Jocelyn and Adam tidying the room up, placing the manageable chunks of the ceiling into a pile next to the window, which was thankfully still in one piece. Sunlight streamed through a rather large hole in, not just the ceiling but the roof as well, but they could just see something sticking through the tiled roof and Gary shook his head.

"That could have been a whole lot more serious!"

"Morning Uncle Gary, Aunty Karen. We wanted to do what we could to help clear up so as we were both awake, we came up and started trying to tidy up."

"You know what you two? You are a credit to both your families. I'm going to make sure they know it too!" Gary replied, full of pride at how resilient they were.

He looked up through the gap in the ceiling and roof and shook his head as Karen looked up too.

"It's my fault. I rushed the repair to the roof tiles. I could have killed Adam!"

An unexpected tear flowed down his face as he walked out of the room with Karen following behind, indicating to the kids not to follow.

He went into their own bedroom and sat heavily on the bed as Karen sat and hugged him.

"Hey, now look here you! You did the best with what you had and if you'd not done the repair the damage could have been a whole lot worse. Think of it like this, Adam would have still been sharing a room with Jocelyn. Without that repair, the whole roof might have come off and then we'd have been in deep shit, buster. So, it's not your fault and I'm sure Adam doesn't hold it against you."

Without really meaning to, the children had been listening in and rushed in and jumped on Gary as they hugged him, telling him how much they loved him and Aunty Karen and that it wasn't his fault.

It was a memory he would treasure until his dying day, many years in the future.

#

Karen cooked a hearty breakfast which they all scoffed down like there was going to be no tomorrow and they marvelled at the bright blue sunny day outside. A complete contrast to the day before.

As they sat round the dining table finishing off breakfast, Gary shook his head.

"Well, you know what this means?"

They all looked at him wondering what was coming next.

"The dynamic duo will have to share a room and bed again!"

In unison from Jocelyn and Adam: "YES!"

Karen and Gary looked at them both and the kids began to study the kitchen ceiling, avoiding the adults eyes on them.

"You know what I think?" offered Karen. "You and Adam should share and I will share with Jocelyn," the sheer look of horror on the kids faces was one to behold.

But Gary was also not having that.

"Share the marital bed with my nephew? No way. He snored like a trouper early this morning! Anyway," he quickly added before Adam could protest about the snoring, "they're perfectly sensible and have shared for most of the summer so what's just a few more days anyway?"

"You'll get us shot you will. What if we get another official visit?"

"Why would they do that? We have a legitimate reason now as the roof damage is quite obvious and we'd just say we had to sort something out. You two are alright if you share again as long as you are sensible?"

Jocelyn glanced at Adam and smiled as they both replied: "Yes Uncle!"

"There you are then. Adam can't go back into his room with all that damage and I noticed the bed now has a crack in it so we're going to have to replace it and a lot of other things too. Shame really as that bed and the others have been in this house for over a hundred years, built from wood from Ashton Wood no less. I'll put a tarpaulin over the roof hole for now but it's not safe for anyone to be in that room until it is properly repaired.

Aunty Karen shook her head as was her wont and finally agreed much to Jocelyn and Adam's delight.

After breakfast, they carefully rummaged

through what had been Adam's room and found most of his clothes were still dry, having been in the wardrobe which was on a side of the room that had not got wet.

Karen and Jocelyn made space again in the dresser and wardrobe in her room and his clothes were brought in. Adam was pleased he was getting the side of the bed he'd had previously and Uncle Gary brought back the partition he'd made a few weeks earlier to keep them apart in the bed.

Karen, helped by Jocelyn and Adam, then made up the bed and once done, Karen announced it was time to have a mid morning break, heading down to the kitchen after gathering orders for her lemonade, as they were all warm after their exertions. Meanwhile, Uncle Gary had driven into Louth and just before lunch he arrived back with a large roll of plastic sheeting and lots of other items, mainly for the roof.

The afternoon was a busy affair as Jocelyn and Adam both stood on the bottom rung of the ladder as Uncle Gary set about getting the temporary cover fixed over the hole in the roof. He found that a large fencing post he had been going to take to the bottom field to replace a rotten one had been whipped up and come crashing down on the section of roof he'd done the temporary repair to.

"But Uncle, I thought I read somewhere that

you needed a hurricane to pick up things like that?" queried Adam. Jocelyn nodded as she had thought the same.

"No, we don't get hurricanes or tornados in this country but it was a strong gale last night. We must have been very unlucky for it to have picked up that thick fence post and drop it right on the side of the roof above Adam's room. Let's hope that's the last of these storms for a hundred years eh?"

In unison: "Yes Uncle Gary!"

Finally after a long day, just before dinnertime, they marched in ready for the chicken and bacon pie, mashed potato, peas, carrots and a rich gravy.

It was soon demolished in short order and they all slumped down in front of the TV which in the end no one watched as they all fell asleep.

It had been a strange twenty four hours indeed and one they did not wish to repeat ever again.

CHAPTER 19: THE LAKE
Friday August 22nd

"I think Aunty Karen is glad we've come out to explore, I don't think we were quiet enough first thing this morning playing with the dolls house!"

Adam looked at Jocelyn as they climbed over the stile, retracing their route when they had been playing at exploring the planets the other week. She may had had fun playing with the dolls house but he on the other hand …

Instead he just smiled at her and remembered she had played some of his games. Aunty Karen kept reminding him, play nice!

"So where to today then? We must have done most of the farmland?"

"Not quite. I forgot to ask them about the copse of woodland that was further down the stream we crossed when we played at planet exploring. I thought I spotted an animal track following the stream so how about we see what's along there?"

"OK. You've got the rucksack, as usual, hope there is food in there in case it's a long trek. Perhaps another star trek?" he chuckled at his own joke and Jocelyn just shook her head.

"Of course, silly billy. Aunty Karen wouldn't let us out before lunchtime without sandwiches, pork pies and naturally a big bottle of her lemonade."

"I hope the trees are big enough to hide me then when I need to pee. I love her lemonade but it does seem to go through me," he chuckled as Jocelyn again shook her head but also laughed.

"Hold it in if you need to! There, we've passed the 'rocky' planet but not been attacked so we must have done a good job there."

Adam smiled at how she remembered their afternoon of space exploration and the stories they'd made up.

They reached the locked gate and climbed over, then eventually crossed the stream via the wooden bridge. Jocelyn looked about and then struck off along the side of the stream as it weaved around heading towards a dense looking patch of woodland.

"Can we stop to have some lemonade?"

Jocelyn stopped and turned to look at Adam. "What about not wanting to drink too much in case you needed a wee?"

Adam kicked at a loose sod of grass and it flew past Jocelyn who just stared at him in a mean way.

"I'm glad that didn't hit me or you'd be in trouble!"

Adam looked down at his feet. "Sorry, I'm just getting a bit bored and thirsty. It's a bit warmer today, isn't it?"

"Yeah, that forecaster did say we might be in for a good week into next week," she sighed. "You realise that's our last week on holiday here. Uncle Gary did say a few weeks ago that if we weren't careful it would be gone in a flash. I'll miss being here ... with you."

Adam was quiet as they continued to walk along the, almost impossible to see, animal track. He'd been thinking the same but didn't want to admit he'd miss her once he went back home.

They approached the edge of the wood which started out with just a few scattered trees, mainly deciduous, but as they headed in, still following the stream, the wood got denser and they had to wind their way between the trees, then something glimmered up ahead.

Jocelyn was the first to spot it. "Wow!"

The trees suddenly stopped as the stream to their left discharged into a small lake. Adam looked at it and sized it up.

"That has to be a hundred feet across and wide!"

"And probably deep too so we'd best be careful. It's really secluded, look, off to the right hand side there's a small wooden jetty over there."

With Jocelyn leading the way they circled to the right around the lake until they reached the jetty which, on closer examination, was somewhat run down and the hand rails had fallen into the water.

Jocelyn tentatively stepped on it and edged towards the end testing it as she went along.

"This is still sturdy. She did a little jump, then a bigger one. "Yes, it'll hold us both. How about that picnic here?"

"Yeah, I love it. This can be a water planet, with aliens that only live in water!"

"Trust you to come up with something like that! So, alien mermen and merwomen!"

"Ahh, yes, guess so."

Jocelyn walked past him and sat down on a nearby log, looking thoughtful.

"What's the matter?"

"Nothing. Well, it's quite warm and it's pretty secluded, I haven't seen or heard anyone since we explored this way."

"So?"

"Have you heard of skinny dipping?" she nonchalantly asked.

"Eh?"

"I'm, well, put it like this, when you had your accident and I had to, you know, see your bits as you were in pain and I fetched some cold water in the bottle and put it on your, err, balls, to cool them ..."

Adam, slightly flushed. "Yes ..?"

"I'm like you in that I like to be fair and I've felt guilty since then. So why don't we go skinny dipping in the lake for a while to cool off and then when we're dry, have our picnic?"

"Skinny dipping?"

"Yes, we both take our clothes off and swim naked."

Adam stood looking at her open mouthed.

"Adam, we'd be even then and after that we wouldn't need to speak about it again."

He was still a little speechless.

"OK, you don't agree so it can stay one sided, that I have seen your meat and two veg as Uncle Gary called them and you haven't seen me."

"You'd allow me to see you?" he asked incredulously.

"Adam, you're talking too much again!"

Jocelyn loosened her blouse then took it off revealing her vest then took that off too. Adam just stood there not sure how to react.

"Well? I'm going for a swim regardless so why not join me?' she teased then unbuttoned her skirt at the side and let it down. She stepped out of it and looked in the rucksack as Adam took in the sight of her in her underwear and socks and shoes.

He took off his shirt and unzipped his shorts as Jocelyn rummaged in the rucksack and brought out the ground sheet for them to sit on, but instead, she took her shoes and socks off and stood on the sheet then smiled at Adam.

"Put it like this, we're friends, aren't we?"

"Yes."

"And I'm hoping we'll be able to come back next year but, and this is really important, I will be what mother calls 'developing into a young woman' so this is the only time I will do this for you. So …" she took down her pants and Adam took off his shoes and socks and followed suit as they both stood on the sheet, naked.

Jocelyn stepped up to him and crouched down looking at his groin intently.

"What are you doing?" he asked, nervously.

"Checking the bruise. It's pretty much gone and you can barely see any mark where that stick pushed up through your shorts and pants. You were very lucky. The rest look ok too!" she grinned and then looked to one side, suddenly embarrassed at what she'd done.

Adam was also looking down at where the bruise had been and nodded. "Yeah, it and they don't hurt anymore. It was your quick thinking that helped, thanks."

"I'm glad. Come on, lets get in and have a swim, but not too far from this jetty and keep an eye on the lake bottom. If it gets too deep then we head back and stay near the jetty. Got it?" she asked as she held out her hand. Together they walked along the short jetty, sat dangling their feet in the water to become acclimatised then Jocelyn slipped in followed by Adam.

For half an hour they swam, splashed each other and had fun. Adam completely forgot about being naked although a few times he did feel his extremities were getting a little cold. Something brushed past his belly and he realised it wasn't Jocelyn, then spotted what it was.

A large, silvery dark fish, then he spotted several as he heard Jocelyn calling to him.

"Adam, you've gone a bit too far. Come back here to this end."

He swam over to her and pointed back to where he'd been.

"There's big fish in here!"

"I'm not surprised. Anyway, I think we should get out, we haven't any towels except that little one for our hands and that's no good. It's warm enough if we just sit on the jetty to dry off."

She swam to the jetty but Adam raced her and pulled himself up as she watched his cute bottom and accompaniments before he turned and sat down.

"Help me up?"

He put out a hand and she hauled herself out and sat next to him dripping wet.

They looked at each other.

"Sorry, I shouldn't stare." Adam said. Jocelyn took his hand and held it.

"Well, I'm looking at you. So what's the big deal? I find adults funny. We all know what each other has got so why the big fuss? I feel safe with you," she said.

"I wish you were my sister!"

Jocelyn put her wet arm around his shoulders.

"I do too. But we are sort of related aren't we? Aunty Karen and Uncle Gary are my godparents and they are your true aunty and uncle, so to me that makes us related, in a way if you get my meaning. Hey, didn't we get married a few weeks back!"

"Trust you to remember that!" Adam reached back and grabbed the small towel and dried her back.

"Thanks, but not the front, seeing is one thing but touching …"

"Yeah, understood."

They sat and gradually dried off enough to get dressed. The sandwiches and lemonade were just what was needed after their exertions and soon they had everything packed up to head back for the farmhouse.

"Let's explore round the lake edge as it should bring us back to where the old track was," suggested Jocelyn and the began to work their way round, just keeping the lake edge in view through the trees.

Adam was deep in thought after what had happened at the lake so didn't realise Jocelyn had stopped suddenly until he bumped into her.

"Hey up, what's up?"

She pointed ahead. There was a small rough parallel set of tracks that suggested a vehicle had been down it, but a long time ago, the track that had seen better days and was becoming overgrown.

"Wonder where it leads?" she asked as Adam stood next to her. He looked about, then up at the sky and found the sun as a few clouds flitted past it. Looking off to their right it disappeared into the denser part of the wood extending along the shallow slope up the other side of the valley, whilst the other way it looked as if it led to the lake end.

"When Uncle Gary took us up to the highest part of his fields, past the old cottage, he pointed out another farmhouse across the valley. I reckon this leads in that general direction. Do you think we're on someone else's land?"

Jocelyn looked at Adam a little alarmed. "I never thought of that, I just assumed we were still on Uncle Gary and Aunty Karen's farmland, but what if we're on someone else's?"

"We'd best follow the this back to the lake and see if we can get round to where we first came in. Hope we don't meet anyone otherwise we're in big trouble!"

They turned to the left and followed the track until they reached a small clearing that had been left to become rough ground where there was a sign erected with red painted letters on it:

PRIVATE PROPERTY.
DANGER:
NO SWIMMING OR FISHING IN THIS LAKE.

Jocelyn looked at Adam and shrugged, "Oops. Looks like we were right. Lucky we weren't caught skinny dipping, by the way, don't say a word to Aunty or Uncle or our parents about what we did, OK? Best get moving!"

They spotted a small animal track and began

to follow it. Fortunately for them it seemed to follow the other side of the lake then, abruptly, they came across the continuation of the stream as it carried on from the lake through the woodland.

Adam kept noting where the sun was and every so often took his bearings and pointed the way forward. Jocelyn didn't argue, she'd noticed he was good with navigation, so put her trust in him. Eventually they rounded the lake and, crossing the original stream again, they found the first animal track they'd used at least a couple of hours earlier.

It didn't take too long for them to make their way back to the farmhouse, but before they entered, Jocelyn indicated for them to go through into the walled garden and she headed for the bench.

Sitting down, she patted the seat beside her and Adam did a quick salute and sat as she shook her head at him.

"Silly boy!"

"What are we doing here?"

"I think we have to be careful what we say about today, don't you? I mean, although we share a bedroom and bed, we're still separated by Uncle Gary's barrier and we have to change in separate rooms. So we'd best not mention we went skinny dipping in the lake, just that we had our picnic at its side before coming back. You agree?"

"I guess so, I don't want to get into trouble, even though, well, I enjoyed swimming with you, and, and I'm still amazed you suggested it."

"Remember, we're even now. But best keep it to ourselves. Oh, look, Aunty Karen is waving to us from the landing window. I hope she can't lip read!"

They both waved back and headed indoors to find Aunty Karen down in the kitchen with two glasses of lemonade ready for them.

"Had a good day then?" she asked.

"Yes, we've been down to the lake."

"Lake? Hang on, to the south of us, bottom of the valley between us and farmer Edwards land?"

"Err, yes, it's past the fields with the pits and hollows in and off to the left, surrounded by a wood."

"Oh. Did anyone see you there?"

"No, well, we didn't see anyone. We walked round the lake and had a picnic close to the jetty we found there. It's a bit old and broken."

"That's not our land, its Mr Edwards. You didn't go swimming did you?"

"Oh no aunty, of course not," Adam however made it sound almost like a confession. Aunty Karen looked at Jocelyn.

"Did you go swimming?" she asked pointedly.

Jocelyn squirmed at this as she could see a change in Aunty Karen.

"W, why?"

"You did, didn't you. I bet skinny dipping eh?" Aunty Karen indicted for both of them to sit with her at the kitchen table and they did so now, concerned at what was to come. Both lowered their heads.

"Sorry, Aunty. We aren't bothered and it's only the once and it was fun as it was warm." Jocelyn offered.

"There were large silvery black fish too!" added Adam as Karen eyed them both.

"What am I to do with you eh? So, you've seen each other - "

"But it's only fair as I had to help Adam when he hurt himself and I saw his willy and balls so we're even now!" defended Jocelyn as she began to wonder what punishment they would get.

Karen shook her head then started to laugh quietly which threw Jocelyn and Adam as it was certainly unexpected.

"I, I do understand and there are aspects of your two adventures that, well let's say mirror what happened to me and Gary when I came up visiting.

Look, Uncle Gary and I did the same thing a long time ago when we also discovered the lake, but also got into trouble as farmer Edwards, senior, caught us and gave us a right telling off I can tell you. Somewhat embarrassing as we'd just got out the lake so there was nothing left to the imagination you could say.

I'm not condoning what you've done, as kids will be kids and I applaud you for being fair to each other. You mention the farm track down to the lake looked old and not used in a long time and there is a reason for it.

Did you see the sign that was put up?"

Jocelyn nodded. "Yes, but only after we'd dried off and had our picnic. Then we set off to go round the lake when we found the track and followed it back down to the lakeside, we saw the sign so decided to come back here."

"There's a very sad reason why it's no longer used. Two boys and a girl drowned there. In fact they froze and, well, let's start from the beginning.

Five kids aged around fourteen or fifteen from the village were exploring one winter and tracing the stream back from the village. It was a pretty harsh winter, it was February 1963 and most of the country, not just Lincolnshire, had very heavy snow falls and a lot of drifting. The kids shouldn't have been out, but had got fed up of being stuck indoors and they managed to get out and meet up. One of them knew of the lake so they followed the course of the stream which of course lies at the bottom of the valley and so they eventually found it, except it was frozen over. The one who knew about the lake had expected that so thought they could walk on it.

It was protected from the drifting snow by the trees. Foolishly two of the boys and the girl went out onto the ice, which in most places was thick and did support them. However there was one spot which was thinner and as all three met up together as they were messing about, the two boys fell through the ice. The girl screamed and tried to help them but was pulled in by one of those in the water. The other two boys came over to help but they had to leave them as the three kids had disappeared under the thicker ice, being taken by the current.

They raced up to the farmhouse and old man Edwards did his best with his tractor but the girl and boys couldn't be found. A large contingent from the village was assembled and they also failed to find them."

"What happened to them?" Adam and Jocelyn looked shocked.

"Their bodies weren't found until a month or so later when the weather began to improve and better equipment was brought in. It was a terrible tragedy. After that Mr Edwards put the sign up and in fairness it became a story to warn anyone about the dangers of the lake.

So under no circumstances do you go back there. Understood?"

In unison: "Yes Aunty."

Jocelyn looked at Adam and held his hand then a thought struck her. "You somehow knew we'd been swimming didn't you?"

Aunty Karen reached to Jocelyn's hair and plucked a small thin bit of almost dead green weed and showed her."

"Pond weed. Doesn't grow on land does it!"

"Oh!"

"If I hadn't spotted that then I wouldn't have known, but you two have to promise me something now and be serious about that promise otherwise I'll be very upset and it will spoil the remainder of your stay with us."

They looked at each other then nodded quietly, not sure what was coming.

"Promise NEVER to lie to me again? OK?"

"Yes, we promise." Jocelyn flung her arms around Aunty Karen as Adam also promised and did likewise.

It would be late at night once they had gone to bed that Karen told Gary what had transpired that day and he just shook his head.

"Brings back a few memories eh?" was all he could say before grinning at Karen.

CHAPTER 20: AN UNWELCOME ENCOUNTER
Sunday August 24th

"But Adam, it's a nice day and we'll soon have no more days to go out exploring and playing together!"

Adam shrugged. "I've been out down the fields, in woods, tree climbing, on the swing, exploring other worlds, swimming with you with no clothes on and so I just want to have a read of my book today."

"But I thought we were friends?"

"What's that got to do with it? I just feel like a quiet day and have missed reading my favourite book."

"Huh! You can do that after dinnertime in the evenings!"

"You don't understand!"

"I do, you're being a spoilsport that's what. Right, I'm going out this morning whether you come or not, but I'll be back at lunchtime and after that we go out exploring together, right?"

"That's bullying!"

"Huh! Boys!"

Jocelyn walked through to the kitchen where Aunty Karen had heard them.

"Boys!"

Karen sighed. "Jocelyn, I know this is difficult but you don't seem to grasp how much Adam has changed since meeting you. Think about it. He was a nerdy type, a bookworm and preferred to stay indoors even on a lovely warm, sunny day. But you've done him wonders. He's done far more things that you wanted to do than the other way round. Just the other day he spent the morning with you playing with the dolls house. You may not have noticed but he hated it. But you know what? He did it out of respect, and dare I venture, love, for you.

Sometimes we all need to have a bit of time for ourselves to do the things we want and just this once, let him have his time to be a bookworm again, OK?"

"Alright. I guess so. I just, I just like having the company exploring the countryside. You're so lucky living here and both Adam and I live in built up places, so this farm for me is like heaven!"

"I know love, but once he's back home, he'll begin to appreciate what he's missing out on and if we're lucky, you both can come back next summer, maybe even sooner, say in the spring?"

"Wow, that would be wonderful. Yes, I hope we can as well."

"Here's a thought for you. He likes reading, I can tell you that, although he won't admit it, Gary couldn't wait to get a letter from me after I had my first holiday up here and met him. So perhaps you two should keep in touch once you go home by writing occasionally to each other.

I'm not saying you two are old enough to be courting like Gary and I were but it'll give you clues as to if, in a few years you two might become, say, more than friends?"

"Aunty Karen, you are so wise." Jocelyn hugged her. "I'm going up to the top field to enjoy the view but I'll be back for lunch. Midday?"

"Yes dear, remember, not the cottage mind! You never know, Adam might miss you and go with you in the afternoon."

"Yes, fingers crossed. Bye."

Jocelyn fetched her shoes and, as it was a warm day left her coat as she headed outside.

Meanwhile, Adam was busy reading, at least to everyone else it looked that way but ever since he and Jocelyn went swimming , something had changed in him and he was struggling to work out what it was …

#

The farm track which led away towards the main road around a mile and a half away was dusty as she walked along it. Jocelyn was still deep in thought and really wished Adam had come along with her but Aunty Karen was wise and perhaps Jocelyn was a bit pushy and Adam did need his own space.

But she too had felt a change in herself since they had gone skinny dipping in the lake just a couple of days earlier. She kept pondering what it was as she came to the spot where she had to go through the gate and walk up the rough track way towards the old cottage. She didn't relish passing the cottage, memories of finding the dead tramp still haunted her but sometimes you had to push past those memories and feelings of trepidation. She did so want to go sit at the top of the hill and look over the countryside.

She had a thought, damn! She should have asked for the binoculars, but Adam always seemed to have those and it was too late now.

The cottage slowly appeared as she walked further up the track and hill. She thought she heard voices and for an instant spotted some movement up ahead near to the cottage. Her heart seemed to stop, but she shook her head and carried on. No good her telling Adam to be brave and be adventurous if she wasn't!

There it was again, boys voices as far as she could tell. Her thoughts flitted back to Adam and she wondered if she was indeed beginning to have feelings for him, despite him being three years her junior.

She put them aside as she closed in on the cottage and suddenly saw a tall-ish looking blonde haired boy climb out of the top right hand window and lower himself down, dropping the final few feet.

He hadn't seen her and he went round the back out of sight, but her curiosity now took over and she walked briskly up to the cottage as three sets of eyes peered out of two windows watching her approach.

"Stop! Who goes there? Friend or foe?" came a voice from the downstairs front window.

She briefly hesitated thinking to her self it was typical she'd run into boys interested in the late war.

"Friend! I'm Jocelyn, on holiday nearby."

"Go on your way, there's no fun in playing with girls," came the reply. That irked Jocelyn.

"Not even one who found a dead body in there just a month ago?"

There was a mad scramble and the three boys came rushing out to stand before her.

"*No way!*"

"Yes, way. My boyfriend and I were exploring the back room and it was dark, but as our eyes adjusted, we spotted him. He was a tramp so we told our uncle and he got the police and ambulance out and they took the body away. He'd been dead for a few days, the smell was awful!"

"Whoa, really?" said the shorter of the three and it was then she noticed two looked as if they were twins with only slight differences, one being a little shorter than the other. The tallest boy, however, was not impressed.

"Nah! She's having us on. Girls are scared of dead bodies and she'd be crying all the time if she saw summat like that."

"That's where you're wrong pal, my uncle

and boyfriend would confirm it if they were here."

"Oh, you have a boyfriend, lardy dah!" the tall boy said sarcastically as Jocelyn realised what she'd said and blushed.

"Well, he's my friend anyway. You three have names?"

"I'm Stuart, my twin is Philip and our leader is …"

"DON'T TELL HER! She's the enemy!"

"It's Eddie, isn't it?" she asked catching him by surprise.

"How di …"

"You three were a bit loud and didn't know I was here until almost too late. I heard, Philip, I think, say something to you and call you Ed. Makes sense it's Edward or Eddie."

Eddie smiled, twiddled with his neckerchief and relaxed a little. "You're clever. I like that. Want to join in then?"

"Yeah, alright, what shall we do?"

"Stu, Phil, arrest this person for impersonating an officer and a man!"

The twins walked forward, smiling as Jocelyn feigned mock outrage.

"Oh no, they've caught me, the heroes of Britain. What shall become of me now I've been unmasked."

"Hey up, I'LL make up the story if you don't mind, this is my gang alright?"

"Yes boss!" she replied but with tongue in

cheek.

"We've unmasked her as a traitor so we shall march to that there wood and tie her up for questioning!"

The twins stood either side of her, nervously wondering what to do. She leaned into the one she thought was Phil, "You can hold my arms you know as long as you're gentle!"

"Oh, right ho. I'm Stu by the way, he's Phil!"

Eddie just shook his head at how poorly his 'soldiers' were conducting themselves. Nonetheless they walked together past the cottage and towards and into the wood, Ashton Wood, the end that Jocelyn and Adam hadn't explored yet. She made a mental note of this and hoped she could get Adam to come up with her to explore before the holiday ended.

Onwards into the wood which on this side was quite thinly spread out and Eddie pointed to a tree. "Tie her up there, ready to be questioned."

Stu produced a thin bit of twine from his pocket and gingerly went up to Jocelyn.

"Can you stand with your back to the tree and put your arms behind the trunk?"

She smiled at him and he blushed as she did as he asked. The tree wasn't very wide so easily accommodated her arms as Stu then tied her hands together but Jocelyn winced.

"Hey, not too tight!"

"Sorry."

"Soldier. Don't be sorry," barked Eddie as Stu

then tied her feet together and to the tree but a bit looser this time.

He and Phil backed away whilst Eddie stood in front of Jocelyn.

"Now, prisoner of the allies, give me your full name, rank, and where you hail from!"

"Jocelyn, code named Seagull, spy, and from Berlin!"

"Oh, that was a bit easy! You're supposed to resist. Not very good at this are you?"

"Sorry but it won't be long before I have to be back for lunch."

"LUNCH? LUNCH? Prisoners don't get lunch!"

"Aunty won't be happy if I don't get back."

"Ahh, now we're getting somewhere. So 'Aunty' is your commandant and gave you orders to spy on us, didn't he."

"She. She's a she and is my aunt after all. That was the clue, *aunty* ..."

"SILENCE! Private Stu and private Phil, find us some ferns so we may torture the prisoner for information!"

"That sounds fun!" suggested Jocelyn and giggled as the twins raced off in search of the ferns.

"Stop it, you're supposed to be playing along!" Eddie was getting a bit annoyed with this girl that had intruded on their war games. He also recognised her from a few weeks back.

"So, you escaped from my clutches once

before but not this time. We saw you go into the tunnel. Dangerous it is, especially if it gets sealed up again when someone is inside.

"YOU!" Jocelyn's eyes widened at this admission and suddenly didn't feel too enamoured with the game, or Eddie.

He walked behind her and the tree and whipped off his neckerchief and surprised her by rushing round and tying it around her head across her mouth, gagging her. She tried to struggle to call out but couldn't speak except in a very muffled way and the twine was painful when she tried to wriggle loose.

By now the twins returned with several fern fronds looking worried at what had happened.

"Eddie, I don't think y ..."

"SHUT UP! Do you want to be in my gang or not?"

"Y, yes, but this isn't right."

"We're only going to tickle her then let her go, OK?"

The twins nodded despite the clear look of terror now on Jocelyn's face. They each took a fern then began to tickle her on her legs and arms but Jocelyn was now too upset to laugh or see the funny side.

"So, you resist our torture." Eddie now looked more menacing and he stepped forward and glared at her.

He reached forward and undid her blouse, loosening it up to reveal her thin vest and began to stroke her chest with the fern, before stuffing it into the neck part of her vest and she winced. The twins stepped back a little, but were too weak to say anything.

"You will give up your secrets or you shall be tickled more until you do."

Jocelyn tried shouting through the material that it had gone too far but Eddie was now obsessed. He went behind her and unbuttoned her skirt and slowly pulled it down as Jocelyn tried to scream and tears began to trickle down her face. She kept looking at the twins for help but they were now mesmerised by seeing a girl in her vest and panties with her skirt round her ankles and so were frozen to the spot.

Eddie wasn't finished. He walked over to a large stone set in the ground and lifted it up, smiling in a maniacal way, he picked up a large earthworm and walked back round to face her.

He pulled her pants open and dropped it in them and let go. "You want to squirm, this'll make you squirm."

Just then a loud, deep voice boomed out and the trio looked terrified and bolted in different directions …

#

"Adam? Adam? I thought Jocelyn was coming back for lunch but its quarter past one and she's not back yet."

Adam looked at the wall clock, saw the time and sat wondering what could be keeping her away. Perhaps she'd found someone else to go off exploring with, he mused then found he was upset by that idea, that she would indeed go off with someone else.

It was his fault.

She was right, he could read in the evenings and should have gone with her.

"I've finished my sandwiches so will go out to find her. She won't be far surely?"

"No, but knowing you two you have gone further than when she were here two years ago. Be a love and see if she's alright? She said she was going to the top of the hill not far from the cottage, but don't go in it this time, OK?"

He quickly donned his shoes and ran out as he wondered where she might have gone. They'd explored everywhere that Aunty and Uncle owned.

Everywhere except they'd not done much at the wood past the cottage. She'd mentioned it a few days earlier but instead they'd gone and found the lake.

He walked quickly out the gate then remembered he'd spotted an animal trail cutting across the field north of the farmhouse so he changed direction, climbed over the stone wall and set off directly for the wood.

It took him ten or so minutes to get to the wood. He remembered it was the thinner end of Ashton Wood, the one he and Jocelyn had explored further to the east when they were exploring in the direction of the village.

He was about to call her name when it struck him, if she were playing with someone else then she might not want to be disturbed by him, especially as he'd refused to go out that morning with her.

Adam worked his way through several thick clumps then heard voices in the distance up ahead. One sounded like a bully, ordering people about. Perhaps local boys playing at war, he never understood that, war was horrible and people had died! How could anyone enjoy doing that?"

He crept nearer to the sounds then caught sight of something that made his blood boil.

He was side on to the scene where a tallish blond haired boy with two others standing back from him, had Jocelyn tied to a tree and she was clearly upset. What was worse he saw her blouse was undone and a piece of fern had been pushed in at the top and was sticking up against her face. Then the bully walked round and did something that horrified Adam, He slipped her skirt down as all three then tapped her with the ferns. She was writhing and clearly crying and he stood frozen, not knowing how to tackle three older boys at once and save her.

Then the bully went way beyond anything acceptable as Adam saw him pick up a worm and put it into Jocelyn's knickers as she squirmed and tried to cry out.

That did it. Thinking on his feet, he cupped his hands. He'd been practising on the quiet for a couple of weeks and it was the only thing he could think of that might make the bullies run away.

"WHAT'RE YOU BOYS DOING TO THAT GIRL, LET HER GO NOW!" he shouted in his best Uncle Gary impersonation in as deep a voice as he could muster.

The three looked wildly around and bolted in different directions and Adam sprang into action, racing over to Jocelyn untying her gag, pulling up her skirt and untying her hands and feet as she wobbled forward. She pulled the skirt up, pulling down her pants and threw out the worm in disgust before pulling the skirt back up again.

She pulled the fern from out of her vest and threw it angrily at the ground. Her face was streaked with tears as she buttoned up her blouse then wrapped her arms around Adam, squeezing him tightly.

"Let's get away from here!" she said through the tears.

Hand in hand they raced through and out of the wood using the route Adam had taken to get there, Jocelyn crying all the way until they reached the stone wall. She was shaking and Adam threw his arms around her.

"I am so sorry, I should have been with you, I was selfish and could have stopped it from happening. I won't let anyone hurt you again, I promise!"

He too was crying as they held on to each other and gradually Jocelyn settled down and caught her breath.

"You came for me and saved me from them, Adam, I'll always love you for that. You're the best. I need to get home and get changed out of these clothes and have a bath as I feel so dirty," she paused then began to sob again, "he, he touched me and opened my blouse, he took my skirt down. He, they touched me in places no one should touch with those damned ferns. The worm, THE WORM!

I HATE THOSE BOYS!"

He held her gently, not knowing what more to say. He knew one thing, he wanted to find them and make them pay, but just then they heard Aunty Karen's voice calling out for them and so they clambered over the stone wall and went running into the farmhouse.

Aunty Karen took one look at Jocelyn's tear-streaked face and looked shocked.

"What, what's happened?"

"Aunty, it was awful, three boys. I started playing with them and it was nice but then the leader, someone called Eddie was mean. They tied me up to a tree and at first it was OK as I was their prisoner but then he seemed to change and started unbuttoning my blouse, …"

Jocelyn sobbed for a few minutes then continued, "He shoved a fern down my vest and it hurts where it went, then he surprised me and put something round my face and I couldn't talk. I tried to bite through it but couldn't. Then, then he, he, …" she burst again into tears and buried her face into Adam's shirt as he hugged her. She regained a little composure, "he took down my skirt then pulled my pants out and dropped a worm into them telling me to squirm," she took a deep breath amidst the sobs but Adam jumped in.

"I'd reached the woods and realised they were bullying Jocelyn and saw what happened and I was really angry. So I did my impression of Uncle Gary's voice and they ran away. I untied Jocelyn and we came back here as fast as we could."

"He's my knight, my hero and I'll never go anywhere without you ever again," she again flung her arms around him and squeezed him, but Aunty Karen could see she was squeezing him too tightly and gently pried them apart.

"I need a bath Aunty, now, I need to bath, I feel so dirty and crawling and …" she sobbed again as Aunty Karen indicted to Adam to stay downstairs as she gently led Jocelyn up to the bathroom.

Adam was angrier now than when he'd first seen what was going on and stomped around the living room muttering to himself that he should have gone out with her.

Neither Jocelyn nor Karen heard him go out the front door.

#

It had been a fairly routine day and, as Detective Constable Freshman took his regular short cut across the fields to get home to Scrawford, he thought he heard distant voices up ahead off to one side. They seemed to come from Ashton Wood, normally he'd skirt round the north of the wood but the voices seemed to lure him towards them.

It sounded like some boys and possibly a girl, but he couldn't see them as he was still in a dip before reaching the field bordering the wood.

The voices didn't seem right as the girl went quiet but one voice stood out as dominating and he realised who it was, young master Edward Edwards. He was known to be a bit of a bully and if there was any rowdiness then there was a good bet he would be involved in it one way or another.

It didn't sound right, as if he was taunting someone, then two other voices piped up but were quickly silenced by Edwards. Ahh, it had to be the twins, Freshman though, Stuart and Philip Boardman. He couldn't understand why they hung out with Edwards. As he reached the brow of the hill he looked for where the voices were coming from but initially couldn't see them.

He fished his small but useful 7x42 binoculars out and scanned the edge of the wood then quickly swept back as he spotted them.

"Oh heck! That's going too far even for them!" he saw the young girl with her top undone and her skirt down at her ankles and she was clearly tied to a tree. Then he was horrified as he saw Edwards put something, presumably a creepy crawly, down the poor girl's pants and he was about to reach for his whistle when a deeper voice bellowed out and the three boys ran in different directions.

He spotted where Edwards was running and began to run on an intercept course as he caught a glimpse of another smaller boy seemingly helping the girl, perhaps a younger brother. Satisfied she was being looked after, he caught up and brought down Edwards in a spectacular rugby tackle that his old school's games master would have been proud of.

"Right Edwards, I saw most of that and you have a lot to answer for."

He grabbed the boy by the ear and twisted it so the boy understood he meant business, but by the time they got back to the tree, the girl and boy were gone.

He noted the twine and remains of several ferns on the ground, the discarded neckerchief and gathered them up.

"You're in deep trouble now boy. So are your two stooges so you know where we're going don't you?"

Eddie knew he was in real trouble now and sullenly walked with the policeman across the fields, past the old cottage, down and across the valley to his father's farm.

#

Meanwhile, Adam stormed back up the route he'd used to find Jocelyn and began to look angrily around. He'd never felt like this before but he didn't stop to analyse the feeling. There was no sign of the bullies and as he walked round the tree, he was puzzled to find no trace of the twine or ferns or neckerchief.

It was a mystery.

A voice called out in the distance. At first he couldn't quite make it out, but it got close as if someone was returning to the scene of the crime and Adam hid behind as large a tree as he could find.

"Stu? STU? You there?"

Phil was wandering around, trying to find his brother as they had all gone off in different directions, he and Stu deeper into the woods but on separate blind paths. He retraced his steps until he found the tree but was shocked to find no trace of the girl or that anything had happened there.

He smiled, at least there was no evidence but he knew the trio, more specifically, Eddie, had crossed a line. He didn't mind teasing the girl, what was her name? Jocelyn, but undoing her clothes was going too far. Then doing what Eddie had done to her, Phil shivered at the memory.

He was so wrapped up in his thoughts that he didn't see Adam's fist until it was too late and incredibly Adam floored the boy who was at least four years older than him. Without letting up Adam furiously kicked at Phil as the boy screamed at him to stop and he finally did so.

Just as Stu rushed up and knocked Adam to the ground, winding him briefly. Before he could get up, however, Stu hauled him to his feet and punched him in the face, just missing Adam's left eye. Adam struggled and kicked out but now Phil had recovered enough to seek his own revenge.

Normally the twins were reasonably placid and didn't like fighting but they were now fired up and began to roughly push Adam from one to the other until suddenly Stu was lifted up by the scruff of his neck as Uncle Gary threw him hard to the ground and wheeled about grabbing at Phil who looked utterly shocked.

"WHAT THE HELL ARE YOU DOING BEATING UP MY NEPHEW?" Gary shouted at them and the twins cowered as he stood over them. Adam stood unsteadily up and spat at them.

"They and another bigger bully were

stripping and hurting Jocelyn until I scared them away and managed to free her. She's back home with Aunty Karen, but I don't know where the other boy is, he's got away!"

"Well, not so fast sonny, afternoon Gary." DC Freshman had heard the commotion as he returned to evaluate the scene and look for any clues, "I apprehended Eddie Edwards after seeing some of what transpired and catching him as he ran away. He's with his father and I dare say getting a right beating with the belt. Serves the rascal right too. I came back to see what I could find and heard the commotion, so someone tell me what's been happening here?"

Adam jumped in. "I came up to find my friend, Jocelyn and saw the three of them bullying her and doing things they shouldn't. To be fair, these two didn't do much as it was the bigger boy who was really bad. I called out in a mean voice to let her go as I hid behind a tree and they all ran off and I helped her back to the farmhouse."

"Oh, so it was you that called out. Gary, did you know that 'un could do a pretty mean impression of you? Did well he did. I saw what must have been you helping the girl so I hot-footed it after Eddie as I figured the girl was in safe hands. So you two, what have you got to say for yourselves?"

"That boy came out of nowhere and attacked me he did."

"And I'll do it again if you hurt my girlfriend!"

"Listen twins. You don't need to hang out with that trouble maker and you are both involved in what happened to the girl, so you don't have a leg to stand on. The boy had every right to be upset as does Mr Ashton here so, Gary, what would you like me to do with them?"

"If you would, I think it better for you to take them to their parents, it'll be more official if a policeman escorts them home and they have to explain themselves. Philip, you got what you deserved from Adam. Look at him, nothing like your size, yet you two thought you could rough him up. Shame on you both. Take them away Mike and call round once you are done as we'll have to decide if we want to prosecute them."

The twins looked horrified.

"No, no, we can't go to jail!"

"You two, with me." Mike Freshman ordered and the twins looked aghast, lowering their heads.

"If you'll excuse me and Adam, we need to get back and see how Jocelyn is doing. Sounds like there was no physical damage done but I'm guessing it's traumatised her, so she'll need our love and support."

"Indeed. I'll drop by later then. Right you two, MARCH!"

DC Freshman frogmarched the twins away as Gary took Adam by the shoulder and they walked down the hill towards the Farm.

#

They walked through the door as Karen and Jocelyn came out of the living room and they gasped at Adam with his clothes torn and a bruise growing just below his left eye. Jocelyn ran up to him and hugged him tightly whereupon he had to ease her away as he was sore after the fighting.

"Adam, oh Adam what happened?" she asked looking worried.

"He found one of the twins and gave him a right sorting out I can tell you. I could see it happening from way back and was rushing towards them when the other twin turned up and they both set about Adam. I'm proud of you son, you were prepared to take on lads that are much older and bigger than you and you did yourself proud."

"Come on, let's get you cleaned up and let me look at your face," Aunty Karen gently took Adam by the arm as Jocelyn followed them up to the bathroom. Karen was going to close the door but Jocelyn was having none of it.

"It's alright Aunty, I don't need to strip off, just my shirt as I hurt in my ribs."

With that Jocelyn helped him off gently with the shirt as Aunty Karen filled the basin with warm water and she fetched a flannel and carefully wiped his face then examined his chest. Jocelyn all the while held on to his hand tightly and smiled at him.

"You alright Jocelyn?"

"I will be. I have my very own knight to thank for that. He's a real hero isn't he Aunty?"

"He is indeed, who'd have thought it. Brave little soldier aren't you!"

"They hurt Jocelyn and I had to do something."

"It takes a special sort of person to take on those sort of odds, also someone who is prepared to try to right a wrong. I wouldn't recommend you do it all the time though, at least not to boys bigger than you for the time being!" Karen said as she smiled at him and gently ruffled his hair. "Right, doesn't look like anything is busted, but reckon you'll be sore for a day or so if not longer. Try to stay out of trouble you two, this summer is becoming like a battle ground what with having an argument with a tree branch, falling ceilings and getting into scrapes with the local bullies!"

"Jocelyn?"

"Yes Adam?"

"Promise you won't go exploring on your own again?"

"Promise."

"And I promise if you ask me, I will always be there with you and not be selfish and want to read during the day."

They hugged and Adam winced a little but put up with the pain. Aunty Karen eyed them both and left them as Jocelyn ran into their room, fetched a fresh shirt for Adam and helped him carefully into it.

Karen was just about to walk downstairs when there was a knock on the door and Gary went through and opened it.

"Oh!"

Mr Edwards and his son were standing there as Gary tensed ready for an argument.

"Afternoon Gary. I've brought this miscreant of a son of mine over to apologise. DC Freshman explained what had happened and I can only say I am truly sorry for what he has done. Is the young lady alright?"

"She's settling down but naturally very upset. I don't think she'll want to see him after what has happened today."

"Well, what are you waiting for? Apologise to Mr Ashton!"

"I'm, I'm really sorry. Things got out of hand and I am sorry and I hope she is OK."

"I will pass that on to her. Just so you know, DC Freshman caught the twins too and they told him everything. That is, after my nephew, Adam, fought with Philip but then Stuart turned up and together they started beating Adam up for wanting to avenge Jocelyn. He's at least four years younger than them, yet still took them on. I'm proud of him. I arrived just in time and shortly after so did DC Freshman. He's taken the twins to their home so no doubt they'll be dealt with in similar fashion to Eddie."

"Good, the three of them are bad news and I've been getting fed up apologising to quite a few parents of kids bullied by them at school. So as far as I am concerned this is the final straw."

"Yes, this has gone too far. Look, Bill, I know we don't always see eye to eye on some matters, but I have to tell you now that I don't ever want to see Eddie on any part of my land or the twins either, and I'll be letting their parents know. I will be pretty harsh if I find them trespassing, is that fair and understood?"

"Indeed, no problem and I'd do the same thing if the shoe was on the other foot. We'll be off and, well, it's up to you if this does go further when Freshman arrives. I just hope that you understand, Eddie here has certainly been dealt with before we came here and I hope this might be the end of the matter?"

"Yes Bill. I won't take it any further. However, Karen and I will have to tell Jocelyn's parents and I can't be held responsible if they take matters into their own hands. OK?"

"OK, understood. Right you, back home. No tea tonight for you, me lad!"

With that Mr Edwards and Eddie walked back to their car.

Karen had been listening from the top of the stairs and came down to stand and give Gary a hug.

"What a day eh?"

"Tell me about it. I could have told him that I suspect it was Eddie and the twins who blocked Adam and Jocelyn in the tunnel, but I reckon the boy has been punished enough. Bet his bum is sore from that belt! By the way, Adam let something slip when we were walking back, he said he had to do something as they had attacked his girlfriend …"

"Told you. They're meant to be together they are, it's in the stars."

"Oh don't give me that drivel about it being in the stars. But you are right, they're incredibly close and it's clear Adam would have killed for her, he was pretty intense when he took on Phil despite the clear size difference! We'd best keep an eye on them. Heaven help us when they have to go back to their normal lives!"

"Yeah, that's crossed my mind too, I'm just hoping the small bruise will have gone by the time Marion and Bob come to pick Adam up!"

With that they walked into the kitchen to sort out a drink and what to have for dinner.

#

DC Freshman returned just before dinnertime and after a chat with both Jocelyn and Adam, he had a quiet word with Gary and Karen in the kitchen.

"Basically as they are minors, there is little that can be done. I was off duty but if you are happy with the punishments dealt out to Eddie and the twins by their parents then I don't see a need to make an official report."

"We agree Mike, Jocelyn is settling down and Adam is enjoying being a bit of a bruised hero. I've also had Mr Edwards round with Eddie earlier and Eddie apologised, but I've made it clear he and the twins are not welcome on my property from this day forward."

"Very well, I'll be on my way, don't be surprised if you get a visit by the twins parents to apologise for their sons. They were angry and humiliated that I brought them to their door in plain view of the neighbours. I suspect they had a good hiding after I told them what I had witnessed."

"Many thanks and do take this the right way, but I hope we don't see you again in any official capacity."

"Indeed Gary, hopefully it's under better circumstances. I'll take my leave of you and give my best wishes to the two love birds. Quite a strong bond there is you ask me when one will go out of their way to defend the other's honour!"

"Tell us about it. Started off not on the best of terms and now look at them. Puppy love, but you never know if these things will blossom in the next few years."

"Time will tell, well I'll be off. Good evening

to you."

With that Mike Freshman took his leave.

#

Late that night, Jocelyn struggled to fall asleep after her ordeal and occasionally cried, so on that first night Adam crept round and asked if she wanted him to lie next to her to keep her company.

She didn't refuse so it was a surprise to Karen when she popped her head round the door in the morning to see them together on Jocelyn's side of the bed, fast asleep with Jocelyn's arm slung over Adam. She figured why and Gary's words from the other week echoed in her mind: *'Look Karen, he's nine and she's twelve, not exactly raging teenagers are they! I doubt Adam has any feelings yet, or dare I say it, fully evolved equipment to do any damage!'*

Well some of it was no longer true considering each had said the other was boy/girl friend but they did seem to be responsible and Gary was probably right about Adam, so Karen shook her head and decided to leave them be for now.

CHAPTER 21: HOT
SUMMER BLUES

"Forecasters suggest the heat wave is building and may be with us until late September so we shall wait and see if their predictions come true."

Uncle Gary turned the TV off and sighed. "It's gonna get hot kids! Good for my crops as they're ripening but I'm going to have to keep an eye on my sheep and cattle in case the streams run dry if it's going to be that bad."

They didn't need telling as they'd spent a lot of Monday trying to forget what had happened to Jocelyn on the day before and so had helped Aunty Karen in the walled garden, weeding, watering and generally sticking close to each other, never letting each other out of sight.

Aunty Karen had been true to her word the other week and when she had bought Adam extra shorts, she'd had the thought to also buy dainty shorts for Jocelyn and some summer tops, so she didn't have to wear dresses all the time. She'd also thought to get some hats for them, perfect for giving them some respite against the hot sun.

Jocelyn loved them, so both were out enjoying the warm weather but for now, staying close to the farmhouse.

That afternoon, Adam surprised Jocelyn by bringing down the dolls house and setting it up in the walled garden on the small patio section next to the memorial bench. After helping Aunty Karen, they played with it on the grounds that it could also be a space station and that some of the small figurines that came with it could be either aliens or spacemen and spacewomen exploring it as if it was a planet.

Jocelyn didn't object. She was happiest when they were together, but was conscious of the fact they were in their last week of being on holiday. It saddened her but she tried not to show it.

Aunty Karen could tell but at least she was happy that Gary had done a complete circle and now wanted to see them both back for the next summer, if not earlier. He was, after all, actually a big softie at heart.

Monday night and sleep was difficult, although it did eventually come to all in the farmhouse.

Tuesday was even hotter without a cloud in the sky. Uncle Gary took them in the tractor with a water bowser in tow as they helped him fetch water from the stream and take it to fill the water troughs for the sheep and cattle. But it was hot, even for the time of year.

There was no wind to help either and so by the time they came indoors for dinnertime, it was decided that each could enjoy a cold bath to help cool down before going to bed. Karen's salads were refreshing and with most ingredients taken from the garden very satisfying for her to hear them say how good it was, glad they didn't have to have a cooked meal.

Jocelyn and Adam played with the board games, then Uncle Gary once again took them out for a few hours to look at the stars. Jupiter was too low by the time they reached the brow of the hill in the car, but Mars was in the south west and the almost full moon lay over in the southeast. It's light affected the view of the Milky Way but the summer triangle could still be seen and as the next two hours went by they spotted Saturn rising in the east just as Uncle Gary decided they should head back.

Aunty Karen pointed out it was too late for the kids to have cold baths so they headed up to their room, Adam going to the bathroom once he'd got his pyjamas on then Jocelyn going in to do her teeth before getting into her side of the bed.

"Night bro."

"Night sis."

They giggled feeling they'd become family, but sleep was hard to come by. They dozed in fits and starts into the early hours.

Jocelyn was aware the bed rocked slightly but it was nothing unusual as they each knew when the other turned over on their side of the bed, but this was a little more pronounced. She drifted off again but found sleep wouldn't come as she was sweating profusely and the air was still, stuffy and it was so warm in the room.

Finally she had had enough and as gently as she could sat up. In the dim light of the full moon pushing through the curtains she realised looking over the barrier that the jiggling on Adam's side was because he was now naked and sprawled out on top of his side of the bed. She stifled a laugh but understood why he'd abandoned his pyjamas and so she took the plunge and carefully pulled off her nightdress as well and lay out on her side trying to cool down.

It seemed to only last a few minutes as the air was so still and hot. She looked again over to the window and had a thought. Getting up as carefully as she could, she walked over to the window.

Unlatching the right hand window she opened it, cringing when it made a little squeak. She looked back, but from this distance the barrier hid Adam. Opening it wider, she had thought the cooler night air would have helped but it was so still even outside that there was no change and no refreshing breeze.

A scurrying sound came from behind her and next thing she knew, Adam was stood next to her hoping for a cool breeze as well but to no avail. He put his arm round her waist and she did likewise, not bothered they were both naked.

"It's too hot, can't sleep!" he moaned.

"I know, me too. I thought opening the window would help but it's just as warm outside!"

"I've had an idea. Come with me," he suggested quietly and crept towards the door. Jocelyn wondered what he was thinking. If Aunty Karen and Uncle Gary found them creeping about naked then they'd be in deep trouble. She had a brainwave in case either of the adults came to their room to check on them.

"Adam," she whispered but loud enough hoping he would hear. He stopped and in the dim moonlight shrugged as if to say *what?*

Jocelyn quietly walked round to the wardrobe and gingerly opened it. A slight creaking sound but no noise otherwise, she sighed with relief. Jocelyn carefully removed the large and medium sized dolls from it, closed it up and took them over to the bed. As she put the medium sized one on Adam's side as he realised what she was up to and he came over starting to tuck in the bedclothes and bunching them up to look like he was still sleeping on his side.

Jocelyn placed the larger doll on her side, noting it's hair was very similar colour to her own and making sure there was just a tuft visible as she tucked her side in to complete the illusion. Adam's doll had quite curly hair, unlike him, so she pushed it a little further down in the bed with the bedclothes covering the head.

They both looked at their handy work and stifled their giggles as they looked at the two apparently sleeping kids in the bed, then Adam indicted to the door, opened it very slowly and pointed to the bathroom.

Creeping in, it was a bit darker as it was on the opposite side of the farmhouse to the moon but there was still enough light for them to see where they were going. Uncle Gary had called it something like averted vision, but it didn't mean much to them, only that they found they'd soon become adjusted to the darkness.

Adam slowly turned on the cold water tap and took a flannel from the towel rack and soaked up the cool water then indicated for Jocelyn to turn her back to him and he slowly wiped it down the small of her back.

She gave out a little sigh of relief. What a great idea, she thought. She turned to him and took the flannel and did the same to him and he too couldn't believe how good it felt. Then she put the flannel back in the basin of cold water and wiped down her chest and handed it to Adam for him to do the same to himself. They appreciated it would not be wise to wipe each other down, so Jocelyn rummaged in a drawer and found another flannel. Together they continued to wipe themselves down with the cool flannels.

Jocelyn put the toilet lid down and sat there watching as Adam wiped down his groin.

"I'm glad I'm not using that flannel now!" she quietly quipped and Adam grinned and raised an eyebrow making Jocelyn chuckle.

"You looked like Spock just then when you

did that!"

"That was my idea," he whispered back.

"Only trouble is we can't just stay here all night wiping ourselves down."

"No, but it was a good idea wasn't it?"

"Yes, genius, nice one Adam. Pity the house is so warm though, there's nowhere to escape the heat!"

Adam leaned against the wall and closed his eyes knowing they would have to go back to their room, but at least it had helped for a short while. Then a thought occurred to him. "What if we filled the bath with cold water and both got in?"

"I think the noise of filling a bath would wake Aunty and Uncle up. Good thinking but, but …" Jocelyn looked as if in deep thought. "The pantry! It's always cold in there, something to do with the thick walls and no windows so it's always cool!"

Adam put his thumbs up and together they crept out of the bathroom, keeping an eye on the adult's bedroom door, almost terrified that it would suddenly open and they'd be caught out.

With no slippers on, they made their way carefully and silently down the stairs, avoiding the squeaky step and walked along the hallway and through the kitchen door which was always left open. The living room and dinning room were originally two separate rooms, but Uncle Gary had taken down the dividing wall and done something to stop the ceiling collapsing in without the wall there to support it. The two rooms however, didn't take up the full length of the farmhouse on the north side and it left a rectangular smaller room with much thicker walls that helped keep it cool, the pantry. Access was from the kitchen and there were two doors side by side, one was always locked but the other was the pantry.

Adam looked at the small fridge. "What about opening the door on this?"

"No, we can't get in can we and it'll make the food inside go warm if it's left open too long. We can go into the pantry and close the door behind us," the pair walked up to its door and opened it.

Oh, the cool air flowing out was such a welcome relief as they entered, closed the door and turned on the light, which was dazzling at first until they became adjusted to it.

Jocelyn and Adam revelled in the much cooler air, turning on the spot and enjoying the refreshing feeling for almost ten minutes.

"We'd best not stay too long otherwise we'll actually get too cold," observed Jocelyn then looked at Adams arm, "You've got goose bumps already we sho …" she stopped short, put her finger to her lips for them to keep quiet and stood very still indicating to Adam to do the same. "Oh no! We're right under their bedroom!"

There was a faint creak directly above as if someone was moving about. Horrified, they looked at each other, then Jocelyn slowly opened the door, indicating to Adam to switch out the light and they slipped out. They crept down the hallway looking up expecting a light to go on, but they made it to the living room and hid behind the door.

Hushed voices wafted down and Jocelyn thought she made out words like 'I think they're sleeping, they're in bed, come on.'

Faint footsteps came down the stairs until someone stood on the squeaky step and the noises halted for a moment or two. A whispered giggle from what sounded like Aunty Karen, then they continued as Jocelyn and Adam awaited discovery, dreading their fate with bated breath.

Somebody was walking down the hallway, it had to be their Uncle and Aunt and the sound stopped somewhere further down which suggested they had gone into the kitchen, then its light came on. Perhaps they were doing the same as they had, Jocelyn wondered and indicated to Adam for them to creep out and get back upstairs to their room.

They daren't look down the hallway and took a couple of steps towards the bottom of the stairs when the sound of padded footsteps came from the direction of the kitchen. Instantly they made it to the bottom of the stairs and carefully peeked back from around the bannister.

Open mouthed they stared at the naked forms of Uncle Gary and Aunty Karen who hadn't spotted them, so they crept up the stairs, avoiding the creaky step and dived under their bedclothes awaiting punishment.

"Did you hear something?" Gary asked Karen as they tilted their heads to listen for anything untoward.

"I have a feeling we may have been spotted, but can't be sure."

She promptly went up the stairs into her room, grabbing her dressing gown before heading into the kids room whilst Gary followed but stayed in his own bedroom.

Meanwhile, Jocelyn lay under the bedcovers then slowly realised someone else lay next to her and as she turned to look, a faint pair of eyes stared back at her and she bolted upright and screamed. Simultaneously, Adam became aware there was something cold lying next to him and he reached out and touched a cold hand and he too sat bolt upright and shouted out in panic just as Aunty Karen walked in wearing her dressing gown.

"So, there's four of you now?" Karen noted they'd been in such a rush they'd still got the dolls in the bed with them.

Jocelyn and Adam were shaking a little, firstly in shock at what they had seen downstairs, also with what was still in the bed next to them and finally to the upcoming lecture they knew they deserved.

Karen eyed them. "That was a clever idea.

The dolls. Bet you were going down to the pantry. You two naked?"

"We are so hot, it's hot everywhere and we couldn't stand it," blurted Adam and Jocelyn joined in.

"Aunty, we're old enough not to be bothered by our bodies, we don't care and have seen each other when we went swimming. We just wanted to be cooled down and we worked out the pantry was the best place!"

"Harumph! So you deceived us by putting the dolls in the bed, it worked too!"

"Are we going to be punished Aunty?" Adam was almost crying at the thought that he and Jocelyn had let them down, it seemed as though it had been a regular occurrence throughout the summer.

"Aunty, we didn't mean any harm but didn't expect you to come down to do the same thing! And naked too!"

Karen looked from one to the other and she could see they were both about to burst into tears. She gently laughed.

"You two, oh well, I have to give you credit for ingenuity. The dolls were a stroke of genius. Have you slept at all tonight?"

In unison: "No aunty, it's been too hot!"

"Neither have we. Look, the genie is out of the bottle, your Uncle and I are far more broad minded than either of your parents and we know you are still at, what you might call an innocent age, although you mi'lady, are going to have to be far more careful in the next year or so as you'll be changing lots I expect.

If we tell both your parents what's happened then I doubt you'll be allowed to come back. So it's down to you, however certain things will need to be kept quiet and not talked about to them, understand?

I, and I think Uncle Gary, understand about tonight as we've not been able to sleep either and we had the same idea as you and it really was a stroke of genius using the dolls to fool me, as I was the one who looked in to make sure you were asleep.

I think we are more shocked at being discovered ourselves than embarrassed at being naked. You see we rarely ever have anything on when we go to bed, that's why we always told you to knock on the door and wait until we say it's ok to come in, so we have to have time to put something on. We're not ashamed of our bodies but we're the exception, rather than the rule and I'm sure your parents don't do as we do.

I need you to promise, a cross your hearts and hope to die sort of promise, that nothing else is going on between you and that we can trust you for the last few days of the holiday as Saturday, Jocelyn, your parents are due to come and pick you up."

Both jumped out of bed and hugged Aunty Karen.

"I promise, we know we can't do anything adult, don't we Adam?"

"I promise too. We're bestest of friends and won't say anything. I want to come back next year and explore the farm more with Jocelyn."

"Same for me too, but we'll be good Aunty, we love you and Uncle Gary too much to spoil things and won't tell our parents, will we Adam?"

"No, I can keep a secret!"

"Good, now back to bed but get those dolls out of there, they spook me out!"

In unison: "Yes Aunty!"

Karen left them as they put the dolls away, turned the light off but the moonlight still lit up the room and they looked at each other and nodded before getting back into bed on their respective sides.

Adam began to giggle under the bedclothes and Jocelyn sat up and uncovered his face, "What?" she asked, puzzled.

"Hairy Uncle Gary!"

"Hairy Aunty Karen!"

They burst out laughing then dived under the bedclothes again as a voice came through the closed door.

"I heard that!" Aunty Karen said, shaking her head and chuckling as she finally went back to her own bedroom to put Gary in the picture.

CHAPTER 22: THE
FINAL DAYS …
Wednesday/Thursday August 27th/28th

The next morning, Uncle Gary was still in the farmhouse when Jocelyn and Adam came downstairs for breakfast; they stopped and looked at him then lowered their gaze, awaiting the worst.

"Right you two. Aunty Karen is out in the garden so time for a talk about last night. Go into the living-dining room and sit at the table."

Sullenly, they did as they were told and sat in their usual places, heads down, knowing that Uncle Gary had a reputation for being strict yet, for most of their time at the farmhouse, he had been a great, fun loving uncle.

He entered with a tray laden with two plates of bacon and eggs, a large pot of tea and cups and plates for all three of them along with their cutlery and a bottle of tomato ketchup.

"Tuck in, breakfast is served."

They did so cautiously and he waited until they'd all finished. It was all cleared away promptly and he came back in and sat down at his usual place, looking from one to the other then he spoke.

"*Hairy Uncle Gary?*"

They both looked at him horrified and immediately looked like they were going to burst into tears, he'd found them out.

Uncle Gary looked again at each one as they nervously awaited their punishment. Then he burst into loud raucous laughter which subsided into a more gentle chuckle.

"Seriously? I guess it is appropriate and I suspect stems from almost at the start of your stay here when I caught you one morning standing outside the bathroom with Adam inside when I had overslept. I came out only in my pyjama bottoms so, yes, I have a somewhat hairy chest. Your Aunty likes it like that and we don't argue with her now, do we?"

They shook their heads but were not sure how to respond, was it a trap to lure them into saying something he wasn't going to like? What could possibly be worse than their nickname for him?

"It's alright you two, don't look so glum. Look, I know you are aware I was not happy when Aunty Karen said Jocelyn could stay, knowing we didn't have a spare bedroom and, at first, I didn't agree with her plan. But you two have gone from you, Jocelyn, almost badly injuring Adam pushing him off the swing on the very first day, to being two of the closest friends I have ever had the good fortune to meet.

I know you have feelings for each other, for now, it's clear it's a close bond and not of the other kind. I believe Aunty Karen explained a lot to you about our views on life and everything else after the little misadventure last night.

We think the world of you two and I get it, I really do, you don't see the problem with being naked in each other's company. We're the same, but the big difference is that we're adults and we've got married, we've made an official commitment to love and cherish each other until the day we die. And that makes it OK by the laws of this land in our own home, but the law doesn't see it that way with your ages and innocent world view.

We were incredibly lucky a few weeks back when we were visited by the local authority investigator that we'd managed to sort out the second bedroom. If they had thought we were letting you two sleep together, even with the barrier and however innocent it was, we'd have been in serious trouble. Even though we had confirmation letters from your parents, that didn't extend to you two being in the same bedroom, let alone bed, despite the precautions Aunty Karen and I took with the makeshift barrier between you.

But by and large, you've shown a lot of maturity for kids of your ages. You have to level with me now or otherwise you'll never be allowed to come here at the same time ever again. So please tell me, you haven't erm, well, err, say, done anything wrong have you?"

The look on Jocelyn's face told him she understood what he was asking whereas

Adam looked puzzled. Jocelyn leaned over and whispered something in his ear and Adam's face told Gary what he wanted to know but Adam was almost apoplectic.

"Eww! No! I wouldn't, she's my friend and, and ..."

"Exactly, Uncle Gary, we'd never do that, we know not to do that, we just care about each other and we look after each other and, and, ... we're not old enough to do it anyway! You can trust us, we won't do anything silly, you have our word."

"I know, I had to ask and I'm sorry to have done so, but as adults, Aunty Karen and I are your guardians during this time and so anything that happens could have serious consequences for us. We love you both and want you to come back next year but I need you to understand that what happened over the last few weeks and especially last night CANNOT be told to anyone beyond ourselves. I daren't think what either of your parents would say or do to us if they caught wind of events."

Jocelyn and Adam both crossed their hearts. "We promise."

"Good. Now, are you two up to helping me again with the water for the animals? It's going to be another hot day again and they don't expect it to end until late tomorrow evening."

They both nodded and with his waving of a hand, they rushed out into the hallway to get their shoes on. Aunty Karen had come in via the back door and went in to Gary.

"So?"

"They're good kids at heart and I'm sure nothing too serious has happened. We have to bear in mind that if they both come back next year then we will have to be more vigilant as Jocelyn will definitely be blooming into a young woman by then."

"Yes hubby, quite agree. Now, it's going to be another hot day so have them back by lunchtime, we don't want them wilting out there just because you have slave labour to help you! And make sure they have their hats on too!"

"Yes, love, will do."

With that Gary went out to find them already by the tractor outbuilding waiting for him to get it out and hooked up to the bowser.

#

They came back suitably tired out as well as hot so the home made lemonade with ice cubes in it, then a light lunch went down a treat. Both flaked out afterwards on the settee slumped together for a good hour before Jocelyn woke up and nudged Adam in the ribs.

"We'll not sleep tonight!"

"I know but it's not fair being this warm," he replied.

Aunty Karen came in with yet another jug of

lemonade and set it down before them.

"Don't drink it too quickly, savour the coolness whilst it lasts. If you want you can stay in here as I'll be upstairs tidying up and making the beds. OK?"

"Yes Aunty."

"So, Jocelyn, what shall we do? Nothing that makes us hot though!"

She looked around then smiled. "I spy, with my little eye, something beginning with C."

"Ceiling."

"Yes, your turn."

I spy with my little eye something beginning with … D."

"Door!"

"Oh, yes, obvious really! I spy, P"

"Toilet is upstairs or outside!"

"Oh very funny. Give in?"

"Nooo. Picture?"

"No."

"Photo?"

"No."

Jocelyn kept looking round the room intently. "Portrait?"

"No." Adam was amazed, he'd picked a good one.

"Paper?"

"No!"

She spotted something on the mantelpiece, "Pebble!"

"No. Give up?"

She scratched her head and took another look round but had to shake her head. "OK clever clogs, I give up."

"Paint!"

"Oh for goodness sake!"

"My turn still, I spy erm … C"

"Eh?"

"Wrong!"

"I didn't say what I thought! We've had a C!"

"Not this one!"

She looked around and was about to give up when it hit her, "Chimney!"

"Ha, ha, yes!"

This went on for another half an hour when Aunty Karen popped her head quietly round the door and smiled at the harmless fun they were having.

Eventually, Jocelyn tired of the game and she turned to Adam.

"I'm going out to the walled garden, coming?"

"OK."

They walked out but Adam could tell something was on her mind as they wandered along and sat down on the memorial bench. With the hot weather, Uncle Gary had set up a sun shield canopy which at least gave them some shade from the direct sun, even though it was still hot outside.

"Pity we can't go down to the lake and have a swim, that'd cool us down." Jocelyn remarked.

"Yeah, I know, but now we know it's on that Mr Edwards land we'd probably get Uncle Gary in trouble with him and I'm not doing that," he paused, "Something bothering you?"

"It's, well, it's just that suddenly it's almost over. I can't believe it really. Adam, it's been the best holiday I've ever had, anywhere. With you. It's going to be really hard going home, I can tell you."

"Same here. Aunty Karen told me this morning that she's had a letter from my parents and they'll be delayed by a week so they asked if I could stay here until they get back. It's going to be quiet without you."

"I'll take that as a compliment."

"I thought that's what I meant …"

"Oh Adam, yes, it is a compliment, perhaps we can write to each other?"

"I'm not good like that, I mean, I'm bad at writing things down, my teacher says I'll never be literater, sorry, literate, oh, I remember now, I'll never be able write literature?"

"That's the right one. I'm good at writing so I'll let you know how things are going with me at school and what it's like at home and you do the same."

"OK, I'll try. But I don't know your address?"

We'll get Aunty Karen to write them down for each other. Look there's a red butterfly just landed on that pink bush."

They got up and carefully walked up to it.

"I know that one, I watch out for butterflies in our back garden, it's a red admiral. The bush is a buddleia. If we keep watching we might spot more types," remarked Adam and they returned to the bench.

"There, that's smaller but still red, no, more orange I think."

"Comma, look for the small white mark that looks like a comma on the underside, - at least something from literature I can get right, a comma!"

"That bright yellow one - I know that one, a brimstone."

"Male. The females are more creamy/light greenish."

"You know a lot really, don't you?"

"I just like to know things, that's why I read. Mum and dad are scientists so sometimes it can be a bit much when they keep insisting you find out everything you can, but I try to stick to some insects and butterflies in nature along with space and astronomy in science. Sometimes though, I wish I could just play without having to learn all the time."

"Which is why you've had more fun this holiday with me!" Jocelyn cheekily smiled at him and as they sat together he leaned in and nudged her and she nudged back.

"Yeah, best holiday ever, thanks Jocelyn."

"We're a team."

"*Yes you are.*"

They looked at each other in surprise.

"Sorry, why did you say it like that?" Jocelyn wondered.

Adam looked at her perplexed but before he could say anything the voice spoke again.

"You do make a good team. We know, we've been watching you."

They looked around and then saw them.

Geoffrey and Mollie appeared. Gary's deceased parents drifted forward and stood next to them.

"Kindly move into the centre and we'll join you," Mollie said and obediently they did as they were told, whilst remaining silent at what seemed to be going on.

"Don't be alarmed, you weren't last time. You know, when you were stargazing. You've both come a long way haven't you," Mollie observed.

Adam and Jocelyn looked at each other but stayed where they were sat, not daring to move or even breathe.

"Cat's got their tongues Mollie, you'd think after seeing us the first time they'd be able to cope with seeing ghosts!" suggested Geoffrey and Mollie admonished him.

"Now, now, don't be like that, it's natural to be scared. Last time was late at night, this time it's broad daylight so a little more unexpected.

"We didn't dream you then last time?" asked Jocelyn in a rather nervous, quiet voice as Mollie looked at her sweetly.

"Of course not. We sensed you were in the garden so came to see how you are getting along. You've both changed a lot since you arrived, haven't you?"

"I think so, we didn't get off to a good start as I accidentally pushed Adam off the swing and we had to take him to hospital."

"Yes, quite a spectacular fall my young man," observed Geoffrey.

"Jocelyn didn't really mean to do it though. We're best friends now."

Mollie looked at him and smiled. "Yes, we can see that. Good thing too otherwise the summer would have been awful."

"I'm sure we would have been alright," Jocelyn added but Mollie just chuckled.

"I was thinking more about Gary and Karen. It put them under a lot of stress in the first few days as I'm sure you know and your Uncle Gary wasn't happy. My, how he's changed his tune."

"He, he's very hairy!" blurted out Adam and Geoffrey laughed.

"Family trait, takes after me you see and I take after my father and his father and, well you get my drift. It was bit of a rum do having to share a room and bed, no Mollie I don't mean like that dear, you two know what I mean, but you've been on reasonably good behaviour."

"Except of course for skinny dipping in old farmer Edwards' lake, oh, and of course being naked last night and seeing each other as well as your Uncle and aunt, I bet that was a shock?"

Both kids looked down but Jocelyn took note of the implications.

"So have you two been spying on us all the time then?"

"No, of course not. Well, not all the time. But you see we sort of tend to find ourselves drawn to some situations and occasionally lend a little hand shall we say."

Adam seemed thoughtful. "The cottage and the tramp?"

Geoffrey turned to Mollie. "Now he's getting it."

Jocelyn now looked deep in thought. "In the tunnel when we were trapped. I felt drawn to the middle right hand side wall and that was where the ladder and vertical shaft were."

"That was us. As for the cottage, we were saddened at the death of the tramp and wanted him to be found. It barely took any effort to influence you to want to explore round the back of the cottage, Jocelyn. He received a good burial because of you two," Mollie smiled at her.

Geoffrey took up the story. "Did you know he was a war hero? No, of course not, many suffered much tragedy whilst fighting so that you two and everyone that came after the war could lead a good life. Sadly he was one of those who society didn't thank and help when he needed his country to help him when he fell on hard times.

Also, Mollie here guided you to look for the

dolls too!" added Geoffrey.

"I did feel a little odd when I was in that room by myself."

"Yes, it seemed sad that they'd not been out for several years, shame Karen didn't let you carry on playing with them, but I understand her reasons. Adam nearly fell from the tree too, twice, and Geoffrey managed to stop you falling," Mollie remarked as Adam's eyes went wide.

"I told you Jocelyn, I said it felt like someone stopped me falling down!"

"We also urged you to get under your bed just before the roof came in during the storm."

Adam's eyes went wide and he smiled at them as Jocleyn looked sweetly at them.

"Thank you, both of you. We try not to be any trouble."

"We know dear. We can't always be here for you but all we'll say is look after each other, and remember, don't tell your parents what's been going on, they'll never understand."

With that Mollie and Geoffrey faded from view.

#

Jocelyn awoke to find herself and Adam side by side on the bench and for a moment she was confused.

Adam snorted then opened his eyes.

"Thank you Mollie, thank you Geoffrey," he

mumbled as Jocelyn stared at him and looked around.

It was still sunny and hot but at least the shade of the canopy Uncle Gary had erected gave some relief from the sun.

She gently nudged Adam as he came fully awake.

"It happened again, we fell asleep but it sounds like you also saw and heard Mollie and Geoffrey!"

"They helped us, didn't they?"

"Yes, seems like it, doesn't it!"

"Wonder if Uncle Gary and Aunty Karen have seen them?"

"Don't know, but I'd be surprised if they haven't. Let's go inside as I need some lemonade!"

"Good idea, me too."

They walked back along the path and entered the back door into the kitchen which was a little cooler but not by much. Aunty Karen wasn't there but they knew not to take things without asking so whilst Adam sat on a kitchen stool, Jocelyn walked through into the hallway to find Aunty Karen just coming down the stairs towards them.

"Let me guess? A nice hot cup of tea?"

Jocelyn's eyes widened at the awful prospect of something hot to drink, then Karen smiled at her. "Oh course not, I'm guessing you two want my refreshing homemade lemonade?"

"What makes you think that Aunty?"

"That little trickle of sweat on your temples!"

They walked through to join Adam and as Aunty Karen opened the small fridge they were lucky enough to own, Adam whispered to Jocelyn, "Have you asked her about Mollie and Geoffrey?"

"No," she whispered back as Aunty Karen stood behind them listening in.

"You have something you want to ask me then?" she asked a little mischievously knowing what she'd overheard.

Jocelyn took the plunge. "Erm, do you, do you see the ghosts of Uncle Gary's parents here, as they lived here so long?"

"Well, that's an interesting question now isn't it? The short answer is ….

… yes. We both have. And before you ask, we both saw you that night you sat out watching the stars and you seemed to fall asleep. But not before we saw Mollie and Geoffrey appear to you and you made room for them on the bench. Then both of you had quite a conversation with them before you fell asleep and they faded from view. You woke up and looked quite puzzled, I can tell you.

That's happened a few times to us too. I also saw you both just now with them. I hope you weren't too scared?"

"Oh no, we found out they've helped us a few times." Adam said as Jocelyn nodded at him.

"That's nice of them, I'm not surprised as

they were really nice people. For me they were great in-laws, that's not always the case I'm afraid. As long as you are not scared of them then that's OK. Anyhow, it'll soon be time for our meal so let's go get some salads from the garden, I'll need lettuce, radish, carrots, cress and cucumbers from the greenhouse.

They'll go well with the thick ham farmer Edwards gave me the other day. Ever since the incident with his son he's been rather good to us, keeping us on his good side, so although it was a nasty business it has had a good effect on our working relations with him."

#

After the meal Uncle Gary asked them if they wanted to help him take some more water to the sheep and cattle fields as it was expected to be a couple more degrees hotter overnight and into the next day.

They did so and got back around nine thirty pm all three flaking out on the settee and chair in the living room as Aunty Karen brought them tumblers of cool lemonade pointing out that she was going to run out soon as she had not been able to get any more lemons from the market earlier in the week.

At ten pm Jocelyn and Adam said goodnight and went upstairs, did their teeth and went into the bedroom.

Adam grabbed his pyjama bottoms and was about to leave the room when Jocelyn chuckled at him.

"What?" he asked.

"Adam. What's the point of going to change in separate rooms? You really want to wear anything in this heat? We've seen each other and I don't care, as long as we keep to our sides of the bed."

She began to strip off then plopped down on her side of the bed and sighed.

Adam shrugged stripped of and did the same, but wondered if they would be able to sleep at all as it was so warm and the air so still.

Sleep came in fits and starts to the kids; they didn't hear Karen and Gary come up the stairs trying to talk quietly as they could as they went into their room.

Once again Jocelyn sighed, got up and opened the window, there was a slight breeze, but of warm air so there was little respite from the warm night. A rustling from the bed and then Adam stood next to her and took her hand.

"I thought last night was warm!"

"I wonder how they manage in really hot countries?" Jocelyn asked and Adam just shrugged.

"Guess they're used to it."

They heard a faint noise, the bottom step that squeaked on the stairs; they rushed back to the bed and dived under the sheets. A light knocking on the door, then Anty Karen crept in and they peered over the top of the sheets and stared in shock.

Aunty Karen was in just her bra and knickers.

"You saw the same when we were on the beach! It's too hot again tonight but your uncle has had an idea and gone downstairs. I'm going to take a wild guess here and suspect you're not wearing anything are you? You little rascals. BUT, get something on to cover your modesty and come down stairs," Aunty Karen closed the door and they heard her head downstairs.

They got out of bed and looked at each other, wondering what was going on, then Jocelyn rummaged in her drawers and fetched out a clean pair of knickers and her light vest and put them on, then looked at Adam.

"Well? Find some underpants!"

He did so and quickly got them on, almost falling over in his hurry. They walked cautiously down the stairs and could see the kitchen light was on and the back half of Aunty Karen was visible. They walked in to find Uncle Gary just finishing putting the four kitchen stools in the pantry. Jocelyn looked at Aunty Karen not quite sure of what to say or think as Uncle Gary wasn't wearing underpants. Instead, he was in his swimming trunks which didn't leave much to the imagination. She remembered covering him with sand on the beach and having to avert her eyes that time, but it was more difficult now.

"OK, this time we're at least covered up and we can sit in here for a bit until we start to feel cold," Uncle Gary said as he went in and sat at the far end. Aunty Karen ushered Adam next, then Jocelyn, before she also stepped in and closed the door.

It was soooo cool and refreshing compared with their rooms and the rest of the house. It was Adam that broke the ice, so to speak.

"Uncle Gary ..." Jocelyn froze, wondering what he was going to ask as she kept looking at Aunty Karen and trying to keep her composure.

"... How long do they think this hot weather will carry on for?"

"There's some good news Adam. Looks like there is a vicious weather front going to sweep in tomorrow afternoon and they reckon we could have another heavy storm and downpour. The good news is that should clear the air and cool things down.

Not a moment too soon as did you notice the stream wasn't as full this evening when we went to fill up the bowser?"

"Ahh, I was wondering that," Jocelyn said as she thought about earlier that evening. "This is much better."

"Yes, better than all of us sneaking around the house at night in the emperor's new clothes!" added Aunty Karen.

Adam snorted as he remembered the sight of Aunty and Uncle in the altogether, then he stopped himself as the other three were looking at him.

"Sorry."

Jocelyn then burst out laughing and ended up bent over as they all began laughing. Gary nudged Adam and whispered in his ear.

"Now you know why your Aunt fell for me!"

Adam creased up as Jocelyn nudged him having caught what he'd said, tears streaming down her face. Karen shook her head. "GARY! I hate to think what these two think of us now!"

"The best Aunty and Uncle in the world!" stated Adam and Jocelyn together and Aunty Karen shook her head at them.

"You two, anyone would think you were twins the way you seem to think and speak alike!"

"Well, you did marry us a few weeks back," observed Jocelyn whereupon uncle Gary peered down the line at Karen.

"*What?*"

"You knew, I told you, typical man, they forget anything we say Jocelyn! Goes in one ear and out the other with nothing in between to keep the thought in place!"

"It was only a play marriage uncle Gary, not real." added Adam as uncle Gary shook his head and closed his eyes enjoying the cool air.

It was getting a little too cool for Jocelyn, however, she carefully nudged Adam with her arm and as he turned to look at her she mouthed,

'Are you cold?'

He nodded.

"Aunty, we're getting goose bumps now on our arms and legs and beginning to feel cold so can we go back upstairs?"

Of course dears, off you go. I expect we'll be up soon too," Aunty Karen opened the door and the rush of warm air was more intense than they'd expected. Uncle Gary indicated for them to go quickly so they scrambled out of the pantry and Aunty Karen closed the door.

They didn't wait and quickly ran upstairs and into their room before falling on the bed in hysterics.

Catching her breath, Jocelyn lay there then looked over the barrier at Adam.

"That was so embarrassing! Uncle Gary, I didn't know where to look!"

"But he wore those when we were at the beach."

"And trust me, they don't leave anything to the imagination. I was less embarrassed when we saw them naked last night!"

Adam was confused but then leaned over to Jocelyn. "Aunty Karen's bra and knickers didn't cover much either! Her bikini covered more when we were at the beach!"

"I saw! But I have to admit, we're right, they are the best. We've done more things, broken more rules, done things we shouldn't, it's been fun!"

Suddenly they went quiet as that sunk in.

"I'm going to really miss you," Adam mumbled but Jocelyn heard him and leaned over and gave him a peck on the cheek.

"I'll miss you too. But we did promise to write and we can look forward to coming back next year."

Adam smiled and they settled down to try to get some sleep even though it was still quite warm in the room. They again ended up on top of the bed but fell asleep before either of them thought of undressing.

CHAPTER 23: OF A STORM AND A LETTER

For once, that Thursday morning began with a few sunny breaks but as the morning progressed, the clouds thickened and the sky grew darker.

For a while that day it grew even hotter, then just after dinnertime, the heavens opened and it began to pour with rain as the weather front moved through. Uncle Gary had wisely decided to stay at the farmhouse all day and set himself upstairs in the damaged bedroom so that he could try to deal with any problems if the tarpaulin was to be ripped off the roof when the storm approached.

Adam and Jocelyn kept out of the way and played with the board games, but around eight pm the lights flickered then went out. Jocelyn grabbed her small torch and they made their way downstairs. Uncle Gary had beaten them to it and was in the hallway with a small door open they'd not really noticed before. Adam looked, then realised.

"Ahh, the electrics must be under the stairs."

"Quite right young man," as the lights came back on, Uncle Gary emerged and closed the door. "That hopefully will be OK, there must have been a bit of a surge on the mains and it tripped the fuse. That's a good thing as that's why there are fuses in the first place. You'll have all this to come when you get older, you mark my words."

Aunty Karen called to them from the kitchen and they all wandered in to see what she wanted.

"Drink?"

"Mine's a coffee, nice mug of Maxwell House will do me just right," answered uncle Gary. Aunty Karen looked at the kids and knew immediately what they'd say.

"Lemonade coming up. Actually this is the last of it so take your time drinking it, savour it as there will be no more, that's it for this year I'm afraid."

They took the drinks but Adam's curiosity got the better of him.

"Aunty. That door next to the pantry, where's it go and why's it always locked?"

Uncle Gary gave her a glance but let her answer.

"Oh, it is an old cellar, very steep steps down into it. Years ago it became flooded and although we got the water out it's not a nice place, very damp down there. It'll cost too much to have it fixed and we do have more pressing things to spend our money on, don't we Gary?"

"Yes, a roof for one thing, that's a priority, so as it's unsafe down there we keep it locked so no one can fall down and get hurt."

"Oh, good idea," Adam agreed and Karen looked at the kitchen wall clock.

"Anyhow, drink up, and if you want, you can

stay up until ten pm, that'll give the lemonade time to pass through you I hope, so you don't need the privy in the night. Not in this weather!"

"Ooo, good point Aunty, I don't want Adam here to get us stuck outside in the pouring rain just 'cos he wanted a tiddle!"

"Eww, you don't have to go into details Jocelyn!"

"That's alright you two, use the bathroom if needed, just don't pull the chain. Not that I think any of us are going to get any sleep tonight if this storm keeps up. What with heatwave and a storm, I could do with a holiday where I can sleep all the time just to catch up with my forty or so winks!" added Uncle Gary as a loud crash of thunder rolled over the farmhouse.

It startled both kids as they almost jumped out of their skin.

"It's the lightning that's the baddie, if you hear thunder then you're OK."

"How do you know uncle Gary?" asked Jocelyn, keeping away from the windows of the kitchen.

"The lightning is the static electricity with lots and lots of power that can kill you, but the thunder is just the sound of it crashing through the clouds. Lightning is faster than sound so we see a flash before we hear the sound of it," Adam jumped in before Gary could say a word.

"Not bad Adam, guess all that reading does have its use after all. Yes, it's static electricity that builds up in the cloud when suddenly it is released and it always heads for the ground, but sometimes not directly. If you see a flash, count how many seconds it takes before you hear the thunder and that tells you how far awa ..."

There was a bright flash that lit up the kitchen window curtains and Adam began counting as uncle Gary finished what he was going to say, "divide the seconds by five and you know how far away it is."

There was the sound of thunder and Adam stopped, "Eight seconds."

"So it's ..." prompted Uncle Gary.

"A mile and a half away," Jocelyn said and Adam screwed his face up at her for beating him to it.

"And seems to be coming from the east as they predicted so the storm will have picked up lots of water from the North Sea. Oh well, hope the tarp holds out!"

They all walked into the living room but Jocelyn and Adam went and sat at the dining table whilst Uncle Gary and Aunty Karen settled on the settee. Karen had found some writing paper and at Jocelyn's suggestion she convinced Adam they should try practice writing to each other.

"I'll start so I'll write a short letter and give it to you then you write down your reply and hand it back to me, got it?"

"Well, yes, I'm not a dummy you know."

"You did say your weren't good at writing so do it for me?" Jocelyn put on her nicest voice and Adam glanced at Aunty Karen who just winked at him.

"OK."

Jocelyn quickly began to write and a few minutes later she handed the letter to Adam who read:

Dear Adam,

Since I went back to school, all I can think about is being on the farm with you, Aunty Karen and Uncle Gary. It feels like a long time ago now even though it is only a couple of weeks.

Mum and Dad say they enjoyed their long holiday in the Caribbean and have just got back the pictures they took. But as I look at them I can't help but feel they had a good time without me and wonder why they had me?

So I think about the adventures we had at the farm and it makes me feel good.

I hope you are alright and that you too enjoyed the summer at the farm with me and of course Aunty and Uncle.

Write soon.

Jocelyn x

She handed it to Adam and sat back as he read it then his eyes widened when he got to the end.

"Why is there an x at the end?"

"It's a sort of sign that you like someone."

Jocelyn answered, "so, start writing your reply to me."

Dear Jocelyn,

Adam stared at the paper and Jocelyn could see he had drawn a blank and was stuck. She whispered in his ear and he nodded.

Thank you for your letter, I liked it very much.
   Adam.

He handed it to Jocelyn who was a little stunned he'd finished already so she read it and grimaced. Not even an x at the end.

"Really Adam? You need to write more than that. Tell me what you thought of the holiday and what school and home life is like that sort of thing. Try again."

He shrugged and picked up another piece of paper.

Dear miss mardy pants!
I told you I am not good at writing.
Can I be excused?"
   Adam x

He handed back the 'letter' and Jocelyn buried her head in her hands in despair. Aunty Karen saw this and came over to them and saw Adam's two, so called, letters.

"So, Adam, not really a good try. Do you think that starship captain would write like that?"

"He has someone to do it for him."

"Some things, yes, normal run of the mill sort of things that just need a signature, I agree. But like any good captain he would have to fill out a mission report and send it in. So you could see these letters as mission reports to your very good friend Jocelyn at command whatever it is, starfleet headquarters," Karen went back to cuddle up to Gary and Adam looked thoughtful. He took another sheet of paper and began to write.

Dear Jocelyn,

Six weeks ago, I started a long voyage to the planet Ashton Wood Farm where I met the custodians of the galactic gate, Aunty Karen and Uncle Gary. They were their code names given to us and proved correct.

They had arranged for me to meet ambassador Jocelyn who at first I did not like as she tried to kill me.

However I survived and it turned out it was a test of me and I passed. We became good friends and took many missions together, some of which we did undercover as Parker and Lady Penelope from Thunderbirds.

Sometimes we were in danger and sometimes we were hurt but we looked after each other and learned lots of new things. We explored the stars with Uncle Gary who it turns out was a spaceman with lots of information on the stars around us.

The chief cook on our spaceship farmhouse was Aunty Karen who made very good lemonade and looked after us when we were hurt so she also was a space doctor.

I enjoyed my time with you at the farm and hope we can do it again next year.

Your very best spaceship captain friend
Adam xx

He handed it to Jocelyn who eagerly read it, paused then burst into tears and ran out dropping it on the floor before running upstairs and to their room.

Aunty Karen and Uncle Gary stared at him.

"*What?* What did you put to make her do that?" Aunty Karen was shocked and rushed over to pick up the letter, read it then gave it to Uncle Gary as she rushed upstairs to find Jocelyn.

"Wow, way to go Adam. That's really nice. I think you touched a nerve as I honestly think she's going to miss you badly."

Meanwhile as Karen reached the top of the stairs she could hear Jocelyn crying and found her lying down on the bed on her side.

Karen sat gently next to her.

"I read his letter," Karen said as Jocelyn tried to dry her eyes. "Why the tears Jocelyn? It was a really nice way to sum up the holiday with you."

"I know. I know, I don't know why I'm crying

but it got to me and I didn't expect this."

"Adam is full of surprises isn't he? You see, he does have the ability to write and express himself but sometimes you have to find the right way for him to do it. You have completely changed him since he came to us on that first day, all quiet, wouldn't say boo to a goose and all that. But being with you has made him tougher, more confident, self assured, adventurous, the list goes on.

You've done that and that letter was his way of finally being able to say thank you in a way he could express and understand it.

But I don't think the tears are because you don't understand him, I think they are because you don't think your parents love you. You've had more love and affection in these few weeks than you could possibly have ever hoped for.

I read your mock letter to Adam. You wrote as if they don't love you and preferred to go away on holiday without you. But I remembered after they had left you here that your mum and I used a good amount of paper writing to each other back in April and that she was worried you would feel this way.

You won't know this, and you can't tell them I told you, but in her letters it turns out they initially said no to the holiday even though there was no cash alternative. However, did you also know that when they got married, they never had a proper honeymoon? They couldn't afford it and indeed neither had ever travelled anywhere except to Skeggy or to come up to us at the farm.

So they saved up for a holiday, but there was always something else to spend the money on, especially when you came along. For them, you were the best thing to have happened to them, so they spent their savings on giving you as good a life as they possibly could.

Then at Christmas they won that holiday and because they had to take it from the last week of July and it was only for the two of them they at first said no, but it was I who suggested that they could let you come to us for some of the summer holiday. Especially as you had to miss last year, it seemed the ideal solution, you get to come here and stay with us and they get to have their holiday, a long delayed honeymoon.

I didn't think they'd take the opportunity to extend the holiday but I did gather that they tried to book the extended holiday with you joining them, but the company said no. So they didn't have much choice."

"But Aunty, why haven't they written or sent us a card to say how they're getting on?"

"I guess it's a long way and that it may take weeks for any post to get here. They won't have forgotten you Jocelyn and I bet you that they're missing you a lot. They said so when you were last here two years ago, your mum especially said it was like an eternity for her those two weeks you were here with us but she knew you were in safe hands.

"I guess you're right Aunty. Adam's letter really caught how I feel about this summer. Best I've ever had."

There was a light knock on the door and Adam asked if he could come in.

"Yes Adam, it's alright."

He gingerly entered and looked really upset.

"I'm I'm really sorry tha …"

Jocelyn rushed off the bed and hugged him.

"It wasn't you, the letter was brilliant, I loved it. I'll explain later when we go to bed, its complicated."

"Talking of which, it's almost ten anyway so go do your teeth and get ready for bed and I'll be up in about ten or so minutes to make sure you're OK."

"Yes Aunty, thank you for telling me about, you know, what happened and I'll be alright now."

"Ok, off now with you, get those teeth cleaned!"

As Karen left them heading towards the bathroom, a roll of thunder echoed through the house, another storm seemed to be coming across the Lincolnshire Wolds.

#

Jocelyn trembled at the large crack of thunder, having been awoken by the bright flash. She could hear the rain striking the window hard and the storm had to be on top of them.

"You OK?" she heard Adam ask.

"Sort of. I know what you and Uncle Gary said about thunder earlier but it doesn't stop me being frightened when it happens."

Adam got out of bed and walked over to the window. In the dim light Jocelyn could see he was in his pyjamas and he was lit up suddenly by a flash, then there was a bang from the thunder. She buried her head under the bed sheets then poked her head out again.

"You're a lot braver than I am," she said and Adam turned to her and walked over, sitting on the bed but making sure he didn't sit on her.

"If you want, come to the window with me and hold my hand and we can face it together."

"I'm not that brave, I'll stay here."

"OK, shift up then and I'll stay with you. I'll face the window if you want and hide you from the flash of the lightning."

Jocelyn said nothing but pushed back until she touched the barrier Uncle Gary had set up all those weeks ago and she opened up the bed sheets for Adam to climb in.

He noted in the dim light she was wearing the nightdress that he liked, the one with several butterflies on, apparently it was a set along with her knickers he'd seen a few weeks earlier. He climbed into bed, made himself comfy as Jocelyn put her arm around his waist and they settled down to go to sleep.

"I'll always be there for you, Jocelyn," he whispered and although he couldn't see her face, she smiled and held him tighter as another bright flash lit up the room, followed by the thunder.

It was a long night.

CHAPTER 24: TIME
TO GO HOME

Friday was a lot cooler with some sun and lots of cloud and they spent the day walking back up past the cottage and to the brow of the hill.

Jocelyn as usual had the rucksack with their sandwiches and drinks in, a flask of tea this time as the lemonade had indeed run out.

With a sheet laid out for them to sit and lie on, Adam and Jocelyn whiled away the day just soaking in the landscape, knowing this was the last time they would see it together.

They had Uncle Gary's binoculars and kept swapping with each other surveying all they could see, identifying birds, butterflies and insects along with wild flowers with the Observers Books they'd carted up with them, they didn't want the day to end.

The evening meal was quite a subdued affair as everyone knew that after the meal, Jocelyn had to pack her suitcase with all she had brought, along with a few things that had been bought for her such as summer tops and shorts. The only things that couldn't be packed were her going home clothes, tooth brush and nightdress.

Adam went upstairs and helped her, she was nonplussed when he handed her her underwear from the chest of drawers and she packed them away, leaving a pair out for the morning.

That night, once Aunty Karen had bid them goodnight, Jocelyn slipped into Adam's side of the bed and they lay there in their PJ's and nightdress knowing that in the late morning, Jocelyn would be leaving.

They didn't want it to come, but morning finally arrived. They got up, dressed together and did the final packing, leaving the suitcase on the bed as they went down for breakfast.

It was a quiet affair despite Aunty Karen's best efforts to cheer them up. Uncle Gary brought the suitcase down and placed it near to the front door in the hallway and then they all waited. Uncle Gary had decided he should be there for when Beryl and Henry arrived just in case they got into an argument with Karen.

They'd decided that Adam shouldn't be hidden away. Him being there for the summer was bound to come out at some stage, so they'd agreed to say he'd slept downstairs for the summer and thought it an adventure.

Mid morning, then almost eleven am. Finally the blue Ford Cortina drove into the courtyard and stopped. Beryl and Henry got out, beaming away, tanned to within an inch of their lives as they walked through the already open front door.

Jocelyn ran to greet them and her father scooped her up then put her down. "My you really are getting too big for me to carry you.

How's our little or not so little girl eh?"

"I'm alright."

Beryl gave her a hug and a huge kiss on the cheek. "Oh my darling, we've missed you so much. If there's a next time then no company is ever going to keep us apart again!"

" I thought you'd send postcards?"

"Sorry? We did! Didn't you get them?"

"No, nothing!"

"We sent loads, must have been at least twenty from different ports."

Uncle Gary and Aunty Karen shrugged. "Nope, not a thing. Jocelyn did wonder, as did we, but we did suspect it might take a long time for them to arrive."

"Honest, we made a point of keeping you informed as to how we were getting on and how much we missed our little girl!"

"That's international post for you," suggested Gary as Adam stepped out from behind him.

"Oh, who have we got here then?" asked Beryl.

Before Gary or Karen could say anything Jocelyn jumped in.

"Mom, Dad, this is Adam, my boyfriend!"

Beryl and Henry just looked at Jocelyn, then Adam then towards Gary and Karen who jumped in to explain.

"Adam is my nephew and we'd forgotten we'd said he could stay over the summer as his parents do important scientific research for a government institution and had to be up in the arctic all summer.

So Adam slept downstairs and Jocelyn had the only other bedroom. Not sure if you could see when you drove up but we've got a big problem with the roof and there was only one bedroom as the other got rain damaged.

"Oh, but err, boyfriend?" stuttered Beryl.

Karen mouthed 'Puppy love' to her and indicted to the two kids who were now standing next to each other holding hands.

"Oh, so have you two got on well then."

"Yes Mom, Adam was, is quiet, but we've explored a lot of the farmland around here and we've really enjoyed it," Jocelyn gave Adam a gentle subtle nudge.

"I always preferred to read and stay indoors but it was Jocelyn who showed me how to enjoy exploring and it's been great fun!"

"Well, will you two be hoping to see each other again?" wondered Beryl.

"We're going to write to each other and hopefully we can come back next year to have the summer exploring again."

"That's if you'll let Jocelyn come back next year. They've been really good and being together has really helped Adam overcome his shyness. Jocelyn now likes some space programmes, so they now have a lot in common," added Karen as they all headed indoors.

Henry surprised them, including Beryl when he said, "Well, Adam, perhaps, if my wife is in agreement, you'd like to come and stay with us another time?"

Both Adam and Jocelyn eyes widened with glee.

"Yes please sir. If Jocelyn want's me to come over."

"Of course Captain Adam, I'd like that," Jocelyn gave Adam a salute and they both smiled.

"Sorry to butt in but just so you know, I've no more lemonade as these two have guzzled the lot over the summer. I don't know if you knew but we've had quite a hot spell the latter half of August, so we got through all I had made."

"Tea or coffee will be fine Karen," suggested Beryl as they went into the living room and sat down, then Beryl followed Karen into the kitchen.

"Err, I have to ask as we know you and Gary are quite liberal and open minded, but you didn't show them the cellar did you?"

"Oh of course not. Kept it locked and just told them it had been flooded and was too damp to use."

"Good. Adam. He, err, seems a nice boy but a bit young to be Jocelyn's boyfriend don't you think?"

"He is a sweet, quite innocent boy and they just happen to have become firm friends. They didn't start off like that, I can tell you, but within a few days they seemed to gel and to be honest, they do seem good together."

"OK. Just thinking, you being his aunty, that means he must be Marion's boy?"

"Yes, Marion and Bob, he's been a good boy all summer and it's done both of them a world of good it seems. You'll probably see a change in Jocelyn as she certainly seems the caring sort. She said she wants to be either a doctor or a nurse. She and Adam were exploring in the woods behind us and he fell but she took care of him and got him back here. She'll do well I think."

"Yes, we had noticed she was always into looking after things and wanting to know how to cure this that and the other. As you say, puppy love, such things never last do they!"

"Perhaps, perhaps they really are meant to be together as it's a strong bond they have."

They smiled as Beryl thought about it and shrugged as they walked back into the living room.

#

Suitcase in the boot of the car, Henry was sitting in the driver's seat having said his farewells as Beryl and Jocelyn stood looking at Adam, Karen and Gary.

"Well young lady, time to go, so say farewell

and thank you to Aunty Karen and Uncle Gary for having you."

Jocelyn ran and hugged both adults tightly then turned to Adam.

They stepped toward each other and hugged but both were strangely quiet, until Beryl, Karen and Gary realised the pair were holding back tears.

"I'll write, good letters, I promise."

"I know you will Adam, I'll write too and we can look forward to next summer or even if Dad is right, maybe you coming over to stay with us."

"I'd like that but I don't know where you are."

Jocelyn laughed and nudged him. "You've got my address silly."

"Oh yeah. I'll miss you, this week will not be the same."

"I'll miss you too. Gotta go," she kissed him on the cheek and turned to go when Adam pulled her back and gave her a kiss on the cheek back, much to the amusement of the rest watching.

Jocelyn got in the car, Beryl did likewise and, as the car pulled out of the courtyard, Jocelyn waved madly at them as she sat looking out the back window. Adam watched the car disappear out of view then suddenly ran indoors, upstairs to what had been their room and burst into tears.

Karen was about to rush after him but Gary held her back.

"Leave him, he needs time to process this and nothing you can say will change what he's going through at this moment. He'll be alright, trust me."

CHAPTER 25: BACK
TO MARCH 2020

"*So, that was the summer we cherished,*" Adam looked at his two old school friends, Mary and Gordon, and chuckled as they'd been hanging on to his every word.

"But you can't leave it there, wasn't that a Saturday and you and Jocelyn watched star trek together."

"Yeah, that evening I watched it on my own, it was part two of the Menagerie. I watched but didn't watch, if you know what I mean. I was lost without Jocelyn. It was good to share something with someone who seemed to understand me. To be honest, the rest of the week I went back to being a nerd and not going out and just staying in, reading.

Mum and Dad came the following Thursday to pick me up but all they saw was the normal nine year old boy they'd left there a few weeks earlier. They struggled to believe I had been out exploring and were a little concerned to learn of Jocelyn.

Aunty Karen gave them the same explanation of how they accommodated us both but as I was there first, she changed it so that I had the bedroom and Jocelyn was downstairs on the settee."

"But couldn't your aunt and uncle have done

that in the first place?" suggested Mary.

"Not really, remember the living-dining room was all one long room and that Karen and Gary were usually up from four in the morning, so anyone in the living room would have been disturbed, no matter how careful and quiet they tried to be. Plus, it was going to have to last for almost six weeks and I can imagine all of us would have been driven mad by the arrangements.

Anyhow, there was no way I could have made Jocelyn pregnant, my equipment to put it politely wasn't developed at that time, was it. As Aunty said, in the past people often slept in the same bed regardless of their sex as it was usually the only bed they had. It's so called modern times, especially the Victorians that seems to have made us more prudish."

"OK, so what happened the next year, did you both go back?" Mary was keen to know everything.

"That's the sad thing. I went back for the next two years but I never saw Jocelyn again in the summer holidays."

In unison: "*What?*"

"I thought you two started writing to each other?" added Gordon, surprised.

"We did, several letters, at least one a week, and sometimes more. We all met up over Christmas and New Year at Ashton Wood Farm, but after about six months, Jocelyn wrote that she couldn't write to me anymore as things had changed, but she didn't say what.

I wrote back asking why but never got an answer. I was devastated. Looking back I realise that we were soul mates and her last letter didn't make sense. Her previous one was all excited because her parents had suggested I have the spring half term holiday with them. Then suddenly nothing.

Aunty Karen later said the family were moving away due to her father changing his job and were having to move abroad but she didn't have their new address.

Life was never the same after that and it took a few years for me to come back out of my shell. She really was my soul mate and all I can think is somehow her parents found out we'd shared a bedroom and bed for the holiday.

I'd have married her, she was the one, but it was never to be. I sometimes wonder what it would have been like, but that's life I guess."

They heard a sniffle come from the person with their back to Adam, sitting at the next table, then an older, yet familiar, voice sent an electric bolt down Adam's spine.

"You remembered it well. I also cherished that holiday."

She turned round, wiping the tears from her eyes.

Jocelyn!

Adams eyes went wide and he jumped up as

Jocelyn got to her feet and they embraced and both began to cry.

Finally they settled down and Jocelyn joined them at their table.

"How?" was all Adam could say as his mind whirled at seeing her after all this time.

"Aunty Karen and I got back in touch and she let me know you would be here today. Your friends didn't know me and I made sure I sat with my back to the door so that when you came in you'd not see me straight away. I was going to jump in at several points as you talked about our holiday together all those years ago, but you were so eloquent that I just wanted to hear your voice. A little deeper than I remember it, but that's not surprising is it?"

"I meant all I said towards the end."

"I know you did Adam, and I feel the same."

Mary and Gordon were open mouthed but then caught their breath.

"You look lovely Jocelyn, I can see why Adam fell for you all those years ago. If you will excuse us two old farts, I think we'll get off now and leave you two to reminisce as it looks like you have a lot to catch up on. Come on Gordon." Mary stood up and leaned over, kissing Adam on the cheek as Gordon realised they would be intruding on the unexpected reunion.

"Err, yes, well, nice to meet you Miss Jocelyn, good to see you again Adam, let's meet up again later in the year and perhaps Jocelyn will join us eh?"

"I'd like that, you two sound like you've been good friends to him all these years."

They smiled and nodded then left, but not before Gordon sorted the bill out and thanked the staff.

Adam looked into the brown eyes of Jocelyn. "Still as beautiful as I remember."

"You never told me I was beautiful."

"We were too young to use words such as that. But in my heart, I thought it, even though I always struggled in those days to articulate it."

"I remember. When you spoke about our mock letter writing and your lovely letter that sent me upstairs crying. The words you used were perfect yet I didn't realise it would trigger something so deep in me that I'd obviously held in all holiday."

"Let's take a walk along the promenade, enjoy each others company and perhaps talk about a few things eh?"

She nodded. They thanked the staff and walked out into the sunshine with a slight chill in the air, it was March after all.

Adam broke the silence as they seemed to each be in a world of their own. "Penny for them?"

"I'm just enjoying our meeting up again. So much has happened since that holiday."

"Well, forty one years this summer."

"Yes. So much time wasted on others when it

should have been us together."

They stopped and looked out to sea at the distant offshore wind farms that now dominated, and some would say, spoiled the view.

"So, what really happened after your last letter to me?" he asked quietly. Jocelyn looked down at her feet and when she looked up into his eyes she had tears in her own.

"I made a ghastly mistake. I was in a mood, perhaps due to puberty, I don't know, but I was arguing with Mum and let slip we'd shared a bed whilst on holiday. She flew into a rage and wouldn't let up until I'd told her everything. Dad was equally angry, not at me, either of them, but at Karen and Gary.

As you know, Karen and my mum had been the best of friends since their schooldays which is why Karen and Gary were my godparents. Mum was chief bridesmaid to Karen at her wedding to Gary, and Karen was chief bridesmaid for Mum.

But when she found out what had gone on, it broke their friendship. Took years to reconcile them."

"So I guess that's when you moved abroad?"

"No, we didn't, we stayed at the same address. I found out much later that was the excuse Karen was told to give to you so you'd stop writing. I was banned from writing to you and once when I tried to sneak a letter out to post it,

Mum caught me and tore it up.

I couldn't tell you what had happened and that I so wanted to go back in time and change things but, well there we are."

She reached into her handbag and brought out a handful of envelopes and Adam caught his breath.

"I kept them, all these years and always read them over and over again. You became good in a short time writing to me."

"I had a little help from Mum who changed after that holiday. Dad hinted that Aunt Karen tore a strip off her and him for how they were bringing me up, sheltered and not getting out and enjoying the 'great outdoors'. It made a big difference as they didn't believe I'd been exploring outside and that you had helped me learn to enjoy life more. They liked you when we all met up for the Christmas and New Year a few months later and tried to console me when you stopped writing later in the spring.

They began to take me on day trips, even a few times when their work took them abroad, they insisted I had to come along. They apparently won as I ended up going with them to Norway, New Zealand, Mexico and the US amongst many other places.

So in the end, I did become a bit of an explorer, which is how I ended up working for the government in the foreign affairs department. I've just recently taken early retirement."

"Did you marry?"

"Yes, I met Tracey at University and we married and had three kids but she cheated on me and ran off with an economics lecturer from Yale, took the boys to the US and I've never seen them since.

Then came Miranda," he went quiet. "Twenty three years then, gone, breast cancer. We found out too late. No kids but I guess she was the closest to a loving relationship I could hope for. That was four years ago; been single since then. You?"

"Three marriages, all disastrous. In the past and best forgotten. Oh, here comes someone you'll recognise."

Aunty Karen hobbled up to them using a walking stick and gave Jocelyn a kiss, then did the same to Adam.

"You haven't fallen out then?" she noted.

"Of course not Aunty. Did you know about this?" Adam looked her in the eye, although she was now almost two feet shorter than he was.

"Of course. Jocelyn and I have been in intermittent contact for a few years, but after I'd seen you at your parents funeral I mentioned to her that you had never forgotten that summer holiday and you looked lonely. She was in the same boat and so, knowing you were meeting up with your old school friends here, Jocelyn wanted to surprise you."

"Ahh, so an ambush."

"Well you could put it that way I suppose!" Karen looked quickly at Jocelyn but Adam gave them both a hug.

"Best ambush ever! I'm glad, but shame it's just a fleeting visit as I hadn't planned on staying more than a couple of days in good ol' Skeggy.

"Well, here's the thing. We know you've retired, you don't have any reason to go home in a rush. So, well …" Karen stalled but Jocelyn spoke for the two of them.

"You know how Carol and Jonathon now run the farm?"

"Yes, and? ..."

"They're in charge now and have diversified into the holiday accommodation business. The outbuildings have been converted into self contained units and Carol, Jonathon and Karen still live in the main farmhouse. Apparently Carol and Jono stayed up in Borrowdale at a place called Fieldhouse and loved what the owners had done up there and came back, putting the idea to Karen."

Karen took up the story, "They're in the final throes of arranging the website to take bookings and Jocelyn here is staying with me as they've gone away to Florida for what they reckon is a final holiday before things really take off. That's the hope. So, now you two have reunited, fancy coming back to the farmhouse and staying there for a week or so?"

He smiled, the biggest smile he'd managed for many years.

"On one condition ..."

Karen and Jocelyn looked at each other wondering what on earth he could ask for.

"Jocelyn and I have our old room and there's no bloody barrier in the bed this time!"

In unison: "Done!"

EPILOGUE

Of course, no one realised that whilst they were staying at Ashton Wood Farm (B&B) that the UK would go into lock down over the pandemic.

Being stuck in their old haunt, but this time as adults, was a blessing as they relived memories, covered old times and remembered Uncle Gary.

But that, as they say, is another story ...

COMING NEXT FOR
ADAM AND JOCELYN

A short story: That Christmas/New Year We Cherished

When Adam and Jocleyn along with their parents are invited to Ashton Wood Farm for Christmas and New Year, Jocelyn and her parents can't get there until after Boxing Day.

With Adam and Jocleyn keen to see each other after several months of writing and looking forward to the New Year's Eve party to see in the new decade, little do they suspect that both mothers are out to squash the budding romance ...

ASTROSPACE FICTION NEWSLETTER

To keep up to date with the novels written by Paul Money under the Astrospace Fiction banner, then why not sign up to the newsletter.

Those signing up will receive a *free* mini novel: "Lord Shabernackles of Grasceby Manor".

So, if you want to know more about the James Hansone Ghost Mysteries or the science fiction novels from Astrospace Fiction (or if there will be continuing adventures of Adam and Jocleyn) such as how to purchase them and where, or when the next book in each series will be released, then simply sign up and you'll be the first to be informed. There will also be occasional competitions or give-aways so it's worth subscribing to see what may be on offer soon. Note your information will not be passed on to third parties.

Just head on over to the following link where you can enter your email to be added to the newsletter list.

Note I will not share your email with anybody, it is only for keeping up to date with Astrospace Fiction books.

https://mailchi.mp/1c69765ddf7a/
jameshansonegm-signup
Best wishes and see you soon: Paul M

PLAY LIST: THE NIGHT
WE PLAYED THE MUSIC

"Those Were the Days" Mary Hopkins
"Boom Bang-a-Bang" Lulu
"Mrs. Robinson" Simon and Garfunkel
"These Boots Are Made
for Walkin" Nancy Sinatra
"It's Not Unusual" Tom Jones

Point at which Jocelyn and Adam interrupt.

"Can't Buy Me Love" The Beatles
"Cinderella Rockefella" Esther & Abi Ofarim
"I Heard It Through the
Grapevine" Marvin Gaye
"Ob-La-Di, Ob-La-Da" Marmalade
"Keep On Running" The Spencer Davis
Group

*Adam enticed back in by Gary and a couple of
instrumentals*

"Telstar" The Tornados
"Peter Gunn" Duane Eddie
"White Horses" Jackie Lee
"Good Vibrations" The Beach Boys
"Blackberry Way" The Move
"All You Need Is Love" The Beatles

"Satisfaction"	The Rolling Stones
"Wipe Out"	The Surfaris
"Lady Madonna"	The Beatles
"San Francisco"	Scott McKenzie
"Nut Rocker"	B. Bumble and the Stingers
"Kon-Tiki"	The Shadows
"Albatross"	Fleetwood Mac

THE JAMES HANSONE
GHOST MYSTERIES

It all started with a simple unplanned diversion, '*A Ghostly Diversion*'.

James Hansone is a computer and IT specialist and a complete sceptic when it came to all things paranormal. Until *that* diversion. It changes everything once he becomes intrigued with a ghostly face at a broken window of a rundown cottage, deep in the Lincolnshire countryside. Little did he know that he would go on to uncover the mystery of a missing girl that would change his life forever.

Now a series of six books, James Hansone unwittingly becomes a ghost hunter roped in to explore further mysteries with more books planned.

A Ghostly Diversion
Secrets of Grasceby Manor
Return to De Grasceby Manor
James and the Air of Tragedy
The Haunting of Grasceby Rectory
Spectre of the Grasceby Flier

All available as Kindle, print on demand and Kindle Unlimited from Amazon.

THE JAMES HANSONE GHOST MYSTERIES OMNIBUS VOL 1

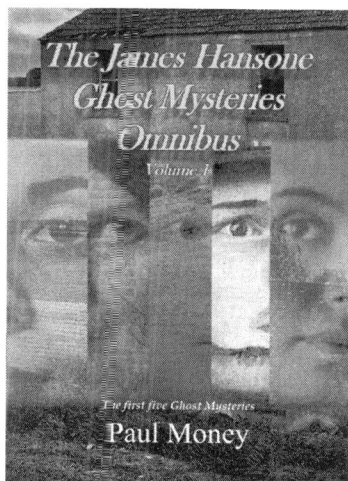

The first five ghost mysteries all in one convenient book.

Available as Kindle, print on demand and Kindle Unlimited from Amazon.

Check out Paul's Amazon author page: https://www.amazon.co.uk/Paul-L.-Money/e/B003VNGE1M

THE JAMES HANSONE
NEW YEAR TALES VOL1

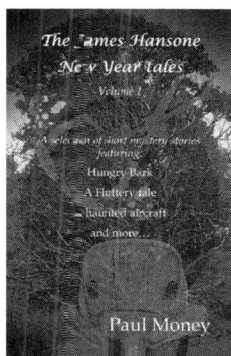

Based on the main characters found in the James Hansone Ghost Mysteries, this is a collection of short stories of ghostly, supernatural and mysterious events recounted by some of the regular characters.

Set in James and Sally's cottage as they see in the New Year by inviting some of their friends to a New Year's Eve buffet but with the condition some of them tell a short story to amuse everyone.

Story's include:
'Hungry Bark', 'A Fluttery tale', 'Out of the Blue… the haunting of Hyperliner One', 'Tales from the diaries…', 'The unreal case of the Mesolithic barrow mystery' and 'I don't want to go…'.

Available as Kindle, print on demand and Kindle Unlimited from Amazon.

THE FRAGILITY OF EXISTENCE

A Sci-Fi/Apocalyptic tale

The extermination of our species was probably inevitable when you look back with hindsight.

Every advanced civilisation has almost always wiped out the resident less advanced occupants whenever they came into contact. So it was the same for us, Homo Sapiens. But it wasn't supposed to have happened. We were not to know that. Perhaps that was a good thing. For the Universe...

Matt and Simone stared out at the devastation and knew it could only mean one thing ...

Humanity was about to become extinct. Could they escape the fate they had seen befall others in their small village of 'Woldsfield'? They were not going to wait around to find out ...

Available as Kindle, print on demand and Kindle Unlimited from Amazon.

THE FRAGILITY OF SURVIVAL

A Sci-Fi/Apocalyptic tale
Book 2 of the Fragility series

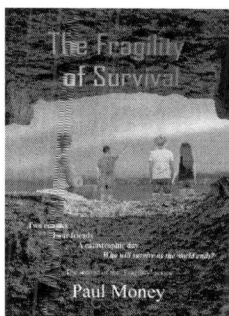

Two couples on holiday in the Algarve
Two couples who like sunbathing on the beach
Two couples who like exploring the region
Scott and Katrina, Danny and Robyn

A simple two week holiday in the sun:
What could go wrong?
How about the end of the world as
we know it for starters?
A desperate plight for one couple
an even more desperate plight for the other
as they discover the fragility of survival ...
Available as Kindle, print on demand and Kindle
Unlimited from Amazon.

THE STARVISTA 4 SAGA
Books 1 & 2 of a trilogy
Book 1: **The last Voyage of the StarVista 4**

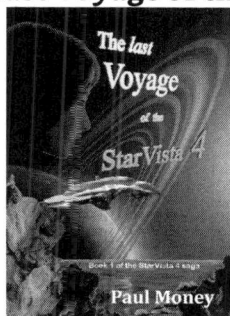

A Voyage of a lifetime.
2700 passengers and crew.

The diary of an eight year old passenger.
Stunning encounters with fabulous
interstellar destinations.
The mysterious multi inclined rings of the gas giant
planet Tianca in the hardly explored Cantrara system.

A 100 year mystery in the making ...

Follow the adventures of Cherice Richmond on board
the luxury star cruiser StarVista 4, with her parents,
Carl and Natalie, the honourable newly appointed Earth
Ambassadors to the Ziancan homeworld.
Little do they know that they will never return ...

Available as Kindle, print on demand and Kindle
Unlimited from Amazon.

THE FATE OF THE STARVISTA 4

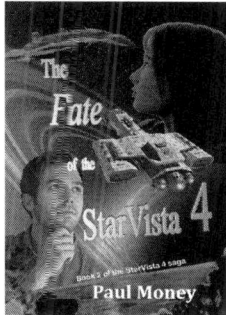

The mystery of the StarVista 4 unfolds in book 2 ...

In book 2 of the StarVista 4 trilogy, 100 years after the disappearance of the passenger liner StarVista 4, Andrew James Hanscne has been fascinated since a boy about what happened to the space liner. Having become highly successful and famous as a space ship designer, with his own construction company, he resolves to solve the mystery once and for all.

But there is more to the disappearance of the StarVista 4 than anyone realises ...

Join AJ as he sets out to fulfil his lifelong ambition and discover The Fate of the StarVista 4.

Available as Kindle, print on demand and Kindle Unlimited from Amazon.

Book 3: Legacy of the StarVista 4 coming soon to complete the trilogy.

ABOUT THE AUTHOR

Paul Money is an astronomy broadcaster, writer, public speaker and publisher. He was the Reviews Editor for the BBC Sky at Night magazine from 2006 until January 2024 before retiring from the role, and for eight years until 2013 he was one of three Astronomers on the Omega Holidays Northern Lights Flights. He continues to give talks on astronomy and space and self publishing astronomy books and articles.

He is married to Lorraine whose hobby/interest is genealogy and family history and she is invaluable with her suggestions involving the historical aspects of all the novels.

As an astronomer Paul has been giving talks across the UK for over forty years and was awarded the Eric Zuker award for services to astronomy in 2002 by the Federation of Astronomical Societies. In October 2012 he was awarded the 'Sir Arthur Clarke Lifetime Achievement Award, 2012' for his 'tireless promotion of astronomy and space to the public'.

Since 2016 he has turned self published author covering ghost mysteries, science fiction/apocalyptic novels and this venture into friendship and adventure with Adam and Jocleyn.

More info can be found at his Astrospace web site: https://www.astrospace.co.uk/Fiction

September 2024

Printed in Great Britain
by Amazon

58727420R00227